Praise for *The English Teacher:*

"The dizzying complexities of melding stepfamilies provide much of the drama in this spare but acutely observed second novel. . . . This fine book demonstrates how a short novel can illuminate difficult real-life issues with sensitivity and insight." —John Marshall, *Seattle Post-Intelligencer*

"Moving and deeply absorbing . . . With the momentum of a Hardy novel, albeit with a more hopeful outlook, *The English Teacher* snowballs to its heartwarming . . . conclusion . . . saved by King's considerable psychological acuity and intelligence." —Heller McAlpin, *Newsday*

"*The English Teacher* has moments of real insight, some sensitive portrayals, and most significant of all, the narrative drive that testifies to a real storyteller at work. . . . Ms. King is a novelist worth watching." —Claire Hopley, *The Washington Times*

"A marriage of single parents is more often the stuff of sitcoms than of serious novels, but King uses it to great effect in this intense character study. . . . King renders Vida's seething withholding in a free, direct style that captures everything. . . . She's also excellent on the children's reactions to each other as the households come together and then separate, dramatically and perhaps permanently." —*Publishers Weekly* (starred review)

"Lily King writes equally movingly and beautifully about both the large, dramatic and the small, seemingly inconsequential acts that destroy and define family." —Lily Tuck, Winner of the National Book Award for *The News from Paraguay*

"King delicately delves into the fragile bonds holding families together, even when logic favors their dissolution. . . . [She] writes with subtle clarity, displaying an intuitive understanding of the vulnerable psyches of teenagers, and with pinpoint perception of her characters' inner lives."
—*Booklist*

"King's prose throughout this fine novel is restrained and powerful, whether she is describing Vida's paralyzed witness of her own life, or tangential class and in-group observations."
—Wingate Packard, *The Seattle Times*

"As intriguing as Lily King's debut . . . King has delved into the depths of two lonely souls and treated us to a wonderful experience."
—Nandini Bandyopadhyay, *The Tampa Tribune*

"This wise and moving novel is much like Sue Miller's fiction, set amid the rocky landscape of family life. . . . The heart of the story is its lovely depiction of wounded people struggling to find solace and stability in each other." —Anne Stephenson, *The Arizona Republic*

The English Teacher

Also by Lily King

The Pleasing Hour

The English Teacher

A NOVEL BY

Lily King

GROVE PRESS
New York

Published simultaneously in Canada
Printed in the United States of America

FIRST GROVE PRESS EDITION

Library of Congress Cataloging-in-Publication Data
King, Lily.
The English teacher : a novel / by Lily King.
p. cm.
ISBN-10: 0-8021-4266-4
ISBN-13: 978-0-8021-4266-5
1. English teachers—Fiction.   2. Remarried people—Fiction.   3. Stepfamilies—
Fiction.   4. New England—Fiction.   5. Islands—Fiction.   I. Title.
PS3561.I4814E54 2005
813'.54—dc22   2005045384

Grove Press
an imprint of Grove/Atlantic, Inc.
841 Broadway
New York, NY 10003

Distributed by Publishers Group West

www.groveatlantic.com

06 07 08 09 10   10 9 8 7 6 5 4 3 2 1

For Tyler, who brought everything to life

Life is beginning. I now break into my hoard of life.
—Virginia Woolf, *The Waves*

ONE

October, 1979

THAT SHE HAD NOT KILLED HIM IN HER SLEEP WAS STILL THE GREAT RELIEF of every morning.

Not that she actually believed he was dead when he slept in on a Saturday. It was merely a leftover ritual, the weak ghost of an old fear from years ago when she awoke and waited, barely breathing, as close to prayer as she had ever got in her life, for a single sound of him: a little sigh, or the scrape of his feetie pajamas across the floor. He'd scuffle into her room still warm and puffy and half asleep, and the piercing relief of him collided with the horror of possessing such a fear and the dread of its return the next morning.

Now here he was at quarter of eleven, finally, his boots whacking the stairs, missing steps, his shirt unbuttoned but with an undershirt beneath (she didn't know what grew on his chest now and didn't want to). He shook out half a box of cereal and ate it in a few loud smacks at the other end of the table. Still, what sweetness flooded beneath her skin! She did not, could not, let him see it, and instead told him to remember to close his mouth please.

His back to her, carrying the empty bowl to the sink, he said he was going over to Jason's. To take apart a television.

She watched him cross the soccer fields diagonally—no home games today, thank God—and disappear down the path to Jason's house. All the delicious, fleeting relief of him went, too.

She returned to the mounds of essays in front of her. Within a few hours she reached the bottom of the freshman papers and moved on to the juniors'. Peter didn't come home for lunch, so she forgot to eat.

Vida began to contemplate canceling her plans for the evening. Tom would want to touch her again, scrape his mustache against her neck. Her armpits grew slippery. The telephone on the wall urged her on—a virus, a migraine. A quick call and it could all be over, the sweating, the rancid taste, and the sensation that she was no longer inside her body but beside it. And yet it was this disassociation that immobilized her, prevented her from getting up from her grading and walking the five paces to the phone. Instead she continued to watch the pen in her hand make small thick checkmarks beside the strong passages, and larger aggressive comments beside the weak, and then, below the last line of each essay, deposit a grade. She always graded more harshly in the afternoon before an evening with Tom Belou.

Peter answered the door. When had he come home? She hadn't heard the doorbell. It would be Lloyd or Wendell, the custodians, looking for an extra hand to move some chairs from one wing to another. But then there was a strange swishing in the hallway, coming at her, and Tom himself appeared in her kitchen. He was wearing a parka. She'd never seen him in any sort of coat. The temperature had dropped twenty degrees since last weekend. It was beige, with a belt he let dangle at the sides.

"You off to climb Everest?" she said, feeling trapped in her seat at the table. She didn't go to great lengths primping before she saw him, but she did brush her hair and her teeth and change out of her old slippers with the stuffing bulging out. Until this moment their encounters had been quite formal, with precise beginnings and ends, no sleepovers, no weekends away. Neither had ever dropped in on the other like this; their children had never met. Their touching was tentative, nearly absentminded, though her memory of it was acute, a confusing ache of pleasure and shame. No intercourse. Miraculously, they were in silent agreement about that.

Her dog Walt nudged Tom's hand with the long bridge of his nose, but Tom didn't respond as he usually did. He just stood there in the doorway, his eyes flicking over her impatiently. He was going to break it off. It couldn't have been clearer to her. This was just the way he would do it, in person, in a parka, perhaps after a trip to the dump. He needn't bother. It was hardly anything to her. She had enjoyed his company, his lack of demands on her, but that couldn't have lasted much longer.

"I'm sorry," he said, pointing to the sea of essays, "I know I'm interrupting." His hands were red from the cold.

Let's just get it over with, she thought, anger and humiliation prickling her throat. Her mind felt calm, detached, but her heart had another engine altogether and thudded painfully.

"I just had this . . . I was planning to . . . but it just made me so crazy, all the . . ." He walked the length of the kitchen, away from her, the bulky parka sleeves squealing as his arms flailed about. She wondered if he'd stitched it himself, this awful coat.

She wished she'd never said she loved him. She was just being polite, returning the compliment late one evening. But now it turned out he'd been mistaken. Of course it had been too soon. His wife had only been dead a short while. She wished he'd just spit it out and go home.

He reached the far counter, spun around, and with three long strides he was there before her, hovering over her and her work. He smelled of something familiar. Maple syrup, maybe. His eyes finally settled on hers. "I love you, Vida. I do. But it's not enough for me. It's not enough to simply love you. I wish for everyone's sake it were but it's not. I want to marry you." A laugh or a sob, Vida couldn't tell which, pushed its way out of his chest. "I want to marry you."

Out of the parka came a ring, no box, that clinked as it landed in her teacup. "Damn," he said, fishing it out with thick shaking fingers. "I'm sure you've had better proposals than this. I'm just not that type."

It was, in fact, her first proposal. Another woman, a better woman, might have confessed this. She never would. She had let him believe, along with everyone else up here, that she'd been married to Peter's father.

The ring hovered now, too, caught in the tips of his fingers. Suddenly she understood the true role of the ring. It forced, as T. S. Eliot would say, the moment to its crisis. Without it, a proposal was just a question, a query, and the response could be the beginning of a conversation that might last weeks, or years. But the ring demanded the final answer within a few seconds. You either reached up and took it, or you kept your hand on top of Hank Fish's essay on Emerson. And once you took it, you'd have an awkward time of giving it back. But to not take the ring, to leave it untouched, to watch it go back into the parka pocket, the proposal marked with a fat F—who could deliver that blow? She heard Peter upstairs, crossing the landing to the bathroom. She'd always imagined these moments filled with ecstatic conviction, but this moment was about ending the embarrassment, stopping the shallow breaths through Tom's nostrils and the little laugh-sobs he was trying to suppress. It was about Peter upstairs and her terror of the mornings and all the years they'd been alone together in this house.

Whether she spoke or simply nodded she'd never know. All she knew was that the ring, several sizes too big, was slipped on her finger and Tom was kissing her, then burying his face in her hair, then kissing her again. Everything felt rubbery. She had the sense, despite his enthusiasm, that it wasn't really happening this way, that they were rehearsing, hypothesizing, and that the real moment would happen later, would happen differently.

Tom called up to Peter, who launched himself down the stairs immediately, his lack of athleticism embarrassing to her in Tom's presence. His face was bright red. He already knew. Even before Tom made the announcement, clutching her at the shoulders, she saw that Peter already knew.

"I am *so* psyched," he said, pumping Tom's hand, then raising both fists in the air as if it were the successful end of a soccer game. "Congrats, Mom," he said to her and pecked her on the cheek. There was a bit of a bristle to his chin. "This has been a long time coming." He was beaming at her, though he barely knew Tom. A handful of hellos at the door, that was all.

They celebrated with cookies and cider. She filled the glasses, passed the plate, but still she was somewhere apart from her body, and this moment was somehow apart from the rest of her life. Again and again she felt they were practicing, all three of them, and each time she smiled at Tom or Peter, she felt they were acknowledging that, too.

She walked Tom out to his car. She hoped that this would serve as their date, that she could have the rest of the evening to herself to finish her work. But he hugged her again and said he'd pick her up at seven.

He got into his car, then leapt out. "I almost forgot." He reached into the backseat. "A little engagement present."

It was a blue box with his insignia on it, *Belou Clothiers.* He had been that certain she'd say yes.

"When I was a very little boy," he said, leaning against the car and pulling her toward him in a gesture of familiarity that was probably familiar only to his wife in the grave, "my grandfather made a dress for a customer, a very simple dress. A few weeks later a friend of hers came in the shop and ordered the exact same dress. She said her friend had told her it was a magic dress. After that he got another request, and another. My grandfather must have made twenty-five of those dresses. I forgot all about them and then when I saw you I remembered. I remembered the dress exactly, right down to the pearl buttons. I don't know why."

She lifted off the top. It was yellow, a color she never wore. She was relieved that it was a summer dress with tiny capped sleeves: it would be at least eight months before she'd be expected to wear it.

"It's lovely," she said, holding it up to herself. Dear God, what had she done?

"It's magic." He kissed her again. The kisses were different now—firmer, possessive.

Tom the Tailor made me a dress, she imagined telling Carol, though she knew she wouldn't.

She watched his car turn off her gravel road and onto the paved school avenue, which carried him past the mansion and all its new limbs, then the tennis bubble, then the hockey rink, in a long arc before finally setting him back on the main road. She would have to leave this campus, this haven of fifteen years, if she actually married him.

"Aren't you freezing?" Peter called to her from the front door. There was a thrill, a wildness, in his voice she'd never heard before.

She opened the trunk of her car and tossed the box in. What's in the box, he'd ask when she got a little closer. He was going to have so many questions this afternoon. She stopped on the path to the house and lit a cigarette to buy herself some more time.

TWO

AT HIS MOTHER'S WEDDING, PETER DANCED WITH HIS NEW STEPSISTER
Fran, whose attention had slid over the top of his head at the beginning of the song. She wasn't focused on anything in particular, which made her lack of interest in him all the more apparent. But he was simply happy to be dancing with her. He might never again have the opportunity to dance with someone so thoroughly out of his league.

This marriage was exactly what Peter had wanted and now it was here, all around him, written on balloons tied to chairs and on the inside of the gold band his mother now wore—the first piece of jewelry he'd ever seen on her. It had all happened so fast, and he was still dizzy with his own good luck. There was something creepy to people about a boy living alone with his mother for his whole life—fifteen and a half years. He'd been embarrassed by it. And now that long chapter was finally over. Tonight they'd go home to a regular house on a regular street, husband and wife in the master bedroom and four kids sprinkled in rooms down a hallway.

The song was coming to an end. He hoped its last notes would bleed into the beginning of the next. But there was a pause as the lead singer, his math teacher, Mr. Crowse, took a swig of beer, and Fran wavered like a leaf in the silence, poised to catch the first wind away from him. He had to secure her in place, and his mind spun in search of the words. After they had lived together for a few weeks, he'd probably have a ton of things to say, but now they were strangers.

He'd already complimented her bridesmaid's dress, as well as her poem the night before. He could make fun of the band, the Logarithmics, which was made up of the very geekiest teachers at Fayer Academy, but he wanted to say something big, something that would intrigue her.

"My mother wanted to marry your father from the moment they met." His mother wouldn't like him saying that. He knew it wasn't true.

"I could tell," Fran said, scrutinizing them, his mother and her father, who stood holding hands and not letting go as the music started up again. It was "Beast of Burden" and they played it much slower than usual, Mr. Crowse practically whispering into his mike with his eyes shut and sweat streaming over his lids. Peter and Fran watched their parents step closer, her father tucking his mother's fingers tight in the dip between his shoulder and collarbone.

Fran turned back abruptly to him. "Shall we dance?" she said in a foreign accent.

At school dances, he headed straight for the bathroom whenever he heard the first languid notes of a song like this. Even a slow dance with Fran did not overpower the urge to bolt. But she'd already looped her arms loosely around his neck, so he placed a hand on either side of her waist. She was a year older but no taller. The fabric of her dress was so thin he could feel the narrow band of her underwear and the heat of her skin where there was no underwear at all. Peter tried to keep all the facts straight in his head: this was his first slow dance and his first contact with the underclothes of a girl; yet this was his mother's wedding and this was his stepsister. He felt there was some secret to this kind of dancing that he hadn't been let in on. Quickly his hands made damp nervous spots on Fran's dress.

Halfway through the song Fran's head, which had been cocked and swiveling in every direction away from him, plummeted to his shoulder. Her eyelashes flickered on his long neck.

"Does your mother dye her hair?" she whispered.

Peter opened his eyes to see his mother floating by. Her hair was longer than most mothers'. Usually she wore it pinned at the back with the same tortoiseshell clip but today it was down, her dark red curls draped over Tom's arm like a flag.

"No," he said, though he sensed another lie would have pleased her more. "She doesn't."

At the end of the song, Peter peeled his palms from Fran's dress. Before he could decide what to say, her father tapped her on the shoulder and gave a little bow as she turned to him. She put her arms out like a professional, the way she had when she'd said to Peter, Shall we dance? But this time her face looked like it had been plugged in. No girl had ever looked at him like that.

Instead of completing the swap, his mother whispered that she had to go to the john, and left him on the dance floor alone. He watched, for a short while, her tall figure try to push through to the stairs on the other side of the room. Every few feet she was stopped by people wanting to congratulate her. They mashed their faces against hers, pawed at her dress, spoke loudly into her ear, and all the while his mother kept imperceptibly moving on. If he held his breath, she would look back at him. But she didn't. She reached the stairs, kept her eyes forward, and disappeared beneath the floor.

He took a seat at a table with some children he didn't recognize and their babysitter. The children were tying her wrists together with the strings of balloons and none of them noticed when he sat down. He swung his chair toward the dancers and sipped on a flat Coke someone had left behind. He felt suddenly grown-up, beside but apart from the screeches of the little boys, his right ankle on his left knee which made a box of his legs, the way most of his male teachers sat during assemblies. The babysitter was pretty and probably thought he'd come over to try and talk to her so he was careful to ignore her. All three of his stepsiblings were out dancing now:

Fran, with her father, still shining like a star; Stuart, the oldest, old enough to be in college but for some reason wasn't, glumly twitching with a fat cousin of theirs; and little Caleb up on the shoulders of Dr. Gibb, who had been Mrs. Belou's oncologist. She had only been dead a couple of years and now his mother was Mrs. Belou.

Peter started to wish he'd invited Jason. His mother had told him to invite as many friends as he wanted, but he thought they'd get in the way of the beginning of his life with his new family. He'd envisioned the whole wedding differently, with him and Stuart and Fran moving through the day together, comparing parents, trading information like spies before a mission. He pictured them all sitting around one table, pointing out relatives and telling their stories. Well, Peter only had one relative there, his aunt Gena, but she had a good story. Years ago, she'd gone into the Peace Corps and fallen in love with a guy in her village in Africa. One of the guy's wives had tried to strangle her with reeds from the river. She still had the scars on her neck.

As if beckoned by his thoughts, Gena took the seat beside him. "You look a little gloomy."

"I'm not."

"Really?"

She put a finger under his chin and guided his face to hers. Even though Gena was four years older, she was like looking at his mother through magic glass, the creases gone, the cheeks soft shiny bulbs above her big smile. His mother once said she wanted to skate on Gena's skin it was so smooth.

"I'm just taking a break from dancing."

"You glad she did this?"

"Yeah."

"You like the steps?"

"I don't know them really."

They were all dancing together now. Stuart had tied a napkin around his head and was jutting his arms out like he was putting a hex on people.

"They must be pretty tough." She meant because of their mother.

"I guess." He didn't like it when people dwelled on Mrs. Belou's death.

Gena looked away. He was afraid she was preparing a move. He hadn't been a great conversationalist, though usually he liked talking to her. He'd only met her twice before, but he felt comfortable with her. She said what she thought.

"What do you think about Tom?"

Gena watched Tom, who was dancing in that shoulder-bouncing way that people who did not grow up with rock music did, then turned back to him, as if he were the real subject of study. Finally she said, "He'll call a spade a spade."

"What's that supposed to mean?" he said with sudden defensiveness, as though they were in the middle of a fight.

"I don't know." She shook her head slowly. "I don't know what he's going to find in there." She looked at Peter and seemed surprised by his disturbed face. "Oh honey, for you this is fantastic. It's a nice family. And you've got brothers and sisters now."

"One sister." He felt sulky. What did she mean by find in there?

"One sister." She looked at Fran, twirling beneath the bridge of her father's arms. "Who will hog the bathroom and torture you with all the gorgeous friends she brings home." Her head fell back, laughing at her vision, and he could see the three ragged white stripes just below her chin.

The bass player, Mr. Carbone, struck the last chords of a song with a long flourish and an embarrassing scissor split, then announced the band would be taking a breather. Peter hoped his stepfamily would join him. There was plenty of room—the children were playing at the dessert table now, smashing pieces of cake faster than the babysitter could push the plates away. But the Belous drifted over to their side of the room where Tom's friends and family all congregated. Peter scanned the top of the crowd for his mother's hair, but she still wasn't up from the bathroom. He had a flash of her climbing out a small window but he knew that was ridiculous. Where would she go? Their house on campus had been emptied out that morning; Mr. Hoyle, with his wife and new baby, would be moving in tomorrow.

Dr. Gibb took a seat on the other side of Gena. He leaned across her to shake Peter's hand for the third time that day, then said something that made Gena smile. He was neither young nor old, but in that long dull part of life Peter dreaded. He had a squat face and an oxbow of hair just above his forehead, cut off from the rest of his scalp by the bald patches on either side.

He and Gena plunged into a serious discussion. Their voices dropped to exclude him. Peter feigned disinterest and slowly turned his back on them so that gradually their voices rose again.

"I don't know about that," Dr. Gibb said. "Youth is very resilient. But it's true that there are easy declines and difficult declines and this was a very very difficult one."

"Slow?"

"No, relatively speaking, it was swift. But she fought it with her bare hands. This was a woman who did not want to die, who did not believe she *could* die."

"My father always told us no matter what, die with dignity."

Dr. Gibb took a deep breath as if to stop himself from saying something more acerbic. "There is not a lot of room for dignity with cancer of the brain." He said "cancer of the brain" like it was a French delicacy. Peter felt a sudden hatred for this man who had brought death to his mother's wedding.

Why did people have such a fascination with death? Once they'd found out Tom was a widower, everyone at school wanted all the details about how his wife had died. Wasn't it wonderful, they all agreed, that Tom had found Vida. Like a rose in winter, his English teacher had said.

Peter had stopped himself from thinking about dying long ago. When he was much younger, for no good reason that he could remember, the reality and certainty of death struck him all at once. He went through a long scary stage of believing he would die in his sleep like in the stupid rhyme Jason's mother always said before bed. Sleep itself began to feel like death, and he would jerk himself awake whenever it came over him. He felt, late at night, the pull of his father, the mystery of him that was as large as the mystery of death itself and all tangled up with it. He began to wonder if his father was dead, dead and wanting Peter to join him in death. It was the winter of fourth grade, with its short bleak days and long nights and everything snapping and cracking outside his window. Finally spring came, with its softening and loosening, and his mind loosened too, relinquished its grip, and he began sleeping again.

He tuned out Gena and the doctor after that, and looked around the dreary room for distraction. This restaurant they'd rented out was one of the summer shacks in Fayer right on the water. It would be a great place to go on a hot August night when you wanted to feel a breeze against your skin. It was not a great place to go in November when all the windows were covered with thick plastic which billowed out and collapsed back in loudly with the wind. He was filled suddenly with a familiar loneliness, and he stood up quickly, desperate to shake it, anxious to find his mother among all these strangers.

There she was, weaving her way slowly back across the room. She looked like another person today, all that hair everywhere and a faintly pink dress swirling down to her ankles. She lifted a flute of champagne gently from a passing tray.

Peter's French teacher, Miss Perry, asked Dr. Gibb to dance and Peter was surprised to see how eagerly he accepted her, leaving Gena's side without another word. His aunt turned back to him without a trace of injury.

"When are you going to come visit me?" she asked. When he didn't answer she said, "I'm not worried. You'll come. Someday, when you're a little older, you're going to get in the car and not even know where you're going, and five days later I'll see you pull up into my driveway."

"I'd call first."

"No you won't. You'll just show up. And I'll be real glad to see you." She gave him a rough hug, clubbing him on the ear with one of her thick upper arms.

What he had wanted to say was that every fall his mother promised they'd visit Gena during spring vacation, but when the vacation drew near his mother always had some excuse for not having bought the tickets—that senioritis was going to be bad this year, that not one junior was going to get into college at the rate they were going, or that it had been years since she'd taught *King Lear* and really had to do some thinking. That was her most frequent excuse for everything they didn't do—she had to do some thinking. Peter understood that they didn't have a lot of money compared with most of the kids at Fayer, since they lived off one teacher's salary, but they'd never taken anything but the same three-day vacation every year. On the first weekend after school ended each June, they drove north to York Beach to stay at the Sea Spray Inn, an aqua-blue, three-story motel across Route 1 from a gray beach and gray water. During the day he would swim, going back and forth between the pool and the beach, while his mother sat upright reading on a towel near the rocks. They shared a room and if he woke up in the night there was often a bright orange circle of ash floating above her bed. He felt comforted by her wakefulness, the smell of her smoke, and the rattling wheeze of the ice machine down the hall. He always wished the trip was longer.

But Gena probably didn't want to hear about almost-visits, and Peter was glad when his mother joined them. He leaned closer to her, ashamed of his need of her, that secret ache he kept expecting to grow out of.

"How much longer are we going to stay?" he asked her.

She turned to him but didn't answer.

"Mom?"

She was looking right at him, with that smile that had been fixed on her face all day, but she still didn't reply.

"Mom!" He waved a hand at her. "I said, how long are we going to stay?"

"You can stay as long as you like."

"But how long are *you* going to stay?"

"I don't know, Peter."

"Are we going to have dinner all together when we get home?"

"We just ate." She spread out her arm at all the round tables still covered with dessert plates and coffee cups.

"Wasn't that lunch?"

"It's past six." She was irritated with him and looked off toward Tom, who was making his way to her. He passed a table of Fayer teachers, all women, and Peter saw them admiring him.

When Tom reached them he said, "I feel like Lindbergh in Paris the way people are carrying on."

"You smell a little better," his mother said. "He was soaked in urine."

Peter noticed how Tom's fingers, like organisms separate from the rest of him, folded into his mother's as they spoke. It was weird, much weirder than he expected, to see his mother standing there holding hands with a man, a husband. And she had an unnatural expression on her face, like she knew the whole thing was weird, too. He wondered, for the first time, if his mother was in love with Tom, really in love, the way he was with Kristina. She couldn't be— she'd only known him since June and he'd known Kristina since sixth grade when she was new at Fayer. They sat together at study hall. They became partners in earth science. Neither was popular; they didn't get asked to meet at the beach on weekends where their classmates smoked cigarettes and made out behind the rocks. In the spring, Peter tried to kiss her when they were alone in the woods, collecting salamanders for their terrarium. He'd caught one, fluorescent orange like a bike reflector, and she bent over to watch it scramble in his palm. Her hair was loosely woven in a braid, strands curling free in the damp air. Even now he could remember how he wanted to press his lips to the pale skin beneath the braid as she stood there so still. But he thought you were only supposed to kiss a girl on the lips so he buried that desire and tucked his head around to find her mouth. She screamed in fright. She said she'd thought he was a bird, a crow come to snatch up the little glowing salamander. She seemed really sorry for the confusion and Peter knew that if he tried again she would have kissed back, but he'd used up all his courage in the first attempt, and they walked back with their salamanders to the science wing in silence. He never got another chance that year, and by the next fall she'd cut off her braid and grown breasts and became the most popular girl in their grade. She still was, and he still loved her.

Peter remained beside his mother and Tom, though they were as far away as stars. Even if they had both been shorter and spoken audibly, he wouldn't have understood half of what they said to each other. It was like that with couples. Kristina was like that with Brian Rossi now. Gena had gotten pulled into a conversation with three tiny old ladies Peter didn't recognize. Beside him, their backs to him,

Miss Rezo and Mrs. Shapiro, two of the other English teachers at Fayer, were talking quietly.

"No, I never did. No one did. When she interviewed she said her husband would be joining her, but then he never came. I don't think anyone dared mention him after a certain point."

"It's like Lena Grove showing up in Jefferson looking for Lucas Burch. Where'd she come from exactly?"

"Texas, I think. I can't recall for sure. But there was never a mention of him, not even to my cousin Lucy who sat for them for years."

"Really? The one with the wired jaw?"

And then they launched into a long discussion of jaw-related dentistry. It seemed to him teachers often did that, picked the least interesting angle of a story and pursued it like bloodhounds, leaving behind all the more promising trails. It's why he hated school, history in particular. The past had to be more intriguing than what they were given to learn.

"He's no longer in the picture" was what he remembered his mother saying the first time he asked about his father. Another time she said, "He was a man," and he waited for her to go on because she liked talking about people and what she noticed about them. But she said nothing else and he knew by her changed expression not to ask more. The two times Gena had visited, he asked, when he got her alone, if she knew anything about his father. She said his mother had never confided in her about things of that nature.

Tom turned to him. "You ready to go home, Peter?"

It sounded so normal, as if Tom had been asking him that for years. "Definitely," he said.

From the backseat of the Belou station wagon Peter could see the heads of his mother and stepfather in the Dodge ahead. It was strange to see her in the passenger seat of her own car, the car she'd had all his life. She looked small. Tom's head was turned to her and he was driving very slowly.

"We might as well get out and walk," Stuart said, slamming his palms against the steering wheel again. "What's wrong with him?"

This was the first time he'd ever been alone with the Belou kids without his mother. He'd imagined this moment differently, too. He thought their stiffness and reserve with him—and with each other— was due to his mother's presence, but except for Stuart's occasional outbursts, no one said a word, and Peter's ears rang in the silence. Fran sat up front, her arms locked over her wool coat. Caleb was with Peter in back, turned away from him, breathing onto the window, then squeaking letters into the brief fog.

The Belous lived across the bridge from Fayer in Norsett. Fayer was technically an island, though no one called it that. Norsett was on the mainland, a bigger, poorer town than Fayer with abandoned processing plants blocking most of its water views. There were a few shabby summer houses on the southern edge, but the year-round residents lived in small capes along an inland grid of streets. To Peter, who had lived in the same cottage in the grass sandwiched between playing fields all his life, a normal road lined with houses was deeply exotic. Even the sidewalks were part of a dream come true.

As they crossed the harbor, Peter felt the same surge of anticipation of the wedding that he'd had each of the times they'd driven to the Belous' house in the past month. But this time it was cut short by the recognition that it was done, no longer something still ahead but slightly behind. It was only now, in the backseat of the Belous' car above the cold black water, that he let himself admit disappointment. Yet, as they headed inland, turning one unfamiliar corner and another, each street looking so similar Peter wondered if he'd ever find his way out, the realization of disappointment about the day (except the two dances with Fran, which he would treasure even if she never spoke another word to him) had no effect on his anticipation of their arrival at 81 Larch Street, where he would begin his life as a regular person who ate his meals not in a cafeteria but in a kitchen, whose neighbors were not his teachers, and who on weekends would not find himself moving furniture or passing hors d'oeuvres to alumni. Most of all he looked forward to siblings, and even their withdrawal in the car now did not chase away his image of what that would be like. There was bound to be some awkwardness at first, but in a few weeks they'd look back and laugh at how shy they'd all been.

He wondered what Tom and his mother were talking about. She would be thinking about their dog Walt and how long he'd been left alone at a strange house. She would be thinking about all the papers she couldn't grade this weekend. She didn't like any disruption of her routine. Even their dinky three days at York Beach threw her. He could count on her being ornery (one of her favorite words to describe herself) for the rest of the month. But what she would be saying was a mystery. He'd never, before this summer, seen his mother in the company of a man.

Stuart pulled into the driveway behind the Dodge. Peter got out last, and waited a few seconds for his mother, but she and Tom remained in the front seat, windows rolled tight. He followed the others into the house.

Not to Peter, not to anyone in particular, Fran said, "Thank God *that* is over." She collapsed onto the sofa in her coat. Stuart, who didn't ever seem to wear a coat, went to turn on the TV. He turned the dial from channel to channel and when he finally stopped, he muttered, "Jesus, look at that," but he was blocking the set and no one cared enough to ask him to move. Caleb snuck into the recliner in the corner, a chair so enveloping and puckered it looked like an enormous cupped palm. He picked up the library book on bats that had been left facedown on the arm, snapped on the standing lamp over his shoulder, and began to read.

Peter stood alone near the door. He heard steps on the porch. Once his mother was inside it would become his house, too. There was shuffling and whispering but they did not come in. He picked up a Lucite cube of photographs from a table next to the sofa. He hoped Fran would notice him turning it over and narrate, but she just stared at Stuart's back, as if she could make out, from the flickering edges of his body, the images on the screen.

The pictures were only of Stuart, all taken when he was much younger. In each one he had the same enormous smile. They were all typical scenes from childhood: riding a tricycle, frosting a cake, building a sand castle, fishing. Peter turned the cube from side to side to side, trying to catch him without that smile. That smile bore utterly no resemblance to this Stuart who stood muttering and shaking his head in front of the TV. This Stuart had no expressions at all. It was as if all his facial muscles had been snipped. His mouth hung flat and motionless, even when he spoke. But here in these snapshots, the smile covered his whole face, a combination of joy and shock and love, his forehead wrinkled in surprise and his head bent to one side affectionately. The pictures spanned seven years or so, and his joyful face was the same in each one.

"There's not going to be a quiz at the end of the period, Peter," Fran said without looking at him.

He put the cube down. Where was his mother? He didn't even know where his room was. He didn't know where anything was, except the kitchen, where he'd had dinner twice. But he liked it here. It was a real home, lived-in, with soft carpet everywhere and lots of places to sit. Even the smell was better.

Something brushed against the front door. Peter waited for it to open, for his mother to help him begin his life here, but nothing happened. Another scuffle—an attempt at a knock?

"Answer it," Fran barked.

Peter swung the door open and found his mother limp in Tom's arms.

"Oh my God," Fran said, disgusted.

Caleb lifted his eyes briefly from the bats. "What are you doing?"

Tom took a few small steps into the house. "I'm carrying my bride over the threshold." His face was flushed from either strain or embarrassment and he lowered Vida feet first to the ground, steadying her carefully as she took back her own weight. It was such a delicate, silent motion, and Peter felt comforted by it. It was, in fact, the first comforting moment he'd had all day.

"Congratulations," he said, the sound lingering unfinished because he'd wanted to add "Stepfather" or just "Father," but at the last moment couldn't say either. *Father* was such an unused, alien term. He thrust out his hand like Dr. Gibb.

Tom encased Peter's hand in two warm palms. "Thank you, Peter, thank you." He, too, seemed to want to do something else then—give him a hug or ask him an important question. Peter waited, his hand hot and buried, but nothing came.

When he was released, he turned to his mother. "Congrats, Mom." He felt, in the presence of the Belous, that he should hug her. They had gotten into a bizarre habit of performing in front of them, pretending they were another breed of mother and son. At their first dinner all together his mother, in the middle of the meal, had stroked the top of his head while bragging about his interest in writing. She'd exaggerated completely—he'd won a stupid poetry contest in seventh grade, that was all.

He stepped toward her and they raised their arms. It was a show; they hugged without pressing. He remembered this from childhood, this weak hug, as if he were made of paper.

"What the hell?" Tom said, stepping toward the TV. "Oh, no."

Peter tried to make sense of what he saw: fires, screaming,

mayhem. Every few seconds the TV camera itself seemed to be struck by a passerby. The jolted footage made him slightly nauseated. Then it rested on one image, a long lean Uncle Sam, his striped pants in flames, surrounded by dancing, chanting men whose robes flipped in and out of the fire.

"Those lunatics are going to burn themselves up, too, while they're at it," his mother said.

"They've seized our embassy," Tom said gravely. "Goddammit they've taken our embassy."

Peter didn't know who *they* were. He glanced at his mother for an explanation but he could tell she didn't know either. She didn't follow the news very carefully. All on-campus teachers got a paper delivered to their door every morning but theirs usually ended up in the trash can, the rubber band still fastened around it.

"Why did they agree to let him in?" Stuart said. "He could have had that operation in Mexico. They knew it would stir up trouble."

"He's been our ally for many years. We owed him."

"Ally? He's been our stooge. Our oil guy."

"What are you talking about?" Fran asked.

Tom began explaining about the Shah of Iran. Peter tried to focus on what he was saying but a man on TV came up to the camera shouting angrily through brown teeth, then spat at the lens. The spit was thick and green. A hand reached around quickly with a cloth and wiped it off. It was eerie to Peter, the hand and the cloth, like a taboo had been broken. He'd missed Tom's explanation.

"Is President Carter in there?" Caleb asked from his chair. Peter was certain that when he was seven he'd had no clue who was president.

"I doubt it," his mother said, though what did she know. "It's probably just a bunch of functionaries."

"What's that?"

"Good decent hardworking diplomats who were brave enough to remain in the country during a revolution." He'd never heard Tom use that tone of voice before.

"Mom?" he said quietly. "Do you know where my room is?"

"I don't even know where mine is."

"I'll show it to you, Peter." Caleb slid dramatically off his chair.

Peter followed him out of the room and down a corridor to the first room on the left.

"We dragged your boxes in this morning."

"Thanks."

Caleb slipped his hand behind a bookshelf. "The switch is a little tricky to find."

Peter waited, surprised by his desire to be alone, when just this morning being alone was what he'd hoped to renounce for good.

"There." A single bulb, painted green, cast the small room in lime-colored light. At first glance, it looked like a decorated storage room. The walls were covered with pen-and-ink drawings of body parts: ears, fingertips, knees. Some had Chinese characters beside them; others had typed-out English quotations Peter couldn't decipher. There was only one full-size poster, also handmade, of a pair of closed eyes and below it the words

> *What is one is not one*
> *And what is not one*
> *Is also one.*

There was nothing in the room immediately identifiable as furniture. It simply looked like a huge mound of junk—notebooks, winter coats, football pads, coin wrappers, a stapler, a fishing rod, balled clothing, a rubber Richard Nixon mask, a bike pump, a rumpled suit—that spread from the doorway to the far wall. As Peter leaned closer, he could see, beneath the only window, jutting out through all the crap, the flowered corner of a mattress.

"So that's my bed?"

"No. That's Stuart's bed. You're here." Caleb pointed to the near wall, which was stacked with boxes—his own boxes, Peter realized. "It folds out of the wall. It's pretty cool. Look." Caleb pushed into the cluttered center of the room all of Peter's boxes, then lifted a metal lever and caught the bed as it exploded out of the wall. "Ta da!" he exclaimed, gazing at the whole room—at the exploding bed, the warty cactus, the burnt thumbs of incense in a dish—with undisguised reverence.

"So why didn't *you* move in here?"

"He didn't want me to."

At this Peter felt a small bit of pleasure mingle with his horror, but it was short-lived. No one had told him he'd be sharing a room with Stuart. Stuart frightened him. Stuart didn't even speak to him.

"Where's the bathroom?"

"Right next door," Caleb said, still eager to please.

Peter stepped into the little bathroom and locked the door. He stood at the sink, a hand on either side of the basin, as if he were bracing himself to throw up. Maybe he'd feel better if he threw up. He tried to coax something out. Then he noticed a tiny little screen fastened to the drain and a clot of moist hair caught in it. With his fingernail, he pried up the screen, tapped it empty on the side of the plastic bucket below, and snapped it back in place. All this he did without thought. He was in a state beyond thought. In the mirror he saw, for an instant, the real Peter, the Peter he was when he was not conscious of looking. But after that all he saw was his mirror face, flattened out by self-awareness. Usually, when he looked in mirrors, he tried to figure out what it was about his face that no longer attracted Kristina. He'd read somewhere that handsomeness was not the result of a certain combination of features but of symmetry. The human eye gauged the degree of symmetry of the two halves of a face because, research had shown, people with symmetrical faces tended to be less prone to disease— thus a better biological choice. But tonight Peter did not try to find the asymmetry in his face. He knew that wasn't it. He wasn't un-attractive. Girls who didn't go to Fayer often thought he was cute at first, before they spoke to him. It was something else. He was undeveloped in some way that was not physical and seemed be-yond his control. He suspected it had to do with being an only child, or having only a mother, and there was a part of him that had hoped the Belous would help him change. Now he feared they would only make it worse.

"Are you all right?" Caleb said through the door.

"Yeah." His voice came out funny, more a breath than noise. He wasn't sure Caleb had heard him, but after a while his feet scuffled away back down the hall.

At the toilet he unzipped his fly. He had already begun to pee when he saw her photograph. She was looking right up at him, grin-ning. Love, she seemed to be saying. Yes, he replied. All this hap-pened in the interval between conscious thoughts, between recognizing that this, this woman tying the shoelace of her sneaker on an overgrown path, was Mrs. Belou, the real Mrs. Belou, and remembering that she was dead. When that last thought came, his stream of urine stopped abruptly, painfully. She had died in this house. She had stood right here, and there by the sink, and in his room. She had touched everything he would soon touch. There was no place he could ever be in this house where she had not breathed. He put down the lid of the toilet seat and sat, the black and white tiles on the floor flashing in time with his slamming heart. He didn't want to live here, in the house of a ghost.

He went back out to the living room.

"Mom?"

She wasn't listening. "We need air in here," she was saying, lifting up a window near Caleb's chair.

"I don't feel well." He didn't know what he wanted, what he expected from her. I want to go home, he wished he could say, even though he didn't completely mean it.

"Go rest on the couch for a bit," she said without looking at him.

"Could have been the shrimp," Fran said. "I spat mine out."

"Maybe that was it." He was unsure which cushion to choose—the middle one right next to Fran, or the far one, so far away it felt rude, unsibling-like. Finally he sat between the two and now they lifted like wings to either side of him and their stiff edges were not comfortable beneath him. But still he felt frozen, unable to choose a direction. Everyone else was focused on the TV. His mother had never allowed TV. Even now by Tom's side she wasn't watching. Her eyes were wandering off—to the lamp, to the curtains, to the little dish on a table in the corner. She wasn't interested in the present. For all her reading, she never bought a contemporary novel. The books she read always had some gloomy old portrait on the cover. He couldn't ever remember having a conversation about a current event with her. And here were the Belous, every one of them, even Caleb now, transfixed by this indecipherable mayhem that had not changed in the hour since they'd been home, Tom looking as if the hostages had been seized from his own house.

Time passed, Peter wasn't sure how much. Fran scooped up Caleb, who'd fallen asleep with his head on the arm of his chair, and took him down the hallway. He could hear the water running and Caleb moaning about having to brush his teeth.

Having been interrupted the first time, Peter still had to go to the bathroom. He didn't want to return to Mrs. Belou, didn't want to run awkwardly into Fran back there. Did you say hello to your own siblings in the hallway as you passed them? He didn't know the first thing about how regular families behaved. So he went down the other hallway instead. There was only one room here, at the end, and he went in. Tom's bedroom, he determined, from the size of the bed and his mother's boxes in the corner. He found a bathroom off to the left, but the light was out. He shut the door anyway and pushed open the curtain of the small window to let in a wedge of streetlight. He peed, then stood at the window. There had been no street lamps on campus. He tried not to miss his house, tried not to think of Mrs. Belou either, that this was her bathroom and she'd stood right here, too, at times thinking about the past, with maybe her hand on the sill just like this. He put his hand in his pocket and looked across the street into another family's life. They had the TV on, too, and there was lots of movement—a woman carried a bowl into the room, a child hopped on one foot, a man stood up and fiddled with the antenna, the woman ran out, perhaps to answer the telephone. Were they friends with the Belous? Had they been at the wedding? He couldn't see them well enough to know. Maybe the phone call was someone wanting to hear all about it. *What was she like? Did they seem happy? And what about the kids, those poor kids?*

When Peter had learned Tom was a widower, he'd been relieved. It meant his kids lived with him full-time, and didn't just visit every other weekend like Craig Hager's stepsisters. It meant, ultimately, a real union, a true synthesis, without any loose ends. He'd put their mother in the same category with his own father: permanently absent, wholly and completely unpresent. How mistaken he'd been. He could *feel* her. It was like she was standing beside him here in the dark, saying, You're touching my flowered curtains, you know. I know, he said back. I'm sorry.

Through the closed door, out in the bedroom, he heard footsteps on the carpet and then breathing, long, whistly, staccato breaths. Inhuman breaths. Then a final heave out, nearly a whimper, and his mother's voice: "I can't do this."

For many more minutes there was only silence. Peter kept his hand on the knob, to prevent her from coming in and finding him lurking in the dark of her bathroom.

Then he heard the bedroom door shut. He relaxed his grip, deciding to wait a few seconds before escaping.

"Hey." It was Tom's whisper, playfully loud and exaggerated. "What're you doing in the dark?"

"I thought I'd get out of this dress."

"Oh no you don't. I've been waiting all day to take this dress off myself."

Please no. Peter looked around for another exit from this room. His bathroom at his old house had had three different doors. This one didn't even have a closet, and the window was too high and too small. He'd make a racket just hoisting himself up. Maybe he should at least hide behind the shower curtain.

"You look so serious." Tom's voice was closer now, on the bed with her, only a few feet from where Peter stood.

"Marriage is serious."

"Not all the time."

"It's like teaching a class. You have to make all the right choices at the beginning or it's a wash."

"Trial and error."

"No, no errors."

He laughed. "Maybe not on your part, but I'm going to make some." Peter heard the beetlelike buzz of the long zipper of his mother's dress. "But not tonight. I'm not going to make one mistake tonight."

"Maybe I should go say good-night to Peter first."

"Not yet." His voice was muffled.

"Quickly, I promise."

The zipper went back up, the door opened and closed. He had to go now. His mother would call the police when she couldn't find him. But Tom was pulling off his shoes. Item by item his clothes fell to the floor. Now he was going to come into the bathroom. Peter held the knob firmly, readying himself for the fight he would surely lose with one shoulder shove from Tom.

Instead, his mother returned.

"How is he?" Tom asked.

"Better."

Better?

"What's he up to?"

"They're all still glued to the tube."

"Where'd you find that?"

"In the fridge."

"Must be vinegar by now. Now let's get this thing off and see what's going on under there."

"One sec." A pause, then a glass being set on the bedside table.

The dress was unzipped all the way down this time. Peter heard it rustle to the floor. He moved in swift silence to the other side of the room and stepped into the tub. His shoes squeaked but the sound was drowned out by Tom, whom he could still, unfortunately, hear clearly. "God, you are beautiful. So long and smooth. You're like an oboe. I'm finally going to learn to play an instrument." After a while he said, "Do you know how long I've waited to have you, have all of you? God, we've been living like teenagers."

At first Peter tried to fight the great and horrifying waves of words, but soon he surrendered and let them crash over him. At least he could hear none of his mother's responses, and it became easy, after a while, to imagine she had left the room. The problem was, once he got his mother out of the room his disgust abated, and other feelings began to creep in.

"God I want to fuck you." Tom started laughing, then said in a wholly different, tender voice, "Oh, Vida, you are the first thing I've wanted in so long." He said other things, some vulgar, some tender,

and suddenly Peter understood the word juxtaposition, a term Miss
Rezo had introduced recently. Juxtaposition of words, of tone, of
mood. He understood it all now. He felt it in his body.

"Are you ready now, Vida? Are you ready for me?" There was
shifting, rustling, Tom laughing. "I can't quite. Let's . . . Is this hurting? Am I hurting you? Let's try a different." More shifting and swishing. "Oh Vida you are so. I just want. I can't seem. Let's try."

Peter didn't know it was so complicated.

"Let's try some of this stuff." It was quiet for a long while, then,
"Oh sweetheart, I am so sorry. It's all my fault. We've got to get you
relaxed. I'm so sorry. We should have taken a honeymoon, a big
fancy hot-weather honeymoon. I did this all wrong. All wrong. Here,
there's a little more wine left. What can I do? Let me give you a back
rub. God, you are all clenched up like a big fist."

When he left the room, he no longer cared if they heard him. He
didn't even try to be particularly quiet. His mother was lying on her
stomach, her arms bent beneath her like tiny wings. Tom's big arm
lay on top of her. Defeated soldiers. He'd never known sex was such
a battle, and that people who wanted to win could lose. He slid out
the door. The glow of the TV, like moonlight along the living room
wall, and the murmur of voices, Stuart and Fran's, and the smell of
something warm like toast or muffins, all seemed like things from
another era of his life. His legs were stiff.

Stuart was sprawled on the floor. "Holy shit, where have you
been?"

There was no hiding where he'd been. There was only that
one room down the hallway he'd come from. "I got trapped. In the
bathroom."

"No way."

"I did."

"We thought you'd gone to bed," Fran said.

"I wish I had."

"They didn't know?"

Peter shook his head.

"That's fucked up." Stuart chuckled.

"Yeah, it was." At the sound of Stuart's chuckle, he felt suddenly a huge well of laughter inside. "It was really fucked up."

One after another they began laughing, and their laughter fed upon itself and slowly became that airless, throat-clicking, stomach-aching kind of laughter Peter had imagined only in the very best of his Belou dreams.

THREE

ON MONDAY MORNING VIDA WOKE UP ALONE. TOM HAD LEFT AT FIVE, off to some fabric sale in Massachusetts. She'd pretended to be asleep while he rose, took a shower, and returned to the bedroom to dress in the dark. The towel fell from his waist. It was like being in sudden possession of a horse, having this tall firm naked man beside her bed. What thin light there was fell on his pale buttocks and upper thighs, and she wished she could reach out and stroke them without him noticing and wanting to stroke her in return.

The loud nearly debilitating question that had pounded through her body like a pulse since the wedding reception—what have you done what have you done—subsided once he was gone, and she was able to fall back asleep until seven. She stretched her limbs in the enormous bed, her left arm and leg venturing across to Tom's side, still slightly warm. She rolled over into his impression, and put her head just beside where his had lain. She thought of the grisly iron-gray hair at the end of "A Rose for Emily." She would learn how to do this properly. "I promise," she said into Tom's absent ear.

The odor of food slipped through the cracks in the door: toast, bacon, something sweet but burned. Then voices, Fran's and Caleb's, not Peter's, and the clatter and ping of utensils. All these voices, all this commotion, after years of waking to a silent house. Peter is fine, she told herself.

In the bathroom water hung in the air and smelled like Tom.

She could see where he had swiped at the mirror to shave. The basin was clean of stubble but on the glass shelf above it a few tough bristles of his mustache were caught in a scissors' bill. If only she were the girl she had once been. He deserved that. He deserved someone who would walk into this bathroom, breathe him in, and cave to her knees with joy and thanks.

But the sorry truth was she was eager to get to school where her life would resume its familiar course after this aberration of a weekend. Her body felt strange, like she might be coming down with something. The *what have you done* hammering was back. A shower and her school clothes would snap her out of it.

But her nakedness beneath the weak drizzle of water only reminded her of failure with Tom, and she hurried to wash and cover up her body again. In his damp towel she leapt across the bedroom to her boxes. Close to the top of one she found her favorite gray cardigan and deeper down a soft shirt and denim skirt. From another she managed to pull out a pair of tights and her moccasins. She was not the flashiest dresser on the planet—no rival for Cheryl Perry, who taught French in clingy pants and short furry sweaters that swung above her perfect little bum. As she dashed across the room with her armful of plain clothes she remembered the sky-blue velvet dress her grandmother had sent her from Boston, the matching hat, and how she'd worn them to threads, despite the teasing and the Texas heat. Back in the wet warmth of the bathroom, she toweled her hair upside down into a damp frizz, tamed it with Tom's comb, then realized she had no clip. She couldn't teach with her hair down. She rifled through every box but found nothing. She probably had a spare in the car, and the thought of being in her car with Peter, headed toward school, was a soothing one.

She moved swiftly down the corridor. They didn't have much time—school was a good fifteen-minute drive from here, not the forty-second walk it used to be. Her wet hair thwacked at her back.

And today of all days she had to start *Tess of the d'Urbervilles* with her tenth graders. And Peter, too, was starting it in the other class with Lydia Rezo. She had always dreaded his reading *Tess*. And here it was.

In the living room, Stuart was curled up sideways on the sofa in a little egg, his eyes fixed on the morning news.

"This is some serious shit," he said to the knees just below his chin.

Weren't high school dropouts supposed to be sacked out until noon, instead of following international crises at 7:22 in the morning? Still, there was something self-pitying in his fascination with this aggression halfway around the world.

"How about a little air in here?" It was always so stiflingly close in this room. Only one of the four windows actually opened. What they need, she thought, shoving it wide open, is to toughen up a bit. People die—and die unexpectedly. Both her parents were dead. That was hardly the worst thing that had ever happened to her. People disappoint and horrify you in a thousand different ways, Stuart, that you cannot possibly imagine. You move on. You move on, she told him with her eyes as she picked up his cereal bowl and juice glass and bade him a good day, whatever that consisted of.

She pushed through the swinging door into the kitchen. Walt scrambled and strained on the slippery linoleum to rise and greet her.

"Here you go. Here you go," she cooed. She got behind him and hoisted his quivering flanks level to his front shoulders. He bristled—he didn't like her having to help him—and headed for the back door as if he'd lived here all his life. Before letting him out she squatted down by his face. "You didn't sleep in my room last night. Why not?" He put his head on her shoulder and sighed. His nose was cold where it touched behind her ear. She ran her hands from his skull down his neck and along his long rib cage. His hair was coarse and camel brown except on his face, which was a silky, distinguished white. No one knew what kind of mix he was, though people loved to toss out suggestions. Shepherd, collie, retriever, boxer, Great Dane—she'd heard it all. He probably did have some Rhodesian ridgeback, because of how his hair tufted along his spine. She'd found him on the way out of Texas all those years ago, in a cardboard box at a gas station. He'd looked at her as if he knew exactly where she was going and why. She didn't have those answers yet, so she paid the man five dollars and Walt slept on her lap as they headed East.

Walt sighed again, then lifted his head and pressed his face to the seam of the door, to the tiny wind blowing through. She let him out and when he just stood at the top of the back porch, she tapped at the window and said, "Go on, baby."

He took the steps slowly, nearly sideways, his hind legs flopping together, then separating once on flat ground. He looked back briefly before trotting forward to sniff the snarled remains of a flower bed.

She had been aware, when she came into the kitchen, of others at the table, but once beside Walt she'd forgotten them altogether. It was as if all their noises had been suspended, and now, as she turned around, the memory of their chatter came back in a delayed but clamorous rush.

She was startled to see Peter among them, dressed, combed, with a plate of something in front of him. He usually emerged at the last possible minute. Relief rushed up, weakening her, relief and the awareness that her fear was just as strong here as anywhere.

Fran and Caleb were studying her, not with the respectful scrutiny of students on the first day of class but with cold, leery observation.

The smell in the kitchen was disarming. It was nothing like the slightly chemical, overcooked smell in the Fayer cafeteria in the morning.

"Good morning, early birds," she said cheerfully, trying to establish that playful authority she found so easily in the classroom.

"How old is that dog?" Fran said.

"Sixteen."

"Same as Peter," Caleb said.

"Peter's not sixteen yet." Children could be so loose with their ages. Peter wouldn't be sixteen until August. "Who's the chef?"

"Fran is. Want some French toast, Mom?"

"Cup of coffee's fine for me."

"It's over there." Fran pointed to a percolator in the corner. "I just made a second pot."

Vida hoped to find the mugs in the first cupboard she opened, but it took three tries. She scanned the counters and shelves for sugar.

"In the canister," Fran said finally. She was clearly enjoying herself.

"You ready?" Vida said to Peter, scooping her schoolbag (the freshman quizzes uncorrected, *Tess* unopened, the junior author profiles untouched) off the hook with her free hand.

He nodded, but took his time with the few bites left on his plate. Fran slapped another piece of French toast on Caleb's plate, then doused it with syrup.

Vida felt she should ask when their bus came and if they'd done their homework, but they'd been carrying on without her inquiries all their lives. She asked instead if they would let Walt in before they left.

Peter walked ahead of her to the car, his knapsack stuffed with books he hadn't opened all weekend. He wouldn't get away with it; he couldn't charm his teachers with an elaborate tale and heart-crossed promises.

The temperature had fallen further and though the ground still gave slightly beneath her shoes, the hard dead smell of winter seemed to be rising up from it. The trees in the yard jerked in the cold wind, trying to dislodge the few remaining clusters of brown leaves. It was a dreadful time of year. She hated teaching *Tess*, though for years

she had been told it was her signature book. The experience of reading *Tess* with Mrs. Avery sophomore year was reenacted in skits and
referred to in yearbooks. It lived on in countless mentions by remi-
niscing alumni in the tri-annual bulletin. But for Vida, the book
was a torture. She had never cared about that overly naive, peony-
mouthed girl who is buffeted by a series of impossible coincidences
from one gloomy town to another and across four hundred and sixteen pages before she gets her just deserts at the scaffold. She did
have an appreciation for Hardy's descriptions and his worries about
the effects of the Industrial Age on the land and its people. She used
to believe it was her discussions of this "ache of modernism" that
made the book meaningful to her students, but she had come to
realize that it was her own lack of sympathy for the girl that galvanized them. By the end their attachment to Tess herself was fierce,
and their devastation at her demise profound.

They got behind a garbage truck. Vida lit a cigarette as the two
men in back leapt from the runner, separated to opposite sides of the
street, hurled bags three at a time up and over the truck's backside,
and hopped back on just as the truck jerked ahead. White steam
streamed from their nostrils. They wore no gloves and drank no coffee
and yet they seemed warm and full of energy. They'd probably been
up since three, and soon they would be done. They'd go to a diner
for lunch—Reubens, french fries, a few beers. Then they'd sleep—at
a girlfriend's, or their mother's, or in their own solitary bed in a one-
room apartment on Water Street, their muscles tired, their bellies full,
their minds thoughtless as cows. The truck stopped again, and the
man on the left, having caught Vida's covetous eye, grinned at her.
She glanced quickly away in what felt like fright. The truck veered off
then, but the acknowledgment made her uneasy for several more
blocks, as if a character in a book had addressed her by name.

The sun hung small and naked above the rooftops, unable to
push itself fully through the pale cloud bank. They passed a 7-Eleven

and a launderette. In both windows middle-aged women stared blankly out. She thought again of *Tess* and wondered whether she might like it better if she assigned it in the spring.

Ahead of them the bridge to Fayer rose up in a high arc, and its sides were a series of thin squat rails, allowing for a full view of the harbor and its boatyards on the right and the open ocean on the left, with a few fishing trawlers heading toward the horizon. There was often heated talk, especially in the weeks following an accident, of building a wall on either side of this bridge, but Vida was pleased the view had remained, unimpeded by safety and common sense.

It ran nine-tenths of a mile and she took it slowly, like a tourist. Light poured into the car from all sides, an opaque blue wavering light, as they rose toward the height of the bridge. She loved the carnival-like ride of it, the web of patina-green supports above and the false yet convincing sense of sheer solidity beneath her tires. She remembered the few times last summer when she had crossed the water back to Fayer after an evening with Tom, and though she had felt at the time confused and conflicted, the memory now was peaceful. She took a long sip of the coffee she'd wedged between her knees. They were falling now, falling through the early light over cold blue water. She felt happy and even slightly sexual until she remembered the two nights since her wedding, and the feeling recoiled.

"Why is your hair like that?"

Damn. Her hair. "Will you check in there for my barrette?"

Peter flipped open the glove compartment and plunged his hand into the mass of candy wrappers and receipts. "Nope. Nothing."

Vida pulled out the ashtray, stuck her fingers into other dark cubbyholes of the Dodge's dash, then slid her hand beneath the seat. "Damn." In nineteen years, she'd never taught a class without her hair firmly yanked back.

"They have rubber bands in the office," Peter said.

It was true. But she avoided the office, and Carol, now.

They drove through Fayer's tiny center, a small deposit of buildings: a brick police station, a white clapboard church, a stone library, and a few green store awnings. Several people were out, tugged along by dogs or children. She had never known these streets well, never seen them at this time of day. And yet they beckoned to her now.

The road out of town clung to the ocean. Even when a patch of woods or a summer estate blocked it from view, it was always with you, in the wet morning mist, the sandy roadsides, and the seagulls crying out.

"Do you think those people will be killed?" Peter said. He reminded her of Tom already, the concern in his voice as if he personally knew each one of those unlucky paper pushers halfway around the world.

"Not a chance. It would be suicide for the Iranians. There'll be some sort of negotiations today and by supper they'll be free. These things wrap up very quickly." She tried to think of an example and couldn't. She was hopeless when it came to historical facts. The events didn't adhere properly in her brain. She never understood why moments in novels were unforgettable, while in real life the details slipped quickly away. A few weeks ago she couldn't even explain the Bay of Pigs to Peter. All she knew was that she was reading *Middlemarch* at the time. She remembered Dorothea and the wretched Casaubon, and how they had just arrived in Rome for their wedding journey when her mother called her in to listen to President Kennedy's speech. But she couldn't recall what he'd said or in what order the events had unfolded or exactly how it had been resolved. All that came to her when she tried was Dorothea and Will's trembling kiss by the window at the end.

They passed through the stone pillars, *Scientia* carved into one and *In Perpetuum* into the other, and followed the slow-moving line of station wagons up the hill. She hadn't been part of this carpool convergence for sixteen years. She glanced over the girls' field to their old house and the path that ran across a ridge to the school. When he was younger, Peter had a small red canvas backpack that was never filled with more than a pencil and a few exercise sheets. He'd run ahead of her on that path to school, the nearly empty backpack bobbing behind him, stopping only to scoop up something from the ground and drop it into her hand, the soft brown ball of a frightened caterpillar or a long, sticky worm.

There was no ancestral tug as the mansion came into view. There never was. The oversized house, with its bays, turrets, and copper-plated mansard roof, was a school to her, just as it was to everyone else creeping up the long driveway this morning.

Vida pulled into her faculty spot beside the cafeteria. Through one window, a few students from Peter's class hunched over their notes, cramming for something, and through another Marjorie and Olivia in their white uniforms and nurses' shoes were already setting up for the lower school snack.

They sat for a moment in the stilled car.

"You have a test today?" she asked.

"Quiz."

"History?"

"Yeah." He was poised to bolt. He didn't like to be seen walking into school with her anymore.

She could tell he was worried, but she couldn't brush his bangs out of his eyes or lift his chin toward her. She couldn't do that anymore, if she ever had. He was changing so fast and she was too scared to look at him for any length of time. "Did you get a chance to study last night?" she said gently.

He gave some sort of stifled snort through his nose and shook his head. It was rude—the snort, the aversion of his eyes, the lack of words. She wasn't used to rudeness in him. But before she could correct him, he got out and slumped away around the building to the front entrance where he would blend in with the rest.

How dare he be disillusioned already. She slid her bookbag from the backseat onto her lap and shoved open her door. Screw it if he didn't like it. He'd gotten what he asked for. Welcome to life and all its shitty little tricks. Her irritation at him rose, chafing hard against her affection. This was the nameless emotion she felt most in life, this abrasion of love meeting anger.

She walked up the scrubby knoll to the basement entrance, her tight fists bared to the cold, her head leading her body like a sledgehammer. She was a hard woman. Yet Tom said last summer, when he first kissed her, that she was like a heron, with her long neck and delicate bones.

In the vestibule outside the auditorium there was a bronze bust of her grandfather. No delicate man, he. His wild wiry eyebrows, suspended at the edge of his enormous brow, and his thick, nearly detached jaw belonged in a natural history museum. He had the childlike impatience of an old man who did not want to sit for a sculptor, who did not care about his house being transformed into a school, despite all the undeserved credit bestowed upon him. He'd been forced to sell because his only child, Vida's mother, had married a dreamer who'd whistled through the family's money within a decade. Though she had no memories of ever having visited this house, she did remember him, a crooked branch of a man, speechless from strokes, tufts of white hair growing from the tops of his ears. He was the one who named her. He hadn't spoken for months but when her mother placed her in his arms for the first time, saying, "It's baby Vivian, Grandy," he smiled so wide her mother said she heard his face crack, and he said eloquently, seemingly proficient in a language no one had known he knew, "No, mi amor, su nombre es Vida." Another crack, then "Life!" That was his final word, though it took him several more years and the loss of his house to die. When Vida left Texas all those years later, without a map or a plan, nothing surprised her more than finding herself in Fayer, at the enormous front door of her grandfather's house. No one had told her it had become a school. Within a few weeks she had a job as a substitute English teacher, and by the next fall she'd been given a full-time contract and the gardener's cottage.

Though she'd requested high school, they started her with the sixth grade and she'd had to push her way up a grade a year until she'd secured herself a spot in the English department of the upper school. Since then, she'd turned down every promotion offered to her: English chair three times, dean of students, dean of faculty, curriculum director, and assistant head of school. The only thing Fayer Academy had offered her that she'd accepted, above and beyond a teaching contract each year, was the Hutchinson Prize, chosen and awarded at graduation by the senior class for superior teaching, which she'd received four times, most recently last June. She didn't know then, as she rose to accept another sparkling silver bowl, that a man named Tom Belou was seated in the seventeenth row. What she did know is that she was a fool at the podium, fighting back tears of all things, tears for the senior class with whom she'd formed a special, unexpected bond, and tears for her dear friend Carol whose son, she had learned that morning, had committed suicide. She'd pushed out a few platitudes of thanks and hurried back to her seat beside Peter, raw and embarrassed. At that moment, Tom claimed, Vida became the first thing since the death of his wife to disturb him, to make him anxious for the passing of time as one senior then another then another rose from a folding chair, ambled self-consciously across the grass to the lectern, received a diploma, and ambled back.

By the end of the ceremony he'd worked his way to her row of seats and was the first to congratulate her on her award. He was the godfather of one of the graduates, he told her. Could she join them for dinner? She didn't like thinking back on this day and the breaks in her voice at the podium. What could he have seen in her then?

Perhaps it wasn't her at all but that crazy senior class whom she'd loved, who'd risen and hooted and whooped as she walked to the lectern, as if she were not a teacher but a stripper in nothing but high heels and tassels. Was it simply the energy of that moment, such a contrast to the wake of death he found himself bobbing in? Here was life, he might have said to himself; seize it now. Oh she would disappoint him. She was not life. They were all wrong about that.

Assembly had already started. On stage, Greg Rathburn, the history chair who took every world occurrence personally, was explaining the events in Iran. Vida remained in the doorway instead of taking her seat with the juniors across the room. Greg asked for a moment of silence for the ninety Americans being held at the embassy. Vida bent her head but did not shut her eyes or think of the hostages. It was hardly silence with the irrepressible hum of four hundred and twenty-four students who had been separated for a whole weekend. It lasted a long time. After a while, she raised her head in impatience. As always, Brick Howells and Charlie Grant, headmaster and sidekick, stood at their podiums bathed in their own private spotlights. When Greg solemnly thanked the school, Brick jerked his head up like a choirboy feigning prayer while Charlie kept his head bowed for a second too long, as if the interminable moment had not been quite long enough for all of his good thoughts. Phonies to a man, she thought.

"On a much happier note," Brick said, glancing down at his notes as young Greg, heartthrob, former Fayer swimming star, swung himself off the stage. "A little bird has told me that our very own Mrs. Avery was married this weekend." Bursts of applause as surprised heads craned toward her usual seat and then, after a struggle, found her at the door. The applause was stronger now, accompanied by repetitive grunts as if she had made a touchdown. Vida endured the attention, wishing she could see through the heads of the upperclassmen to the front where Peter sat with the rest of the tenth graders. What expression would he have on his face? Why had he been so angry this morning? Brick spoke through the clapping: "You will be courteous enough to call her Mrs. *Belou* from now on." More cheers, as if replacing your identity were some great achievement.

The presumptuousness of Brick Howells. What right had he to change her professional name without asking? And here, before the whole school, when she hadn't even thought to mention her marriage to her students, let alone present them with a new label for her person. "Have a fruitful day," the old git concluded. Vida spun away from the auditorium before anyone could catch her.

Her classroom was the only one on the third floor of the mansion. Brick had put her up there nine years ago to teach an unruly group of eighth graders, and the next year she'd insisted on teaching all her classes in the room. Her students made a fuss about the steep climb, but Vida loved those old uninstitutionalized back stairs that carried her from the loud reverberating blend of instruction, curiosity, and resistance that could be heard down the long hall of former bedrooms on the second floor to the musty silence of her attic. All they'd had to do to make a real classroom for her up here was punch out a wall. The ceiling was high, and the series of long lean windows at the far southern end brought in so much light Vida rarely had to switch on the fluorescent bars they'd installed.

The rest of the mansion, despite the sweeping front staircase and many fireplaces, no longer looked or smelled like anything but a school. Up here, however, Vida felt the old house. She could hear the rustling haste of the servant girls as they dressed in these rooms before dawn, just seconds ahead of the summoning bell of her mother's impatient ancestors. Other teachers did not understand her insistence on remaining on the third floor, especially now since the science wing was finished and there were classrooms to spare. She didn't understand how they could bear the distractions of first- and second-story teaching: people idly peered through the eye-level window on each door, interrupted for chalk or Kleenex, or delivered thoroughly unurgent messages, all as if forty minutes were not already a totally insufficient amount of time in a day to plant a few new ideas in the heads of these students. No one barged in on her classroom up here unless it was dire. If one of her colleagues ever made the journey up, they would inevitably complain about the smell. It was so moldy, they all said, like a wet wool blanket left for about a hundred years. But Vida loved that smell. It smelled the way Texas never could. And most important, she had her own private bathroom with a dead bolt she installed herself.

It was a dark morning and Vida reluctantly turned on the overhead. She pulled out *Tess* from her bag, set it on the desk, then went to the board and wrote

> Sir John
> green malt in floor.
> blighted star

It was all completely rote. This was her thirteenth year of teaching the book. The bell rang. Up here it was more a vibration than a noise, followed soon after by stronger tremors as every student in the building headed to their first class. Soon she could hear her tenth graders heckling each other up the stairs.

"Nice boots, Frizz."

"He parked his Harley out back."

"Walk much, Lindsey?"

"Eat much, Tank?"

"Jesus, Michael. Quit touching me."

Slowly they began to fill the room with their insults and self-consciousness, their collective hours at the mirror, and all their elaborate, transparent airs. They exhausted Vida with their attempts at self-possession, the boys and their cynicism, the girls and their shiny smelly lips.

She heard a girl whisper to another, "'Green malt in floor'?"

The second bell rang and by the time it had finished the great mass of them had divided like cells into individual seats.

Harry Knox, an earnest young man with a feeble frame and large head, addressed her. "Forgive me, Mrs. Avery, but I'm not sure I under—"

"Mrs. Belou!" someone bellowed beside him.

This gave Harry pause. He looked at Vida, then down at his notebook. He seemed to have forgotten his point. Then he flipped his head back up at her. "How do you spell that?"

She sucked in a breath and wrote Tom's name on the board. BELOU. Then she put a MRS. in front of it. It seemed to stare back at her, mocking her in some way. *What had she done?*

They were all looking at her, not as their teacher but as a woman who had just gotten married. *Married.* She felt heavy and mealy, like there was wet sand beneath her skin.

"Hey, now you're like Vida Blue, the baseball player."

"She's Veeda, not Vyda."

"Why aren't you on a honeymoon?" someone in back asked.

"Let's talk about Tess. She's far more interesting."

"So far in this class I've liked what we've read." Amy said.

"Everyone struggles with *Tess* at first," Vida said.

"When do people start liking it?"

"Around page four hundred and sixteen."

Amy flipped through the fat paperback. "I knew it. The very last page."

"*Tess* is a rite of passage," Vida offered, and they wrote it down in their notebooks. Only a few would know what she meant, but she felt impatient with them for stepping behind the curtain of her private life. They could look it up themselves.

"Why do they have to describe everything so vociferously?"

"First of all, Andrew, who is 'they'?"

He looked on the front of his book. "Thomas Hardy."

"One person, singular. And do you really mean vociferously, or might you be referring to another word in the V section of your PSAT study guide?"

Vida could see the long lists of words twisting around in Andrew's head. The class offered him other choices.

"Verbosely."

"Voluminously."

"Vacuously."

Andrew nodded. "All of the above. They go"—she gave him her eye—"*he* goes on forever."

"Example, please?"

"Here. Page twenty-two. 'The village of Marlott lay amid the north-eastern undulations of the beautiful Vale of Blakemore or Blackmoor aforesaid'—if he already said it why's he saying it again? 'The Vale was known in former times as the Forest of the White Hart, from a curious legend of King Henry the Third. . . .' Oh my God, the guy can't stop himself."

"Okay, Hemingway, I want you to remember that paragraph when you get to page four hundred and sixteen."

"I can't conceive of getting to page four hundred and sixteen in this book."

"You will, because you're going to need a good grade in this class to balance out your abysmal verbal test scores. And when you get there, I want you to go back and read that passage and you'll see

Hardy has managed to stuff most of the plot of this novel into that description of Tess's hometown."

"Does Tess die like the white hart?"

You couldn't get much past Helen Cavanough. You could only throw her off with a flat-faced lie. "Of course Tess doesn't die. Now take out a piece of paper." The class groaned. "Not for a quiz. I want you to write four interesting detailed sentences about your hometown."

They liked this kind of exercise, and began writing immediately.

Vida moved to the other side of her desk. She sat in the uncomfortable captain's chair with the school's insignia stamped in gold at her back, and opened her own notebook to a blank page. Lydia Rezo, who also taught the creative writing course, always did the exercises she assigned her students and even read what she'd written aloud to them. Vida never did, but she felt agitated today, and the act of sitting and holding a pencil was soothing. *Norsett.* Though it had been her town for less than forty-eight hours, as she began writing the word she felt she had a lot to say; but once it was there on the page her thoughts evaporated.

"Don't think, Mrs. Belou, write," said Brian, mimicking her when she caught her students staring into space for too long during essay tests.

Vida wrote. *I got married yesterday. I am married. Hello my name is Vida Belou.* She stopped again. She was a hopeless writer who taught writing. She was like Joe Cox, Fayer's beloved lacrosse coach, who'd never heard of the game when he took the job. Like Mitch Calhoun, who taught *Moby Dick* year after year having only read the first page. *I am a fraud.* She wanted to try and write one beautiful sentence. What to her was beautiful? *This morning the bridge stretched out over the Atlantic like a* . . . Some kind of bird? A diver? Something more abstract like a promise or a long-awaited answer? Her mind burned in frustration.

Michael cleared his throat and Vida looked up to find every student watching her. How long had it been? She had no idea.

"Okay," she said, closing her notebook, rising. "Let's hear a few."

No one raised a hand. She was used to this. She scanned the room for a solid start. Danny had his head tucked into his neck, which meant he liked what he'd written. She nodded at him. "Let's hear it, Dan."

The boy looked stricken, as if he never imagined having to share these words. He wasn't the kind of student who would ever dare refuse, though his eyes begged her to choose again. On another day she might have relented and shifted her request to Helen beside him. But today she did not. Danny was from Norsett, too, and she was curious to know what he'd say about the place. "Go ahead."

His face splotched red and he inched closer to his page. "Norsett is an old fishing port from which in the nineteenth century sailors traveled as far as the Bay of Fundy to bring back tuna and cod. Behind the old white church lies the graveyard, the flattest patch of land in town and enclosed by iron gates with iron roses on each handle, where the town's seafaring dead are buried." He took in a wobbly breath. "My mother's body is an anomaly there, a thirty-two-year-old woman who never learned how to swim."

She had known this child since he came to the school in fifth grade. She had taught him three years in a row. How did she not know that his mother had died? Had she once known, then forgotten? She was aware of the spreading length of her silence.

"It's only three sentences," he said.

"Three incredible sentences," Helen said.

Nearly everyone in the class grunted their agreement. Vida knew something more was needed, something that recognized the quality and sophistication of the writing. She felt incapable of those words. She hated it when students got so personal, and she never expected it of Danny. She hoped Fran and Caleb weren't writing things like this in their English classes, tying up the tongues of their teachers. "Most of those fishermen didn't know how to swim either." she offered.

"Oh," Danny said, without looking up.

"Would anyone else like to read?"

"After that? No thanks," Lindsey said.

Perhaps it was cruel to have forced only Danny to read, but the thought of another soul bared this morning was more than she could tolerate. "Hold on to these descriptions, and when we're done with *Tess* we can go back to them and see if you can see how you've been shaped by your geography the way Tess was shaped by hers. Now, let's look at all that voluminous verbiage again." She looked down at her copy of the book and the twelve years of notes crammed into the narrow margins in different colors and shades of ink. "Can you describe the Vale, or as we say, Andrew, the valley?"

Heads bent over books. Then a hand shot up. "It's different from other places nearby."

"How?"

"It's nicer, prettier."

"Where does it say that?"

"Page three. 'Here, in the valley, the world seems to be constructed upon a smaller and more delicate scale.'"

"Okay. Different from others, nicer, prettier, more delicate . . . ?"

"He's describing Tess, too," Helen offered.

"How do you know?"

"When he introduces her he says something about her lack of experience. She's sort of sheltered like the valley."

"Good. What else?"

"At the dance, that boy notices her and then at the end regrets that he did not dance with her," Danny said. "She stands out to him."

Vida felt there was forgiveness in his voice. "Like the Vale of Blakemore stands out among the others."

"Excellent," she said, thanking him for understanding her. "What about Hardy's insistence that the Vale is not brown and dry but green and fertile?"

Heads dropped again, even Danny's and Helen's. They were deliberately avoiding this part. Pages rustled, but no one responded.

Vida lifted her chin to the back of the classroom. "Kristina? What do you think?" Here was a girl who should know. She'd been caught this fall in the shower of the boys' locker room.

But Kristina was saved by a knock. Vida's students sat in perfect stillness as she went to the door. Whatever it was would be serious, and the only way to hear the whisperings between teachers was to stop breathing.

Vida stepped outside the classroom to find Charlie Grove in the dim attic corridor.

"Jesus, Vida, it's like the House of Usher up here. I can't believe you actually choose—"

"What's going on, Charlie?" She was aware of noise coming up from the bottom of her stairs, some sort of clanging down on the second floor.

"We've just had a call from the hospital. It's Lydia. She fell getting into the bathtub this morning and broke her leg and I don't know what else."

"In the tub? She broke her leg in the tub?"

"There may be some head injury as well," he said, as if to preempt further ridicule. He didn't like ridicule, probably having suffered, like most teachers, so much of it in school as a child.

She realized that the clanking below was from the chairs that Lydia's students were already carrying up her stairs. "But Peter's in that class."

"It will just be for a few days at most. It's the only thing that makes sense. Why have them disrupting the library when you're teaching the same thing up here?"

It was hardly the same thing. Lydia didn't teach, she *emoted*. She was incapable of thought. She was only interested in the characters' *feelings*, particularly the female characters' feelings as they related to their oppression by men. Lydia was Fayer's lone feminist. But arguing with him about stylistic differences would just mean losing more minutes. "Okay," she said. "Send them up."

And so the other section of sophomore English staggered in, lugging their chairs with the thick flat right arm that served as a desk. Lydia liked to arrange her students in a horseshoe, but Vida kept hers in rows. She maintained it was in nobody's interest to allow teenagers to ogle each other's bodies. She directed the newcomers to the back and had them make three new, albeit tight, rows. Peter was the last to come in, and put himself at the end of the back row, the farthest point possible from her. The only thing she had ever asked of Brick was that she never have to have authority over Peter, not even for forty minutes, not even for a study hall. How do you break your leg in the tub? She was careful not to look directly at him and yet she was aware of his every movement. He leaned down and tugged a notebook impatiently out of his bag, then the book. He hadn't even started it; the binding was unbroken. He got a pencil out of a side pocket, then slumped even farther down in his seat. They were equally miserable that he was here.

"What page are you all on, Caroline?" Vida asked one of her best students from last year.

"Forty-six."

She couldn't resist. "And what have you been discussing?"

"We talked about upward mobility and downward mobility, how some families are on their way up, like a lot of ours, and how

the Durbeyfields were on their way down, having once been rich
d'Urbervilles."

"I see," she said, chastened. Maybe there was more teaching
happening in Lydia's classroom than she had realized. "Well then,
you'll be able to help us. We were just talking about the parallels
between Tess and the Vale of Blakemore, the way she emerges as a
sort of living doppelganger, if you will, to the land itself. The Vale is
sheltered and set apart, constructed on a more delicate scale, and—
this is where we left off—not dry but green and fertile. Kristina,
you've had a few extra minutes to think about that, what say you?"
She didn't know if it was Peter or a sudden sense of competition
with Lydia that was making her show off a bit.

Kristina peered into her book.

"Let's hear one of Hardy's descriptions of her."

She tussled with a few pages but came up with nothing. Here
was an intelligent girl who'd let her boobs grow bigger than her brain.

Vida glanced at the clock. Half the period was over. She hadn't
taught them a thing. "Here. Page twenty-six. 'As she walked along
to-day, for all her bouncing, handsome womanliness, you could
sometimes see her twelfth year in her cheeks or her ninth sparkling from her eyes; and even her fifth would flit over the curves
of her mouth now and then.'" She looked up from the passage to
see if there were signs of comprehension anywhere. A piece of her
hair had fallen across her cheek and she pushed it away. By mistake she caught eyes with Peter, who seemed to be not just looking at her but seeing her, seeing through her taut face to one of
her own younger selves, the seven-year-old who lost her two front
teeth at the same time and never stopped smiling about it. She remembered exactly how it felt, the two tender pockets in her gums
and the noises she could get her tongue to make with them. She
forgot where she was going with this. "Can anyone find anything
else about Tess? Mark?"

"It says, 'She was a fine and handsome girl—not handsomer than some others, possibly—but her mobile peony mouth and large innocent eyes added eloquence to color and shape.'"

"How old is Tess?" There. That's where she was going.

"It doesn't say," Michael said.

"Take a guess," Vida said. She was aware of speaking only to the side of the room Peter was not on. It was utterly unnerving, having him in her classroom. Without saying a word, he seemed to bring a sort of skepticism to the place, the only place where she was truly comfortable.

"Sixteen?"

"Why?"

"You said guess."

"She's part woman and part girl," Helen said.

"Good. And her mouth is a peony. Know what a peony is?"

"A flower?"

"Yes, a fat red flower. This girl is blossoming. She's ripe. She's fresh. She's like those green fields of Marlott." She was trying to look past them all, out the window, but again her gaze fell on Peter's. Why was he looking at her like that? Briefly, unwillingly, Vida saw herself at sixteen reading a book on a porch, and felt for an instant that lost intoxication of youth, that faith in life. Then Peter looked away.

"What about those?" Karen asked, pointing. She was not a strong student, but she was highly organized and didn't like to leave class with any loose ends.

Vida glanced at the board behind her. "Okay, good. I was just getting to that." She'd completely forgotten about the three terms she'd put up there. "Let's start with Sir John. Anyone?" She watched how students like Helen and Danny didn't bother with easy ones like this, waiting instead for the more intricate puzzles only they could solve. "Peter?" She needed to establish to the class that she would not play favorites, even if it meant humiliating him.

"It's Tess's father. He's walking along and that guy"—he quickly corrected himself before she could—"that parson"—(clearly he had no idea what the word meant but pushed on—"passes by and says, 'Good-night, Sir John.'"

"And?"

"And?"

"How does Tess's father respond?"

"I'm not sure." He hadn't even read the whole of the first page.

Without looking at her book, Vida said, "'Then what might your meaning be in calling me "Sir John" these different times, when I be plain Jack Durbeyfield the haggler?'" To a group of tenth graders in New England, her nineteenth-century Dorset accent was quite authentic. Even Peter laughed.

Lindsey raised her hand. "Once he finds out he's a d'Urberville, he starts acting differently, even though he doesn't have any more money than he had before."

"So by simply calling out 'Good-night, Sir John,' instead of 'Jack,' the parson sets the whole novel in motion." She watched them scribble. That sentence would appear on nearly every essay next week. "Okay, moving on. Blighted star."

"But what about 'green malt in floor'?" Karen said in alarm.

"Anyone?" She had hoped to skip over that one. She didn't feel like discussing sex and its repercussions now that Peter was in the classroom.

They all turned to the page and pretended to think.

"Why would someone say that Tess is so pretty her mother should mind she doesn't get green malt in floor?" Let's just say it and be done with it, she thought. But they kept their heads tucked down into their chests like sleeping pigeons. "What would make people in the late nineteenth century worry about a sixteen-year-old girl with a mouth like peony? What was the one thing that could ruin her?"

"If she got knocked up?" Kristina blurted.

Knocked up. The expression startled her, and she only managed a nod.

"What would happen to an unmarried girl if she got pregnant back then?" Jennifer asked.

The whole room began speaking at once, including Lydia's students, who'd been so quiet up to now.

"She'd be a total outcast."

"She'd be like an untouchable."

"She'd never be able to marry."

The class was galvanized by the subject, by its proximity to sex. Peter wasn't looking at her now. Nor was he speaking. He was wagging his pencil between two fingers, making it thump like a tail on his notebook. He was smirking at Kristina. It was something in the smirk that brought it on, or in the steady, nearly hostile whacks of the yellow pencil on the page.

"And the guy? What happened to the guy?"

"Nothing would happen to the guy. He was a stud."

"Just like nowadays."

It began so small, small as a pinprick, in her chest. It was the familiar sting of fear but then it spread, its great wings opening all at once, her breath gone, her mind seized like an animal caught in a trap. It was the terror of the mornings and the terror of dream— a terror that had never ever visited her in her classroom before.

She was only partially aware of a new boy from Lydia's class saying something about his cousin. "She was in eleventh grade. Now she's in a mental hospital." Kevin, she suspected his name was.

"What about the baby?"

"They made her get rid of it. That's why she went crazy."

Peter seemed to love the disruption, the cacophony, the mutiny in the room. The pencil looked so small in his hand. When had his hand grown so big?

"Can abortions make you go crazy?"

She looked at the other hand, nestled near his knee. It seemed smaller, weaker. Like a wave, her fear of him began to pull back.

"This one did her. She's a complete nutcase now."

Her own class was watching her, waiting. Never were they allowed to pursue a tangent like this.

"Oh for crying out loud," she said finally. "That's enough." She could feel cool dots of sweat on her forehead. A warm weakness spread over her limbs like a balm.

"It's true, I swear, Mrs. Avery."

"Mrs. *Belou!*" several of them said.

"It's utter nonsense. Let's move on. Why does Tess claim they live on a blighted star?"

The clock spooled out its remaining minutes as she led them through the thicket of their own language, through Tess's first recorded day and into the dawn of the next when, delivering the load of beehives her drunken father could not, she falls asleep while driving the cart and kills the family's only horse.

The bell reverberated at their feet. Vida marveled at how easily they shut their books, stuffed them brutally back into their bags, their minds having moved on to the algebra test or a crush in the hallway or an urge for a particular candy bar inside the vending machine. Vida bid them good-bye from her perch on the desk, unable to dismiss the image of the girl in the narrow lane beside the family horse, trying to stem with her hand the strong stream of blood spurting from its chest. She had always balked at Hardy's heavy hand, the way he put Tess on a conveyor belt of tightly orchestrated events that led to her destruction. But Vida could not find that resistance now. Hardy had all but disappeared, leaving this inexperienced girl to carry on alone.

Peter left without a glance, in a cluster of boys, their voices like the low grunts of large animals, their laugh on the stairs sharp and sinister. Then they were gone, and silence, having been kept at bay for forty minutes, rushed back in.

As she turned to erase the board for the next class, she was aware of the thoroughly irrational hope that this time it would turn out differently for Tess. When she reread tomorrow's forty pages, Tess might not meet Alec the fake d'Urberville, or fall asleep in the bed of leaves he gathered for her, or allow him to lie beside her. And in a week or so, perhaps Angel Clare would not mind about her past, would not reject her for so long with such dire consequences.

Her seniors came in, the boys with their size 12 feet, the girls in their mothers' expensive blouses, slapping down their copies of *The Sun Also Rises* on their desks. She was grateful for the shift to Hemingway, to Spain, to characters who would remain characters, silly drunken characters who mattered nothing to her.

Vida picked up the eraser. At eye level were the words MRS. BELOU. With one stroke, they were gone.

At break she went down the two flights of back stairs to get a cup of coffee. Once the servants' pantry, the teachers' lounge, with its buckling linoleum squares and wall of tin sinks, was not the coziest in the mansion. There was a couch and an end table and some desks and chairs for the math and science departments, who could easily correct their multiple-choice tests in the midst of gossip and complaint, but it needed a rug and standing lamps for real comfort, and most teachers only lingered for a few minutes to read their mail or wait for yet another pot of coffee to brew. Today, however, the place was jammed. Faculty crowded around a card table, loading flimsy paper plates with smoked salmon, croissants, muffins, and cubes of fruit. It was the time of year, a month and a half before first-semester grades came out, that the mothers of less than stellar seniors grew frantic and tried to bribe the faculty with expensive food and a little place card in the center of the table declaring, above their carefully written names, their deep appreciation for all the teachers at Fayer.

Vida's first impulse was to sneak down to the cafeteria kitchen, where she knew Marjorie and Olivia would have a pot on, but the smell of baked sugar sucked her in with the rest. She'd just slip in, fill up her mug, grab a muffin, and get back to her office.

"Vida Belou!" Brick Howells bellowed from the middle of the room, the great boom of his voice mostly unimpeded by the mini-bagel halfway down his throat. He placed his pile of food on the table, swallowed, and made for her, carrying his weight as if he were a larger, taller man. His arms reached out for her well before she was within reach. Over the years Brick had tried to fix her up with various men: his wife's brother at a Christmas party, his college roommate at a faculty-trustee luncheon, and his freshly divorced physician at an athletic banquet. And then, a few years ago, having given up on his friends, he licked her on the neck while she was pouring rum into their Cokes in this very room during a Valentine's dance they were chaperoning together. She'd twisted out of his grasp and said, "C'mon, Brick, you can do better than me." He was drunk—they both were—but her words seemed to sober him and he withdrew in agreement.

But here he was now, ready to gather her up in a public, avuncular hug. Thinking fast, she clasped his hands in hers, keeping him two arms' lengths away but preserving the facade of a strong collegial bond. Her fellow teachers cheered. Vida flushed in anger—hadn't the applause at assembly been enough?—which they took for embarrassed thanks, prompting them to clap even louder. Heads of curious students appeared in the door's small window.

"Stop," Vida said, more harshly than she would scold a rambunctious class, but to no avail.

After the clapping, she was unable to escape the warm wishes, the hugs, the dreamy smiles. A new teacher, one of the many young hires this year, tossed up Vida's unclipped hair and said, "I like it. Get married and let it all hang out."

They had, every one of them, misunderstood her entire life. She had never yearned to marry as these people apparently thought she had. Brick Howells was hardly the only person to have attempted the fix-up. How many times had she accepted a dinner invitation from one of them, only to find in their living room some recently devastated fellow wiping his palms on his slacks? You have so much to offer, she was often told, as if she had a tray of cigarettes and candy perpetually strapped to her waist. But these setups had stopped a few years back. Vida realized now, from their relieved, astonished expressions, that they had all given up.

Her life with Peter had been enough. It had. Why had she tinkered with it? She felt incapable of piecing the events of the last five months into any fluid, comprehensible sequence.

"So, you married your fighter pilot," Paul Gove said to her at the coffeemaker.

Men chose the strangest ways to debase each other. Tom had trained in the air force, but by the time he got to the Pacific, the Korean War had ended and after a few weeks they sent him home to resume his work with his father at Belou Clothiers. Exactly how Paul had gleaned this information about Tom was a mystery to Vida.

"I did," she said, with far more conviction than she'd had in the past twenty-four hours. Paul always had this effect on her. His confidence with women made her defiant. In all the years they'd taught together, she'd felt like a horse he was trying to break. Her falling in love with him seemed to be his prerequisite for friendship. She had never complied, thus they had never been friends, but now he wanted to play jilted suitor, not because he had loved her, but simply because she had not loved him.

"Short courtship." He took a sulky bite of a chocolate croissant. "You pregnant?"

It should have been funny—a woman her age having a shotgun wedding—but she couldn't muster a small retort or even a smile, and she turned away from him with her coffee to the plate of banana muffins, her throat inexplicably twisted shut.

She felt Paul's hand on her arm. "I wish you and Tom the very best. I really do."

"Good God. All these best wishes. You all make me feel like I'm entering a battle armed with a feather." She tossed a muffin onto a napkin and climbed back to her office on weakened legs, glad for this free period before another set of seniors.

She sat at her desk in her office, unable to touch the coffee or muffin or her work. She was aware of the black phone to her left, which she only used when Peter was home sick or once when a student fainted and she couldn't revive him. It was a direct outside line, with an unpublished number and no connection to the office, so no parent could reach her here. It never rang. She could pick up the phone now and call Tom. She had his work number in her book, though she'd never used it. And he didn't even know she had a phone up here. Just the idea of calling him made her heart race. What would she say? What had she done?

She thought of all those wary smiles at the wedding reception, some guests not even bothering to hide their astonishment. How did this Vida Avery, boyfriendless as far back as anyone could go, how did she receive this stroke of luck? A mere high school English teacher who wore old moccasins and drank too much at parties—who had suddenly aligned her stars? The same surge of victory collided with the same certainty she would fail.

For lunch Vida had to descend the two flights, then cross the length of the mansion and the two added wings to reach the cafeteria. Because there was not the room or the staff to feed the entire school at once, lunch was spread out over the three middle periods, and fifth-period classes had already begun in many of the rooms she passed. Through the window of Sally Haynes's history class, three juniors stood before a homemade map, tracing what looked like the Silk

Road. Next door, Roger Graver sat in the middle of his psychology elective, mouth open, eyes closed, while his students walked around him in a circle. In ninth-grade English, Yeats himself read "Innesfree" from a tape recorder: ". . . shall have some peace there, for peace comes dropping slow, dropping from . . ." His voice was old and Irish and lovely.

Students past and present hollered out hellos in the hallway as they passed, some sticking to her old name, some trying out the new.

At last she reached the theater, her favorite place to spy. She wedged the door open a crack to hear the two actors on stage beside a kitchen table. To her surprise, the girl was Helen from her sophomore class. It was impossible to reconcile the private, contained Helen with the Helen now hollering at her stage husband, slamming cabinets, hurling a pot against a wall. Within seconds, however, the incongruity was gone, for the Helen on stage obliterated any memory of any other Helen, obliterated the stage itself, forcing you to believe that this was the only reality, right here beneath these lights, these acts, this pain.

"Ticket, please." The voice just behind her ear made her leap. Jerry Poulk held up a plate of french fries floating in ketchup. "They don't seem to need to eat, but I was starving." He bit off half a fry, then nodded toward the stage. "What do you think?"

Vida had assumed he was down there in front, but they had been performing alone, for themselves. They still were, sitting at the table now, Helen crying softly.

"It's a one-act for this Friday's assembly. They ready?" he asked. He was standing too close to her, chewing, the odor of ketchup coming out of his nose.

"She is. Adam, I don't know. Maybe it's just that she outshines him."

"Girls always do at this age."

"Do they?" She shot him a sly eye. He was careful to ignore her.

Jerry had come to Fayer six years ago. He became the new novelty with all his energy and charm and the ridiculous little pony-tail that hung over his tweed jackets. From the start, Vida under-stood his game. He made his students need him emotionally. In his classes he churned them up, then broke them down. Within a few weeks of his arrival, he was never again seen eating lunch, walking a hallway, or leaving the building without some student pressing beside him, the two in a deep, closed conversation. He built an extraordinary drama department. The spring musical, formerly a one-night embarrassment, now ran two weeks, attracted audiences from out of state, and earned the school nearly twenty thousand dollars each year. And each year, Jerry Poulk was screwing around with a member of the cast. At first, it was hard to tell which one. But Vida caught on to his method after a few years: it was always the girl in the fall that he was hardest on, the one who didn't seem to be enjoying the class all that much, the one who wasn't ever seen in fierce private talk with him. But by February she'd have a good part in the musical, if not the lead, and she'd often be found alone on his stage or belting out a song at his piano. By graduation the entanglement would be over, Jerry refueled, spouting off about some European vacation he was planning with his wife and children, the girl underweight and withdrawn. Whether Brick was aware of this pattern, whether any other teacher had caught on, Vida didn't know. She'd decided long ago it was none of her business.

Without answering her, Jerry headed down the center aisle with his plate of fries. Helen and Adam moved downstage, where they stood close to each other in quiet conversation. Helen managed to convey, all the way to Vida at the back of the theater, that weary acquiescence in the wake of an argument, the listening and not-listening, the acceptance of the failure of real communication. Then her husband made a joke and she kissed him so impulsively it seemed impossible that even Helen knew it would happen.

"No!" Jerry barked from a seat in the third row, and Vida closed the door before he could destroy what she had seen. She was alone in the hallway with the smell of boiling oils and overcooked meats. Her lunch period was already half over. How she wished she could go back in and hop up on that stage in possession of new words and new impulses, a truly new identity and not just a different name. Instead she'd have to squeeze in at a corner of the faculty table, forced to listen to the petty November complaints about the soggy fields or disgruntled parents, or to her own mind full of yearning for youth and talents she did not have—and the unpleasant discovery that Helen Cavanough would be Jerry's spring victim.

On Mondays, Vida finished teaching at 1:40. She monitored an eighth-grade study hall in the library from 2:25 to 3:05, where she intercepted notes, separated disruptive elements, and corrected a set of Macbeth quizzes. On her way back up to the third floor, where she would work until Peter's soccer practice ended at five, she stopped in the lounge for more coffee. It was empty now. Nearly all of her colleagues had afternoon obligations: coaching, tutoring, supervising volunteer work or independent projects for the grow-ing nonathletic population. It boggled her mind, the extra hours her coworkers would put in for a few extra bucks in their paychecks each month. On weekdays, she liked to have all her work done before she went home.

There were a few tablespoons of slow-cooked sludge at the bottom of the pot. She rinsed it thoroughly and began again. It was a pleasant place to be, the teachers' lounge in the afternoon when the light, too weak to pass through the windows, clung quietly to the panes, and no voices were there to drown out the hiss and plock of the fresh coffee being made. Vida sat on the brown corduroy sofa and let her head fall back upon the soft lip. She was tired.

"Congratulations, Mrs. Belou." It was the one voice she dreaded hearing. "You probably need a little shut-eye after this weekend." Carol, Brick's secretary, slowed but didn't stop her trajectory to the closet, where the extra office supplies were stored.

Vida sat up straight. Had she slept? The coffee was still and silent in its pot. Carol's knees cracked as she squatted to reach the mimeograph paper in the bottom cabinet. It was never too late to offer condolence. She needed to say something. If only she'd been able to finish that damn letter. She thought of the opening line, Shelley's "Grief awhile is blind . . ." What good were her own small words if she uttered them now? The letter had so much more strength to it, centuries of wisdom. She'd worked on it for days at a time last summer; she had pages of notes filled with gorgeous quotes from everyone from Shakespeare to Bishop, but no coherent letter. If only she could just hand Carol those sheets of paper and be done with it.

She watched her old friend retrieve the reams of paper, balancing on the balls of her feet, her camel-colored skirt stretched tight. Her son had died. Her son had killed himself. And yet little about her had changed. Vida avoided the front office now, but she could still hear Carol's laugh occasionally, spilling down the hallway. Within moments she would rise and pass in front of Vida once more. What could she possibly say to her now, now that she'd missed the funeral, neglected to call or write, had been unable, that first week of school, to catch her alone, though she had tried, she really had. Carol couldn't know about the pages of notes, the hours of research, the pleasure she had taken in finding just the right line. Because of this terrible misunderstanding they had barely spoken all fall (she'd sent her a wedding invitation and Carol had checked the regret box, offered no words at all), and they used to be such friends. Carol used to arrange her lunchtime around Vida's schedule. She wished she could follow her back to the office, pull up that green chair in the corner, and gossip as they had before at this hour of day. Carol might even ask about the wedding night and maybe Vida could have implied something, maybe Carol could have given her some sort of advice. She'd been married nearly thirty years. But Carol was rising now, her heels sinking back into her shoes, paper in arms, and Vida had yet to say a single word to her. Something would come, she knew, when their eyes met. Carol backed out from the closet and, a few feet from the couch, looked directly at her with a tight smile. The windows were behind her, two pale panes like wings on Carol's back. Vida smiled far wider, opened her mouth, and heard the word "Angel" come out. Carol nodded and vanished around the corner.

Angel? Had she really said the word *angel* for Christ's sake?

Vida poured herself the largest mug of coffee on the shelf and slunk back up to the uncomplicated solitude of her third-floor suite.

At five, she drove down to the gym parking lot and waited in her car with the other parents for the JV soccer players to trickle out the locker room door. Peter emerged with his friend Jason. Both boys were bent over from the weight of their knapsacks and talking in that way that made boys so distinct from girls of the same age: brief remarks, no eye contact. It was hard to tell, when they separated near the hood of the Dodge, if they had even said good-bye.

The passenger door creaked, the enormous bag thunked onto the floor, and Peter slumped in.

"Hey there, big guy."

"Hey," he said at the end of a breath. He shot her a quick glance, then stared straight ahead as if the car were already moving.

"How'd it go?"

"What—practice?"

"Practice, history quiz, the day in general."

"Okay."

"Just okay?"

She put the car in gear and headed down the school driveway, relieved to be moving away from Carol, from *Tess,* from the classroom in which suddenly Peter was a student.

Peter didn't answer. She was afraid he was going to bring up the class, the way she had let things unravel. That horrible new boy, Kevin, and his cousin in the mental hospital. It was physical, the mortification this memory produced.

"How'd French go?" French was always a safe subject; they could make fun of Cheryl Perry. His mediocre marks in that class never bothered her as much as they did in other subjects.

"It was stupid. She showed us this movie about this sort of lonely kid. One day he's walking through a kind of junkyard and he sees this painting of a girl. He looks at her a long time, and then this real girl just appears out of nowhere. She's supposed to be the one from the painting, but she doesn't look anything like her. Why do they do that, act as if you can't tell the difference?"

"Suspension of disbelief. They want you to use your imagination."

"In a book maybe. But it's so stupid in a movie."

The car weaved through the unlit narrow roads, then the lighted stretch of the town center and on toward the mainland. The black surface of the water held the soft yellow light from shore, the bluish neons on the bridge, and the slow red and white streaks from the crossing cars.

"Where are you going?' Peter said, slicing through their silence when the car didn't take the right toward Larch Street.

"We need groceries." The word was strange in her mouth.

"Oh." A trace of delight in his voice.

She had come into this store only once before, with Tom last summer before a picnic. They had bought egg salad sandwiches and lemonade. Every person in the place had greeted Tom: the teenager shelving soup, the woman buying toilet paper, the old man laying out the fish on crushed ice. The cashier and the bagger barely let him out of the store with all they wanted to talk about. Out in the parking lot Vida had glanced back to see a line of them at the plate glass, gawking, all their mouths moving at once.

"Be right with you," a man shouted above the gnarl of the meat grinder, then, upon recognizing her, quickly cut the machine, wiped his hands on a rag, and hurried up to the counter. "What can I do you for?"

She looked down into the case of purple meats. In fourteen years she'd made nothing more elaborate than a cheese omelet. "Any suggestions?"

He chose a small roast. In one long complicated gesture, he wrapped it in a fresh sheet of white paper, tied it tight with twine, and marked the side with a black hieroglyph only his daughter at the register could read. "I was really happy to hear about you and Mr. Belou," he said, sliding the package at her. "Mrs. Belou—the former—she was a customer of ours from the very beginning. Special lady." His pale eyes swam unsteadily. "He's a lucky man. Twice blessed." He looked unconvinced.

Vida thanked him, set the roast in the child's seat of the cart, and headed for produce.

"You'll want to put that in at three-fifty for an hour and a half," the butcher called out to her before turning on his machine once again.

In the vegetable aisle, she pulled the string off the meat and tied up her hair.

Peter was waiting for her at the magazines. He looked at the roast, the eight potatoes, the bag of string beans, and the bottle of bourbon. "That's it?"

"I need to get the roast in." Maybe tomorrow night she'd have more stamina for all the choices and the scrutiny.

Larch Street made Vida uneasy. All these houses pressed together seemed to demand something of her as she drove past—a normalcy she couldn't deliver. She hated the curtains in the windows, the decorations at the door. She still had to look carefully at the house numbers to find the right one. She pulled in behind Tom's wagon and cut the engine. The car shook a little, then was still. Above the squat little house, long clouds floated pink in the dark sky, as if it might snow. Here, too, lights were on in every window; everyone was home. Her throat had seized up; she couldn't even swallow her own saliva.

"Aren't you getting out?" Peter's voice was shrill. He had some fear in him, too, and she wished she found it reassuring. All those years they had been alone together and yet she couldn't turn to him now and ask, *What have we done?*

They walked up the steps together without speaking.

Walt made happy circles around her as she moved from the front door to the kitchen with the grocery bag. Fran and Caleb were at the table spreading peanut butter and fluff onto eight slices of bread.

"Those for lunch tomorrow?"

"Dinner. Tonight," Fran said, glancing at the clock.

"I've got dinner. I'm about to whip it up right now."

"That's okay, we can just have these," Caleb said, bouncing, all sugared up just from looking at that crap.

"We're going to have a roast."

"But—"

"It will be ready at seven-thirty."

Fran sunk her knife deep into the peanut butter and left the room. Caleb tried to do the same with the fluff but both jar and knife tumbled to the floor.

"Sorry," he said, squatting to pick it up and then, thinking better of such a reconciliatory gesture, scrambling off with a small whimper, as if she might chase him.

Vida piled up the heavy slices of bread and dumped them in the trash. Walt was making as much noise with his arthritic limbs as he could, demanding to be fed.

"You're home." It was Tom. She'd nearly forgotten about him.

"I am. In all my glory."

How had it all led to this, his leaning in the doorway looking as if she had broken in through a kitchen window? She brushed the crumbs off her skirt but didn't know what to do with her hands after that.

"I'm glad." He came toward her with a face she recognized from the beginning of their dates, when she'd answer the door and there he'd be, grinning as if every moment since he'd last seen her had been spent in anticipation of seeing her again. But now that he'd gotten her, brought her to his house to live, how long could that grin—a grin that expected so much—really last? He kissed her, his tongue reaching for hers. He seemed to have no plans to stop kissing her. Hadn't he seen Fran storm off or heard Caleb squeal? And the roast had to get in the oven or supper wouldn't be ready till midnight.

"Later, cowboy." Where did she come up with these phrases?

"Promise?"

He seemed not to remember last night or the night before. He swung a chair around to face her as she unwrapped the roast and set it in a pan. He wanted to talk about her day. He had a thousand questions. She fought them off with short answers as she cut up potatoes, trimmed beans, and boiled water for the gravy mix she'd found in a cupboard. She glared at the clock; at this time in her old life she'd have eaten in the dining hall already. She'd be home in her slippers under a blanket, reading.

By the time she managed to get dinner on the table, no one seemed particularly hungry. Even Tom, who always polished off his meals at restaurants, picked at his plate. Vida couldn't understand it. The roast had turned out well; the slices looked just like Olivia's at school.

"So, Stu, what went on today?" Tom tried to be light, but he was worried, deeply worried, about his oldest son.

"Not much. Got up, went to work, came home. Same as you."

"Where's that?" Peter asked.

"At E. J.'s."

"Are those people free yet?" Caleb asked his father.

"It's a used record store downtown."

"In Iran? No, sweetheart, I'm afraid they're not."

"You have to be really *cool* to know about it. There's no sign or anything outside," Fran said, trying to provoke her brother and insult Peter all at the same time.

"They'll be out of there soon, I promise," Tom said. He was too soft with Caleb, as if he were a girl.

"You don't know that." Stuart glared down at his plate.

"Only druggies go into E. J.'s. Everyone knows that," Fran said.

"Who said that?" It was exhausting to watch Stuart fighting on two fronts.

"Mom did. One time we were walking past it and I asked her what was in there and that's what she said. Drugs."

"She did not."

"Yes she did."

"You're full of it."

"Stuart," Tom said.

Vida got up to make herself another drink. Usually she only had one on weeknights, but there was the problem of that promise. She mixed the soda with the bourbon slowly.

"Why can't we just give them a bunch of money?" Caleb asked.

"They don't want our money. They want the Shah and *their* money," Stuart told him.

"The what?"

"The American pawn who used to rule their country until the revolution."

"Where is he?"

"In New York."

"Why?"

"He's at some hospital."

"Cornell. In the city," Tom said. "He's got cancer."

"What kind?" all three of his children asked at once.

He didn't know.

"Is he having an operation there?" Caleb asked.

"I think so."

Caleb looked at his father until he explained. "Hers was inoperable. They couldn't operate."

"According to one American doctor."

"Stuart, please."

You could see around Tom's mouth the effects of the pain of the last three years. She had found that pain reassuring at first; it had filled her with a sense of security to know that he had been through loss and survived, that he was the type of person who would survive. And wasn't there a sort of lucky protective coating around people after such a calamity? She had believed that by attaching herself to him she would be protected as well. But now, in his house, perched on a hard chair in his kitchen, she felt like she was back in her parents' house with all its claustrophobia, all the old inexplicable resentments pressing down on them. She took a long sip of her drink. It kept her from screaming at the top of her lungs.

Stuart scraped back his chair and stood.

"Dinner isn't over," Tom said.

"I'm just going to the bathroom," Stuart said, halfway there.

Peter doodled with his fork in the gravy. He'd said nothing since they'd sat down. She had done this to his life, bound him to this seat at this table with these strangers. She glanced at Tom again for a memory of why, of how, but he was intent on cutting through a piece of meat.

Stuart returned, not from the bathroom, Vida guessed, but from a little toke beside an open window. His eyes weren't red but his lashes glistened, from Visine no doubt, and he slipped into his chair with the catlike movements she recognized from the students she busted at school dances.

Finally it was over. Fran helped her clear without having to be asked.

"What's for dessert?" Caleb asked.

Thank God she hadn't gotten any. Another course at this table would do her in. "It's probably not a great idea to have sugar so close to bedtime," she said. The clock on the stove confirmed that it was nearly nine.

"We've always had dessert," Caleb said to his father, tears already slipping beneath the round glasses he wore.

Fran, scraping dishes into the trash, said, "I can't believe you just chucked all those sandwiches. What a waste."

"I have a candy bar in my bag," Peter said to Caleb. "You want that?"

Vida opened her mouth to protest, but Tom covered her hand with a squeeze.

Caleb nodded, and wiped his face. Peter got up and came back with a mangled package of Reese's Cups.

"May I please be excused?" Stuart asked Vida, perfectly politely, the contempt well hidden. It was the first time he'd looked directly at her. His eyes were a pale brown set below soft swollen lids. They were the only part of his body he was unable to make hard and angry. She'd had several students like him over the years, seething, humorless, unattractive boys who made few friends and suffered, again and again, the humiliating passion of unrequited love.

"You may."

The rest fled behind him. The TV went on and she imagined Stuart hulking over it even before she heard Fran tell him to get out of the way.

Tom still had his hand on hers. He lifted his face, and for a moment, before he could master it, she saw the question, her own pounding question. She wished she could offer him the answer but she couldn't, and in her fear she turned away, and when she looked back it was gone. Still holding her hand, he asked her to follow him.

He led her past their children to the bedroom. All her boxes had vanished. Her clothes were in drawers, her dresses on hangers in the closet. In the far corner, on either side of her desk, were two tall bookcases. All her books stood neatly on the shelves.

"I knew you needed them, since you had all those built-in ones in your old place. I just put everything in alphabetically, but you probably have a much more sophisticated way of arranging your books."

"Yes, much." She tried to smile at him. She hadn't realized how much she'd counted on her boxes remaining packed, things remaining temporary, reversible. "How did you do all this?"

"I got back from Springfield at three. And I'd already stained the wood last weekend."

"You *made* these?" She ran her fingers along the edge of a shelf. She couldn't identify the wood but it was a lovely burnished color and sanded to silk. Each side of the top shelf had been carved into long narrow birds. "Herons," she whispered.

Behind her he shut the door and flopped onto the bed.

"They're beautiful," she said, still standing.

"You're beautiful." He sat up and pulled the butcher's twine from her hair. He spread the mass of it (how she had always hated this bulk of frizz, so inexpressive of her and her love of order) from shoulder to shoulder and stroked it with his wide warm hand from the top of her head to the middle of her back. He eased her down on the bed and continued to touch her head and face. This time, he didn't speak at all. His kisses were gentle on her cheek, her neck, her shoulder. Even his mustache was soft. She could feel the bourbon in her system protecting her, obscuring the path back. He rolled her nipple between his thumb and fingers carefully, as if it might break, and desire, that elusive bird, fluttered faintly. Then he got up, snapped the lock in place, and everything died inside her once again.

"I love you, Vida," he said when he finally gave up. "We'll figure all this out." He pulled her naked chest to his and closed his eyes.

Maybe she slept, she wasn't sure. The light was still on. Tom was still beside her, though his grip has loosened. His eyes were open, staring straight ahead at a framed drawing on the far wall she'd never noticed before, a pencil sketch of an infant wrapped loosely in a blanket and held low in its mother's arms, its head resting heavily on her bent wrist, her breast depleted at his cheek. The mother had no head; her figure began at the small knobs of her shoulders and disappeared at the waist, behind the blanket's folds. Her hands were her most expressive feature, the fingers longer than possible, spread carefully above and beneath the sleeping child. Vida understood that Tom had drawn it, that the wife and infant had once been his.

Draw him! Draw his face, Peter had cried all those years ago, and when she refused, tears soaked his collar and bright blotches appeared on his neck but he wouldn't give up. Please! She'd grabbed the pencil and made three thick lines of hair then, her fingers shaking by now, smashed the lead to the paper four more times—first the mouth, then a low bent nose, and finally the eyes, two short vertical lines that nearly punctured the page, eyes that conveyed not cruelty or pain or whatever had made that man do what he'd done to her but surprise, as if he himself were startled to have suddenly been drawn by her. She had wanted the drawing to be uglier, more frightening; even if Peter was only five she wanted him to stop asking and understand that this was a man you must forget, not remember. The picture was cartoonish, the head too round, but when she moved to correct it he snatched it from her. She'd never seen it since.

She remained still. If Tom saw that she was awake he might want to try again. He would keep trying. That was the sort of man he was. So she waited for his eyes to shut, his breathing to thicken, before she pulled on her shirt and slipped quickly out of the room.

The rest of the house was dark. Walt's tail pounded the carpet as she crossed the living room, but he didn't get up. He refused to come into the bedroom now that she shared it with someone else. She needed to see Peter, needed to know he was all right. The door was open, the way Peter liked it. The boys hadn't pulled the shade and a street lamp cast a fan of light across the room. Peter was asleep on a narrow bed that came out of the wall like an ironing board. She glanced over to Stuart's by the window, hoping he slept as deeply as Peter. It was empty. The clock on the bureau read 12:52. She moved quickly back down the hall. No one on the sofa; no one in the kitchen. Where was he?

If he was gone, he'd have taken her car; she'd blocked in Tom's. She headed for the window by the front door that was closest to the driveway, already angry. She needed that car to get to work in the morning, to get more groceries, to drive away from here if need be. She pushed aside the curtain. The Dodge was there, behind Tom's, just as she'd left it. The anger clung. Her eyes scanned the rest of the driveway and the small yard. The grass and bushes seemed frozen in place. It was a winter's night. Fall was over. Another season gone. She could feel the cold on her face through the glass.

Then she saw them. Stuart and a girl. Had they just appeared, apparition-like, or were they there all along? Stuart was leaning back on his elbows against the trunk of her car while the girl performed a trick that made her arms momentarily whirl together like a pinwheel. Vida couldn't hear them but she knew Stuart was saying *That's so easy* as he brought his weight back down on his feet, freeing up his weedy arms to show her. But they just flopped in front of him unmagically. The girl was laughing and said something that made him laugh too. He reached out to grasp her wrists but she was too quick and spun a few feet away from him.

She was a lovely girl, the kind Vida remembered from a decade ago: long, untampered-with hair, silver bracelets, and a skirt of printed cotton. She had a small, foxlike face which helped magnify her round eyes. Stuart hopped up on the car and patted the spot beside him. The girl took a few moments to decide, then scrambled up beside him. He pointed up at the heavy pink clouds and watched her as she watched them move. Just like his father, Vida thought with shock, never having seen a similarity before.

She meant to turn away from the window, but the scene was as compelling as the performance she'd glimpsed on stage at lunchtime. Like Helen, Stuart had transformed himself, and Vida could no longer find the sullen child from dinner in this spry fellow wooing a girl on her car.

They played like kittens; she nudged him off the trunk and he feigned injury until she came to his side, then he leapt up and ran off and she chased him, catching him by the shirttail and zigzagging with him across the yard as he tried to free himself from her small clutch. Then he twisted and stopped and she slammed into his chest. Vida thought they would kiss then, but they just stood there, close and coatless on the frost-stiff grass.

When the girl left, she moved in a slant across the lawn as if pushed by the wind. Just before she turned from the driveway she called out something. To Vida it was a thin underwater sound, but it made Stuart laugh deeply as he walked toward the porch. Though he was only a few yards away from where she stood at the window, he was oblivious to an audience, even as he raised his face to the house. On it was Tom's grin but wider, his eyes nearly forced shut by the bulge of his cheeks. She saw them each simultaneously, Stuart and Tom, as they once were: exuberant, unbridled boys, untouched by grief.

And then the faces fell away, instantly, as Stuart's foot landed on the first step. Vida was relieved. They had frightened her, those faces, two ghosts of what had been. The knob on the front door clicked and Vida, having nowhere else to go, fled down the hallway toward the slit of light escaping beneath the bedroom door of the man she'd just married, toward the hope that he'd remain asleep.

FOUR

THEY ALWAYS CAME TO HIM, STUART'S GIRLS. LATE AT NIGHT, ON FOOT, THEY appeared like magic in the window.

"Hey," Stuart said, a long pulled-out syllable that dipped deep down to a voice he didn't possess with his family.

The girl's words were quieter: "Whatcha doin'?" or "Come out and play, sleepyhead." Sometimes all Peter could hear were the soft taps of her tongue in her mouth as she whispered.

Her face hung in the window as Stuart dressed. They were always pretty, prettier than any girls at Peter's school. They were goddesses (he'd studied Greek mythology last year): Athena, Artemis, or Aphrodite nearly every night through a pane of glass.

The front yard, the driveway, and (with the plump one) the station wagon were Stuart's midnight court. He never made a phone call or went on a date. They came to him. He never brought them inside, even when a covering of snow lay rumpled on the grass. Instead they each trod in it, not seeming to notice the frozen footprints of the night before.

The first one Peter saw was small and giggly, with twenty bracelets on each arm. From his perch on Stuart's bed, he watched them frolic like ponies on the lawn. The next one had pale eyes and painted lips and with her Stuart sat soberly on the bottom step of the porch (Peter pressed his cheek hard against the window to see so far to the left), kicking the ground with his boot. With the third, Stuart didn't seem to talk at all. When she came, he lifted the window and the screen in one quick motion and they began kissing right there, the cold air blowing in over his bare torso across the room to Peter, who squinted his eyes open to watch. This one, the one with the thick curves and butterscotch skin, he brought straight to the station wagon, and all Peter could see were their heads before they pushed the backseat down flat. Unlike in the movies, the car didn't bounce or shake. No one could tell that two people were lying down in it, taking off their clothes.

Nights that there wasn't a girl, he and Stuart talked. Around Vida and Tom, Stuart struggled for the fewest words possible, but in his room he had a lot to say. He was a philosopher, a mystic. Peter had never met anyone like him. He had answers to all the questions Peter had only begun to formulate.

"Are you a popular guy at school, Pete?"

No one had ever called him Pete before. He liked it. He saw that Stuart knew the truth about him so he didn't dare lie. "No."

"Good. If others like you, you are weakening your true being." He was sitting cross-legged on the bed, and for a long time he didn't speak, just breathed noisily with his eyes shut. Then he said, "Chuang Tzu says that if you are mourned at your funeral, you've forgotten the gift God gave you. And if you grieve over someone's death you're a fool."

"Why?"

"Because death is unimportant."

Peter wished he could see it that way.

"Death," Stuart continued, "is simply movement from one form to another. But what you want to achieve is formlessness, so that ultimately you don't know—or care—whether you're dead or alive."

"How do you achieve that, formlessness?"

"Here." Without untangling his legs, he reached down into the stack of library books by his bed. "Let me read you a little something." He flipped through a paperback with cracked-off corners. "'His body is dry like an old legbone. His mind is dead as dead ashes. His knowledge is solid. His wisdom is true! In the deep dark night he wanders free without aim and without design. Who can compare with this toothless man?'"

That night Peter dreamed he was losing teeth; he dreamed Stuart was a dry twig on the pillow in the morning.

Another book was about Eastern surgical practices. It had pictures, hundreds of pictures. Stuart showed Peter some of his favorites. "They've taken out this guy's entire GI tract," he said. "No anesthesia to knock him out, just a few needles there and there."

Peter looked at the man—he was smiling at the camera, with his stomach on the table beside him.

"Surgery," Stuart explained, "is their last resort, whereas here they hardly consider anything else. It's all about using the knife. In Asia they have a one-in-three-hundred rate of cancer, and we have a one-in-seven. And for every eighty people they cure, we cure one." To Peter's relief he shut the book and lay back on his bed. "I told him to take her to Taiwan but he refused. He wouldn't even bring her to this acupuncturist I found in Bristol. People would rather let people *die* than change their cramped little view." He put his open hands up to the far sides of his eyes, then turned them in, as if he wanted to play peekaboo. He didn't uncover his eyes for the longest time and when he finally did, his palms had pushed all the blood out of his cheeks. Peter watched how it flooded back in.

"You don't like your dad very much, do you?"

Stuart looked at him with suspicion, as if he were working for the other side. "He's okay. He just dreams the dreams of suburbia. If you asked him what he wants most for his son Stuart, his hair-trigger response would be, 'College.' 'But'"—Stuart's voice became stiff and graveled—"'how do you think the boy is doing since his mother's death?' 'College.' 'Do you love him?' 'College.'"

Peter had heard Tom on this topic, but he didn't want to reveal that. He pretended to be putting together the pieces himself. "Is it because he was the first to go in his family?"

"Thomas Marnelli Belou. Rhode Island School of Design. Class of 1952." Stuart managed to protrude the ledge of his eyebrows to become Tom. The voice and accent were surprisingly accurate. "My father's family came down from Shitsville, Canada, and spent three generations in a paper mill. Sixty years they stunk up their houses with their rotten-egg smell before they figured out how to sew and make the money for you, Stuart May Belou, to perch up in an ivory tower and laugh at your pitiful, smelly ancestors."

Stuart lay in bed in the dark, though Peter didn't think he ever slept. Peter tried to keep up with him but by midnight his body, like a child who wants to go home, pulled him unwillingly away from consciousness. When he woke up in the morning, Stuart was always gone.

"What about your mom's side?" Peter asked the next night. "Did they go to college?" He liked to slip in questions about her. It made him feel closer to the Belous, knowing things about her. It made her feel less dead. Just saying "your mom" brought her so much closer to the surface of life.

"Same sort of thing as my dad's," he said without any attempt to re-create her voice. "She didn't even go to college herself. She got married instead."

Peter knew if he was quiet long enough he'd go on.

"She took me to look at colleges last spring—no, two springs ago. When I was in eleventh grade."

"Where'd you go?"

"California. I had this idea I wanted to go to Berkeley. So we saw that and Stanford and UCLA." The light was still on. Stuart was propped up with a pillow that loomed high over his head and bobbed when he spoke. It made him look a little like Marie Antoinette, and Peter kept wanting to laugh.

"It was a pretty weird place, California. The ocean's a completely different color, like it's been injected with some sort of dye. Mom loved it. She kept saying that if I went to school out there they'd all move. She came back really excited about that plan, but my father shot it down. Then she got sick and that was that." With two hands he shoved the tall pillow under his head. He didn't speak for several minutes, then he said, "Talk about mourning at a funeral. She was too well-liked. She wasted too many words and tears on others when she should have been looking inward."

Peter thought how if Stuart died there would be only girls at his funeral. He could see them in tight black dresses all in a row, crying into soaked Kleenexes. Eventually they'd notice each other and the service would turn into a brawl, culminating at the casket, where they'd tear the clothes off Stuart's corpse. The plump one would confess to her nights in the back of the car and the others would have to bow down and give her the crown: Stuart's underwear.

The laugh he'd been battling exploded out of him.

"What?" Stuart said.

"Nothing."

Stuart didn't press him.

After a while Peter asked, "What does the Tao say about sex before marriage?"

"The Tao doesn't *say* anything. 'That which is sayable is not the Tao.'"

Peter waited for the real answer.

"The Tao doesn't concern itself with the idea of sin. Sin becomes irrelevant when you are using your mental energy in the right way."

Peter was patient. He listened to the metal number 7 slap onto the number 6 inside his clock radio, making it 11:57 P.M.

"Sex can be a form of intense meditation, if you do it correctly. It can be very truthful."

Thinking about being with Kristina in the station wagon, Peter fell asleep with a very truthful hard-on.

Peter tried to explain these theories to Jason. But Jason was un-receptive. "I think that guy has found a way to justify going nowhere fast. He's a total loser, Peter." Jason was still angry he'd moved away. No other faculty kids their age lived on campus.

"The words of broken people come forth like vomit," Peter quoted, he didn't know from what.

On a science test, Peter explained in a long, unrelated essay the story about the search for the Lost Pearl and how Nothingness, who was not asked, had it all along.

Not only was he failing biology, but history and French were in question as well. And now his mother, the hardest grader in the school, was his English teacher at least until Christmas break, and Kristina was in that section.

He hated *Tess of the d'Urbervilles*. There were so many words and so few of them were interesting. He wished for once they could read something pertinent to the life of a teenager in the twentieth century. He quickly fell behind in the assignments, and on the third day of class with his mother, he learned that Tess had had a baby. He searched the book for the scene of conception but found noth-ing. A kid next to him told him it happened with Alec d'Urberville in the woods at the end of chapter eleven. He read the pages, but all he could find was that they were lost in the dark, and Alec made a pile of leaves for her to sit on while he went to look for a landmark. Birds were roosting and rabbits hopping, and Tess was asleep when he returned. Peter waited for someone braver, someone whose mother was not teaching the class, whose crush of four years was not two seats diagonally to the left, to ask exactly what had hap-pened. But no one did.

"What name does she give the baby?" his mother asked. She looked around for other hands, then called on Helen, who had all the answers. She always did; even back in first grade he remembered her lone arm in the air.

"Sorrow," Helen said. And without waiting for his mother to ask why, she continued, "Because he was the result of her rape."

His mother narrowed her eyes and tipped her head. He knew the gesture well, and so did Helen.

"She was raped. Alec raped her that night in the woods," Helen insisted.

"A statement like that is insulting to my intelligence."

From the four corners of the classroom the girls piped up in defense of Helen's theory. "But she loathed Alec d'Urberville."

"And she was asleep."

"She wasn't even conscious."

"She never even wanted him to kiss her."

"But she let him," his mother said.

"That was only because he was making the horse go so fast and only said he'd stop if he could kiss her. And she wiped it off after."

"She let him kiss her, regardless of the reason."

"But Mrs. Belou," Helen began, and Peter could hear in her voice how determined she was to make her point. She'd underlined practically a whole page and was holding it close to her face, her left fingers marking three different spots. "Listen to what it says here: 'But, some might say, where was Tess's guardian angel? where was the Providence of her simple faith?' and then he says she was 'doomed,' that it was a 'catastrophe,' that her ancestors had probably 'dealt the same measure' toward some peasant girls."

"And if you look two pages later you will find Tess herself admitting to Alec that she loathes herself for her 'weakness.' She says, 'My eyes were *dazed* by you for a little, and that was all.' And then, a few pages further on, the narrator says that she had been 'stirred to confused surrender awhile.'" His mother hadn't even taken her book out of her bag yet. She knew it all by heart.

Helen retaliated: "Then why does he say, 'But though to visit the *sins* of the fathers upon the children may be a morality good enough for divinities, it is scorned by average human nature, and it therefore does not mend the matter.' He's calling what Alec did a sin, the sin of rape."

"Don't you have to say no out loud for it to be rape?" Kristina asked. Her boyfriend, Brian Rossi, gave her a nudge and a proud smirk.

"She's been saying no to Alec d'Uberville from the moment she met him!" Helen slammed the book on her desk.

"But she was just doing that thing that girls do," the new kid, Kevin, said.

"*What* thing?" several of the girls asked in the same indignant tone.

"You know," Kevin continued, loving the sudden attention. "Saying no to get you to really want it from them." Peter stole a glance at his mother, thinking she'd be ready to blow. But instead of getting ready to stop him, instead of even looking at Kevin, she was looking at Peter, as if he were the one who was talking. "I mean, how hard is it to avoid getting raped?" Kevin continued. "All you have to do is keep your clothes on. Any girl who gets raped secretly wanted it. She might think afterwards she didn't, but at the time she did."

Peter had always heard that his mother was so strict, so challenging. How had she won that teaching prize last year? Why did so many students write her thank-you notes from college? Why was she just standing there?

A few girls lashed out at Kevin, and finally his mother snapped out of her trance.

"I don't want to hear another word on this subject," she said. "Not another word. I am sick to death of you people coming in here year after year and whining about what happens to Tess. A senseless nitwit of a girl in the woods at night with a proven lecher is not rape. It's stupidity."

Lindsey put up her hand. "But—"

"Goddammit. I don't want to hear your buts. Get out of here. All of you. Right now."

There was a sick silent moment before Peter, knowing his mother was serious and would not back down, began packing up his books. Everyone else did the same.

Before he left the classroom, Peter looked back at her. There was something about the way she'd wrapped her arms around herself, or maybe the color of her sweater, that reminded him of the caterpillars they had in the biology classroom, the way they hung suspended from the neck, forcing their own heads to fall off.

On the stairs, Brian put his arm around Kristina.

Karen said to Kevin, "You're gross."

Kevin smiled up at her. "You won't ever have to worry about it, Karen. No one will ever want to rape *you.*"

Thanksgiving arrived. He and his mother had never hosted a Thanksgiving. They always ate at other people's houses. Last year, like most years, they'd gone to Carol's. Her son had been alive then, and they'd talked about basketball. He hadn't seemed sad at all, and later Peter wondered if suicide could just come over you, like a cold, and the thought scared him for a long time.

The Belous, he learned, always stayed home and had very firm ideas about Thanksgiving. There had to be one of those dried-corn-on-the-cob arrangements on the front door, and a fat pewter turkey that they brought up from the basement on a table in the living room. The sweet potatoes had to have brown sugar and pecans on top;

dessert could only be pumpkin pie. The meal was always served at five.

On Thanksgiving morning Peter woke up and felt it, the tightness in the air. He heard Fran scolding Caleb. He was surprised to see Stuart still in bed across the room. He was lying rigid on his back, arms at his sides, palms up. He was meditating, but his eyeballs were twitching against his lids and nothing about him looked relaxed. In the kitchen his mother and Tom were strategizing beside the raw rubbery carcass of a turkey: who would vacuum, who would do the beans, when the pies would go in, where people would sit. His mother looked like she did when she came out of faculty meetings.

He decided to skip breakfast and take a shower. It came to him that he didn't like holidays. He never had. They bore down on you. Each one always ended up feeling like an exam you forgot to study for.

He stood wrapped in a towel before the photograph. He was used to her presence in the bathroom now. Water slid in beads off of his hair onto his shoulders. The frame was slightly steamed. She grew up as Mary May in Skaneateles, New York, a small town built around a large lake. Peter even knew how to spell it. He'd looked it up. She was an only child. She took piano lessons from her aunt Becky. Her favorite color was green. She met Tom when she was seventeen at a cookout in Plattsburgh, where he was training and she was visiting a friend. The picture had been taken before Stuart was born, Peter guessed. She looked so young, nearly his age, squatting there on a trail in the woods, tying her sneaker. He wiped the steam off of her. She was looking straight at the camera, straight at Peter, pleased by what she saw. "Happy Thanksgiving," he whispered.

After he dressed, he decided to unpack the last of his boxes. Stuart had cleared off a shelf for his books, and the bureau Tom had brought up from the basement still had two empty drawers. He took his time. The energy outside his door made him uneasy. They were all setting up the living room for the guests and the meal. Stuart was moving furniture, Fran fussing about silverware, Caleb folding napkins. Their voices were louder than usual. He could hear his mother coming in from the kitchen to ask Fran something about glasses. She had forced a lilt into her voice. She was faking it, pretending that Thanksgiving was something special to her when all his life they'd tagged along at someone else's holiday. She'd never stuffed a turkey or hung a decoration. It was nothing to her, nothing to him, and all day they'd have to act like it was, act like the Belous, to whom, despite death and rupture, Thanksgiving was still something sacred.

He was sitting on his bed rubbing his knees when his mother came in. "You look squeaky clean."

He nodded. He wished she'd just acknowledge the act she was putting on.

"Could you do me a favor and walk Walt?"

"All right." He was relieved to have an excuse to get out.

"Maybe you could get one of the kids to go with you." She was wearing a tattered apron around her waist. Mrs. Belou's apron.

He stood but she didn't move out of his way. She was looking over his shoulder.

"I can't believe you still have that old train book."

Did she know what he'd hidden within its pages?

"It was my favorite book."

"I remember."

Still she didn't move. He wanted to push her. Why was he so mad at her? She'd married Tom. She hadn't messed that up. She'd never been mean; she'd never hit him or called him names like he'd seen Jason's mother do. She seemed mad at him, too, wanting something from him.

"I put the leash around the knob on the front door," she said, giving up, and left his room.

Walt was waiting for him, thwacking his tail against the door. Fran and Caleb were stacking plates. He waited until Caleb went to get more before he said, "Anyone want to go for a walk?"

She shook her head without looking up, then began counting the number of guests on her fingers. She had the ability to make him feel even smaller and less significant than he normally did. It had been nearly a month. When was she going to start treating him like a brother?

He clipped the leash onto Walt's bucking collar.

"Can I come?" Caleb shouted.

"Sure you can."

"Not too long," Fran said. "We've got a lot more to do around here."

It was typical Thanksgiving weather: overcast, colorless, and colder than it looked. Walt tugged hard to the left.

"He always knows just where he wants to go, doesn't he?" Caleb said. "Can I hold him?"

Peter gave him the loop at the end of the leash. Walt pulled Caleb hard and they both had to walk faster to keep up. After a couple of blocks Walt reached the long row of maples he was most interested in and slowed down.

"Isn't it amazing how he's only lived here twenty-three days and he has his whole routine?" Caleb said. "He loves that little patch of moss right here and next he'll go to the little sap hole there on that one. I love the way that branch up there has actually fused with that one. Have you noticed that before? See? They're two different trees that grew one branch. Isn't that cool?" Walt jerked Caleb over to the next tree, to the sap hole. And then to a cluster of tiny mushrooms. "I think he's like a mastodon, just the way his shoulders rise so high when he bends down like that."

They walked on, Walt tugging then stopping, Caleb chattering, observing everything. He was a scrawny kid, the very smallest in the third grade as far as Peter could tell from the class picture he brought home, with dark blond hair that grew in thick tufts in different directions all over his head. Peter wondered what the other kids made of him and all his thoughts. Since he'd been there, Caleb had never had a friend over. None of them had, except for Stuart and the girls he kept outside.

"I love it when the sun's like this, when you can look straight at it behind a cloud but still see its shape perfectly, like it's naked."

Peter was tempted to ask him about his mother, about how he could be so enthusiastic about the world and everything in it when his mother was dead. When Peter was Caleb's age just imagining his mother's death could leave him weak and shaky. He could remember the terror he would work himself into waiting for his mother to come home from a party, the slow circles of the red hand on his clock as it got later and later, the conviction that the phone would ring, the babysitter would come in, and Peter's life as he knew it would be over. He had nowhere to go. He didn't even know his father's name. It wasn't Avery like his, because his aunt Gena's last name was Avery, too. He realized that that fear was gone now that his mother had married Tom. The Belous would probably have to keep him if she died.

They headed back to the house. Walt was tired. His arthritic back legs bounced lightly behind him, unable to carry the full weight.

"He's an old man, isn't he?"

"A hundred and twelve," Peter said.

Caleb stopped and bent down to look Walt in the face. It was completely white.

"You are a sweet sweet dog. Yes you are." He hugged him tight around the neck. Walt, realizing this would last a while, let his head drop onto Caleb's back. Caleb's eyes were pressed closed as if he were praying for the dog. The hug lasted a long time. Peter waited, and felt ashamed he did not love Walt more. He didn't really care that he was so old. Walt had always been Vida's dog. She was the one who did what Caleb was doing now, stroked him, whispered to him. He remembered watching her years ago through a window once. She was out on the field with Walt, running and laughing, wrestling with him on the ground, then lying there with her head beside his for the longest time. Peter had been so angry he'd poured Spic 'N Span in Walt's water bowl, but nothing happened.

The guests began arriving soon after they got back. His mother had put on one of her school fund-raiser dresses and held a glass of wine, talking to Tom's sister. Dr. Gibb came with a date. Fran sat at the kitchen table with her cousins, Jonie and Meg, who were in college. Tom took his brother out to his wood shop in the garage. Mrs. May called. The traffic was terrible and she'd be late.

Peter and Stuart lay on their beds as if it were nighttime. Their room was eerily tidy now that his boxes were gone. He thought of the picture in the train book. He wanted to show Stuart but didn't know how to bring it up.

"Last Thanksgiving I was high until New Year's, totally wasted, day and night," Stuart said. "It was great."

"Why don't you do it anymore?"

"It shrivels your chi to the size of a fig seed."

Peter snorted, thinking of Brian, Kristina's boyfriend, the pothead.

"Not your dick. Your chi is your energy, your life force. It needs to flow easily. 'The true man breathes from his feet up.'"

Neither of them said anything for a while, just listened to the sealike undulations of the party down the hall. This was a good time to show him, Peter decided. His heart began pounding.

"Want to see a picture of my father?"

"Your father?" Stuart had never asked about his father. No one had.

"Yeah. I found it when I was unpacking today." He hoisted

himself up and pulled out a small piece of construction paper from the book on the shelf.

Stuart started laughing. "This is all you have of your dad? She's never even given you a photo?"

"She doesn't have any. I think they split up before I was born."

Stuart looked at the creased, smudged drawing and shook his head. "Jesus. That's really pathetic."

Peter wished he'd just hand it back. He didn't know why he'd showed it to him anyway. He felt hollow in his chest as he waited.

A car pulled up at the curb and cut its lights. Stuart tossed the paper back to him and swung off his bed. "That's my grandmother!" he called, flinging himself out of the room spastically, like a little boy. Peter put the paper back where he'd always kept it, ever since the day she drew it, and followed him out.

Mrs. May was not old-looking but she moved slowly, as if all her muscles were sore. She gave Peter a nod when introduced but not a hand. To his mother she didn't even give a nod. When it was time to eat, she sat stiffly on the couch in a boiled wool suit while her grandchildren fetched her a glass of milk and another slice of turkey from the buffet. Peter watched the Belou kids hover near, vying for her scrutiny. He thought his mother should make more of an effort with her, but Vida sat on the other side of the room, nibbling and sipping. He hoped she got drunk. He liked her when she was drunk. When he was younger she'd peek in his room when she came back from parties. If he spoke to her, she'd come sit on his bed and tell him all about where she'd gone and which of his teachers were there. She always seemed so happy after a few drinks: she'd smooth his hair and say how lucky she was to have him. And he'd be so relieved she hadn't died that he'd hug her tight and she wouldn't pull away.

She was telling school stories now, the raunchy one about the prank on the school nurse. Her eyes were shiny and overfocused, as if she were on stage.

Tom talked quietly to Mrs. May. They spoke of Skaneateles, and of Connecticut, where she'd just eaten a noontime meal with her sister and her brood of children, grandchildren, and even two great-grandchildren.

Quietly, to Tom, she said, "I never envied my sister her six children. Now—" She threw up her hands, then quickly collected them in her lap again.

Tom's head bobbed in understanding.

Vida imitated the nurse's long shrill shriek when she found the sausage in her purse. A boom of laughter followed.

Peter saw no resemblance in the dull face of Mrs. May to the picture of her daughter in the bathroom.

"Vida's a hoot, isn't she?" Peter heard Tom's brother say to him at the door.

"She is," Tom said, confused, like he'd bought an appliance with too many features.

The hugs with Mrs. May were long and tight. Peter and Vida stayed clear, then joined the others at the door to wave as she moved slowly to her car.

"Funny old fish," Vida whispered loudly.

Then Thanksgiving was behind them, a long weekend ahead. That Friday, a cold rain fell. They played Parcheesi, Yahtzee, Stratego. Peter and Fran made frappes. They drank them in front of an afternoon movie about dolphins. Stuart groaned at all the Christmas ads. At one point they were all—Stuart, Fran, Peter, and Caleb—under the big afghan on the couch. Who knew where Vida and Tom were? Who cared? All his life Peter had always known exactly where his mother was; knowledge of her whereabouts was crucial, like knowing you had clothes on. But now he was free of that.

When the movie was over, Fran studied his profile. "You have that funny kind of earlobe. The kind that sticks to the skin on your face, like webbed feet."

Peter didn't know what she was talking about.

"Look." She batted her mobile lobe. "We all have the dangly kind."

Later, he looked at his ears in the mirror. He looked at his mother's at dinner. It was true. Neither of them had the dangly Belou earlobes.

Before dinner, Tom took him aside and scolded him: the wood box had been empty for several days now. Keeping the box full was one of Peter's chores, but he didn't like it because it meant going down to the basement alone. Mrs. Belou's things were down there, in boxes and garment bags, crouching in the corner.

He couldn't explain that to Tom, so he apologized and picked up the canvas carrier. Halfway down the stairs he saw Caleb in the yellow and blue dress, zipping Fran into the red and white one. Their backs were to him. Fran's bra strap was beige. He didn't want to see them in their mother's dresses. Before he even registered what he was doing he was back in the living room empty-handed. Tom shook his head and took the carrier from him.

Within seconds Tom returned.

"I apologize, Peter," he said formally, as if they had just met. "I didn't know they were playing with"—he paused—"costumes." He sat down on a hard chair in the corner that no one ever used, and looked at his feet.

It was the pale-eyed girl who came late that night. After Stuart had gone to her, Peter got up and eavesdropped through the front door. They were on the steps as usual, arguing about Christ. Peter was disappointed; he wanted Stuart to be talking about him.

"But why isn't there any documentation of the thirty-two

previous years if on the night of his birth the North Star led everyone to his cradle and they celebrated the arrival of the king of kings? If all this Christmas crap actually happened, why do we know so little about his life? Why was he a poor carpenter instead of a beleaguered messiah?"

Peter could only hear a whiny murmur.

"They're feeding you lies, Diane. You're like some peasant in the Soviet Union who believes Lenin is still alive. You're like . . ." and his monologue went on until Peter was certain she was crying.

But she was back again the next night, and Peter heard Stuart telling her about that trip to California. "We rented this convertible in San Francisco. Mom refused to let me drive up all those hills because it was a standard, but she was hopeless. It was like she'd forgotten how to drive. We kept rolling down backwards and stalling and going down one-way streets, the whole town honking at us. One time there was this poor guy on a bike and our car rolled down straight toward him and he had to lift his bike up onto someone's porch to avoid being killed. She kept forgetting where our hotel was. God, we bickered the whole time, more like brother and sister than mother and son. It was really funny."

"My father and I went on a trip like that once—"

"But what was really funny is that we had this one day when we didn't speak. Not a syllable. She was mad, I was mad, and we were both too stubborn to give in. And I had my interview at Berkeley that day. She came with me and after the interview the admissions lady gave us this tour of the place and we all ate together at this fancy dining hall but Mom and I never looked or spoke to each other the whole time. That lady must have thought we were a really screwed-up family. Maybe that's why I got in. Mom was stubborn as a goddamn mule sometimes."

Peter moved quietly away from the door. He wasn't sleepy, but he didn't want to hear any more. He was starting to know more about Mrs. Belou than he knew about his own mother.

Mom wore lipstick called Desert Rose. Mom told me cotton candy was made of ghosts. Mom broke her ankle when when she was eight months pregnant with me. Mom knew French. Mom helped raise four thousand dollars for the public library. Mom hated Spiro Agnew almost as much as Nixon. Mom gave dad a black eye once when they were having sex. With her elbow. She didn't mean to. That's not true! Yes it is, Fran. Remember how she used to say "Holy mackerel?" "Holy mackerel, you look lovely." "Holy mackerel, he's a pig." Mom loved birch trees best of all.

Your mother, they always said in a completely different tone of voice. They never said Vida. Your mother needs a new pair of shoes. Your mother's so bony. Your mother said she's going to replace the rug in here.

Your mother, they always said, as if they were trying to give her back.

On the way to school the following Monday, his mother gave him a lecture in the car. His grades, she said, were abysmal. He had to start trying or he'd flunk out.

"I do try, Ma. I try hard."

"You need to work something out with Stuart. You can't talk to him and do your homework at the same time."

"I like talking to him."

"Fine. But after you've done your work. Should I have a word with him?"

"No."

"Don't start thinking about throwing *your* future away, too."

"He hasn't thrown anything away."

"He's a dropout."

"He didn't *drop out*. He finished and he got into a really good college."

"But he didn't go. I call that dropping out."

"He's going next year."

"Right."

"He is, Ma. He told me. He wants to learn Chinese."

"Chinese," his mother said, threading her cigarette stub through the crack in the window. "And what's this 'Ma' business?"

When he got home that night, Stuart was waiting for him.

"Hello, Mole."

Peter dumped his books out on the bed. Huge French test to-morrow. He'd have to tell him he needed to study.

"How was your day, Mole?" Stuart was lying on his back with his legs straight up and his fingers laced through his toes.

"All right. How was yours?"

"Do you know what 'mole' means, Mole?" He was using a tone he usually used on Fran.

"Yeah."

"I don't think you do. Otherwise you'd already be apologizing profusely for having told my father my plans for next year."

"I never told him," Peter said, indignant, the truth on his side.

"But you told your mother."

Had he? He had. "I—" *was defending you,* he wanted to say.

"I wanted to tell him—at the right time. I never thought you'd go scurrying to your mommy with it. He came in here tonight like I was the Second Coming. It was disgusting."

Stuart sat up and stretched his elbows unnaturally, nearly behind his head. Peter didn't know what to say. His heart was racing.

"If I had told my mother something like that, she never would have told my father. She would have known it was mine to tell."

Peter left the room and found his mother dumping frozen peas into a pot.

"Why the hell did you blab to Tom about Stuart?" He'd never sworn at his mother before.

"You mean about going to college? He's overjoyed."

"I told you not to say anything."

"You did?" She had her fake understanding-teacher voice, like he was telling her the dog ate it.

"I did."

He waited for her to expose him, to give him a speech about the truth and the power of words, but all she did was pitch the pea box in the trash and take a sip of her drink. Then she said, "Let's not get mixed up in other people's battles."

"Let's not blab everything you hear." He turned to leave but she caught him tight by the arm. He could feel her thumb pressing through his muscle to the bone. It burned.

"I'm not your whipping boy, Peter," she whispered. "And you're not theirs."

He let go a few frustrated tears in the bathroom. Mrs. Belou's smile was unsympathetic today. She wanted them out. He took the picture off the wall and put it facedown on top of the toilet so he could feel sorry for himself in peace. He stayed in there until he heard Stuart leave their room. Then he grabbed his French books and bolted down the hall to Caleb's room. Caleb was reading a five-hundred-and-twenty-page book about horse farming.

"Have you heard the one about the horse who walks into the bar?" Peter said.

"No."

"Horse walks into the bar and the bartender says, 'Why the long face?'"

Caleb waited for him to go on.

"That's it."

"Oh."

"It's a short joke. I don't remember the long ones very well."

They both returned to their reading.

At dinner all of his stepsiblings were silent and sulky. One by one Tom tried to draw them out, but they resisted. It was Peter's turn to do the dishes with Tom. When he was through, he found them in the living room, speaking in low voices. They stopped when he came in. He headed for his room, then paused in the hallway. They resumed.

"It's like something out of a bad movie."

"She's sick."

"Totally unsubtle."

Peter had no idea what they were—then he knew. The picture. He'd forgotten to put it back on the wall. The realization was physical, like something shattering inside him, his skin pricked from the inside by all the shards. He'd have to explain, release his mother from blame. He'd wait and tell Stuart later; maybe he'd think it was funny that Peter talked to her sometimes.

But later Stuart did all the talking, his mind whipping around his usual topics like a race car: the body, the Tao, Eastern medicine, college. . . .

"I'm rethinking the plan. My stomach has been sort of sinking ever since it was"—he gave Peter a forgiving smirk—"revealed. I would like to go back to California."

"To Berkeley?"

"No. Just to live. Forget college."

Peter felt responsible for this devastating change of heart. His stomach began to sink, too. "Why?"

"It was pretty amazing there."

"I thought you said the water looked fake."

"It did. Everything did. But that's what's cool about it. Every morning you felt like you were stepping onto a movie set, made especially for you and your day. Mom said the place made her feel twenty years younger. She must have said that twenty times. You know what it was? The place was hopeful. Full of hope." His head fell off his elbow, and he stared up into the swirls of plaster on the ceiling. Peter waited for him to say this place was full of death, but he didn't. In the silence, he remembered again the misunderstanding about the picture. He didn't want them to think his mother would do such a horrible thing, but confessing was impossible. How could he explain the disgusted look their mother had given him?

"I got mad at her for saying it so many times, that stuff about feeling younger. Because each time she said it it was like she was having the thought for the first time. The thing is, she was. She was having the thought for the first time each time. The tumor was sitting right on her temporal lobe, erasing the thought as soon as she said it. My father hadn't wanted her to take me, but she'd insisted. I thought he was just being an asshole. And then he was calling all the time. Practically every time we went past the hotel desk there was another message from him. And then when he met us at the airport she just sort of collapsed into his arms, as if she'd just run a marathon. You'd think I could have put it all together. If it were on TV you'd be screaming at the kid: 'She's got a brain tumor, you moron! Can't you see that?'" He pushed the heels of his hands hard into his eye sockets. "But I couldn't. I just couldn't."

Peter dreamed his first dream of her. The dream had no plot; it was just a moment, her in his room, his old room, in a shiny yellow raincoat. He moved toward her with no idea what he would say or do, with no idea if she was real or imagined. But when he reached her, all uncertainty was gone. He hugged her tight, so tight, and breathed her in and she smelled like flowers and old leaves, and then he was crying, aching, and she held him close until the tears running into his ears woke him up.

FIVE

MEMORY DOES ITS WORK UNDERGROUND. BENEATH CONSCIOUSNESS, A PAST moment finds its kin all at once. Like a fish returned to its school, it frolics in remembered waters, and stirs up others. Above the surface, at first, there are only a few brief innocuous ripples which are all that you can allow yourself to know of the commotion below: a checked shirt, the white rim of a porcelain sink. The fluid sequence of moments seems, luckily, irretrievable; there is no line to follow with a finger, no story she feels able to tell. Yet even awful, unlivable memories want to be relived; the fragments yearn to be whole once more.

Vida stood immobile before the half-renovated house, its windows and doors blown out, and workmen, even today, a Saturday, running their tools within its gutted insides. All it took was this smell—the smell of a freshly built room—for the taste of his mustard breath to come into her mouth.

"It looks like they're going to put a balcony off every bedroom," Tom said.

Dutifully, Vida raised her eyes to the second floor.

"And some sort of turret over there."

She followed his gesture to the left.

"I guess the moat will come later."

She knew from the change in tone that a smile was expected, though his words fell between them unheard. Her ribs seemed to be straining inward, strengthening their cage against the growing panic inside. Her limbs felt light, as if they might break off and float away.

"This whole neighborhood was once just a huge field covered in Queen Anne's lace in the summer and children in snowsuits dragging toboggans up there to Blake's Hill in the winter. We used to take Stuart and Fran here nearly every weekend. And now look at it."

Vida tried to concentrate on the circle of new houses and their even newer additions, their pools of asphalt out front, the freshly raked grass in back.

"What's wrong?" This was a question Tom often asked, as if, having missed so many warning signs with Mary, he was determined to find the first one in her.

She always tried to give him an answer, even when there wasn't one. But now, as they moved away from the house, nothing came to her and she felt depleted by the strain of trying to assure him that everything was fine.

"Hey?" He pulled her by the hands to him, forcing her to face him directly. "What is it?"

This was what he was always asking, in one way or another. What is it? What's wrong with you? Why aren't you who I thought you were?

Her mind scrambled for a way out of a whole day of his scrutiny. Mercifully, something arose, not even a lie. "I completely forgot. I have this miserable computer tutorial at school." She'd never planned to go. She'd gotten the memo and torn it up. "I'm sorry."

She unfastened her hands and resumed the walk home. Beside her, Tom said nothing, though she felt him questioning her. She'd made quite a passionate speech at dinner a few nights ago about the evils of technology in the classroom, how it weakened the already weakening grasp on language, how it was the enemy of creativity and spontaneity and the fortuitous mistake. Tom had been amused by her rant; he'd taken her hand under the table. He'd looked at her for the rest of the evening as if he'd remembered why he married her, and that night she found the right equation of alcohol and forgetting and they'd managed, to his great delight, to have a form of intercourse. But now she was drained of words and she could feel his bewilderment returning. Was this how marriage was, bewilderment giving way to reassurance giving way to more bewilderment? Was it possible in any relationship to not disappoint, to do anything more than only briefly rekindle the initial fatal illusion?

She thought of that Hardy poem, the one with the young man walking at night toward the home of the girl he is to marry the next day. A spirit sidles up next to him, a beautiful woman who resembles his bride. She tells him she is the dream he has dreamed of love, and that he loves only her, not the poor girl he has been projecting his illusions onto. When the spirit finally convinces him, he insists on marrying her instead, but she says she cannot, and disappears. When he reaches the home of his bride-to-be, he finds that all the life has been sucked out of her.

"Vida," Tom said softly, so softly she could pretend not to have heard. He cleared his throat and tried again. "Vida." He stopped on the sidewalk and waited for her to turn to him.

She was still thinking about the end of the poem, straining to remember the last lines.

> Her look was pinched and thin,
> As if her soul had shrunk and died,
> And left a waste within.

"What's that from?"
She didn't know she'd spoken the words aloud.
"A Hardy poem." She felt protective of it.
"Which one?"

She didn't want to explain. She wanted to think about this idea of love's being cast onto someone like a spotlight, making her shimmer and glow for a little while, lending her qualities she doesn't possess. Is this really what we do to each other, find a victim and shine the light of all our dreams on them? Angel Clare places all his fantasies of the pure innocent country girl onto Tess, and when she finally forces him to listen to her story of Alec and the baby, she becomes vile to him and he banishes her. *As if her soul had shrunk and died, / And left a waste within.* She could hear Tom saying her name again, but he seemed so much less important, so much more immaterial than this theory of Hardy's, which she'd always taught to her students, but had never suspected would ever apply to her own life.

The computer room had cost over five hundred thousand dollars. On Thursday evening there'd been an unveiling for parents and faculty, and on Friday the day's schedule had been reorganized to allow every student in the school a chance to sit at the helm of one of these machines. Now, in one Saturday afternoon, the teachers were expected to learn how to integrate them into their curricula.

For two years, the administration had been aggressively brainwashing the school community, producing pamphlets with titles like "The Modern Miracle in Education" and "Learning Finally Becomes Fun!" The need was so great, they said, and money so scarce, that faculty members were being asked to give a portion of their salaries each month to the cause. Vida had heard that some of the younger teachers, in fear of not getting their contracts renewed, had actually agreed to the tithing, poor suckers.

Now they were all suckers, crammed in this room on a Saturday. There were not, thank God, enough computers to go around, so the overflow sat on metal chairs at the back. Vida took a seat next to Cheryl Perry, who smelled like cheese and handed her a few mimeographs, general instructions for the IBM System 370.

Mark Stratton, the computer guru, and Brick Howells stood practically hand in hand at the front of the room. Brick declared, in a voice far too loud for the size of the room, that what they were about to witness was nothing short of a revolution. And that no other school in the area, not even Hunt, Fayer's wealthier rival, had implemented this kind of technology.

To Vida's astonishment, her colleagues clapped. Then Mark asked everyone seated at a computer to turn it on by pushing the large rectangular button on the left. He said something else but his voice was drowned out by the sudden snap and whir of the machines. Vida waited for the noise to die down. It didn't. A smell like burnt hair filled the room.

Then they were asked to divide up into their departments. The math, science, and history departments should all take seats at the computers; the arts and languages should find their own classrooms in order to brainstorm ways in which they could use their weekly lab time. This transition was as difficult and bitter as if they had all been third graders. Jose Costa refused to give up his seat: he'd been the first to arrive. And Leon, the frail Latin teacher, put up an equally impressive fight on the other side of the room. The art teachers seemed to have a difficult time simply identifying each other. When she and the rest of her department finally settled around the thick walnut table in the conference room, Vida added nothing to the list her colleagues chirped out, as she had absolutely no plans to ever bring her students into that awful place.

When her department was called back to the smelly, roaring room, Mark assigned them a computer and asked them to simply type onto the screen a paragraph. "You could begin a letter, a short story, or," he said looking specifically at Vida, Lydia, and Liz, the three women in the English department, "a recipe. Anything. Then we'll go from there."

The first thing that came to her mind was Shakespeare. Even though it had been several years since she'd pulled her college type-writer out of the closet, her hands knew the keys immediately.

> If it were now to die
> 'Twere now to be most happy; for, I fear
> My soul hath her content so absolute,
> That not another comfort like to this
> Succeeds in unknown fate.

How ludicrous to see poor Othello in fluorescent yellow on a little TV screen in front of her. After a few minutes, Mark explained how to check the paragraph for mistakes. Vida's computer bleeped seven times. It had opinions about not only spelling, but grammar and syntax as well.

Mark Stratton moved quickly toward her and nestled his upper body on top of her monitor. "Stumped already?"

"Mr. Computer's style is pretty rigid."

"It will only accept the best configuration."

"You can't expect a machine to have a sensitivity to the rhythms and nuances of the English language. Sometimes the least grammati-cally correct sentence is the best choice. I don't want a computer holding back my students' creativity."

Mark laughed. "In fifty years, these babies are going to be writ-ing better books than anything you've ever taught them."

"You can't believe that."

"I don't have to believe it. I know it, my friend."

Before the creation of this room. Mark had been a part-time geography teacher. Vida watched him now, pacing the length of his royal-blue carpet, gazing with possessive pleasure at his hot droning monsters. She thought of the threshing machine, Hardy's symbol for the Industrial Age, that despotic contraption that forced an inhuman pace on fieldworkers, separating their souls from the land forever. Her chest tightened. She felt it, right here, right now, what Hardy had felt, the ache of modernism.

They had left it that Tom would make dinner, but when Vida got home just before six, the house was empty. She called out into the darkness. Only Walt came, slowly, his back legs reluctant to separate after hours of napping. He sniffed her pants, then snorted out the smell, as if he, too, were disgusted by Mark Stratton and his machines. She called out again. Nothing.

She'd never been in this house alone. She tossed her shoes down the hall toward her room and sat in one of the wing chairs facing the sofa. When she shut her eyes, the head and neck of a computer monitor lunged at her. Brick had drained the scholarship fund to pay for the lab. The board of trustees had just stood back and let him do it. And now she was expected to take each of her classes down there once a week. They wanted her to become the engine man, the half-human, coal-grimed creature who kept the threshing machine running. The undersides of her arms burned with anger. It was time for a drink. But she could wait a little longer, wait until everybody got home.

The mud-gray screen of the TV gaped at her. Had she ever been in this room when it was not on, when it was not blaring its garbage? The hostages. The hostages. How much more could we take of the hostages? Every now and then a few were trotted out onto the embassy steps, a tattered white rag tied tight around each face, beards growing in clumps like bad grass on their necks. Every day the newscasters seemed shocked anew that it was still going on. It irked her how they had begun to count, numbering the days since the takeover and her wedding. Today was Day 33. She didn't even know how she knew. They had programmed her, like a computer. *These babies are going to be writing better books than anything you've ever taught them.* What kind of viper would want to believe that? And where *was* everybody? Fran and Caleb, she remembered now, were at friends' houses for the night, but Peter, Tom, and Stuart? It was too dark to see out to the driveway now. Should she start making something? The thought of making another damn dinner pinned her to her seat. She hadn't realized how good she'd had it on campus. Every meal had been made for them. Except for the first and last weeks of summer and a fortnight at Christmas, she'd never had to cook. And when she did, Peter had expected so little—a bowl of soup, scrambled eggs, he didn't care. But the Belous were different. They asked at breakfast what she'd be making that night. They came in while dinner was cooking to lift up the lids and smell. They had begun to make suggestions, one at a time, choreographed hints about what to cook and how to cook it. They liked to set the table. They enjoyed, in fact, all rituals. They were like some prehistoric tribe, the way they found meaning in the repetition of acts. Once Vida had read "Annabel Lee" to Caleb before bed and now he wanted a poem read to him every night. She had driven Fran to the mall last Friday afternoon and now the girl wanted to go shopping on the first Friday afternoon of every month. Stuart still wanted nothing to do with her, but even that had its own pattern. He always sat in the chair farthest from her, and was sure to be out of the house on Saturday mornings and Sunday evenings when she did her grading in the kitchen. She felt grateful to Stuart for one reason: his presence in Peter's bedroom. If she had that dream, he'd be there—and most likely awake—to stop her from hurting Peter.

She had planned to just turn on a light or two and sit back in the wing chair, but her legs kept moving, into the kitchen, into the pantry closet. She brought out the bourbon, the glass, the ice, then shoved them all away. She sat down at the green table, not in the seat at the far end where she did her grading, and not to the left of Tom's place where she usually sat at dinner, but to the right of him, Mary's old seat. It was an odd choice, pressed in close to the wall. Vida felt a little suffocated in it even without the kids on all sides. Mary, she imagined, was part Mrs. Ramsay and part Marmee March, intoxicated by her role as Mother.

The red hands above the stove were clutched at six-thirty. Where the hell was everyone? She imagined the station wagon skidding into the headlights of a monstrous truck. I'm sorry, ma'am, the cop at the door would say. Her heart raced at the thought of a man at the door with a gun.

She pulled out a saucepan, remembering *As if her soul had shrunk and died, / And left a waste within* and Tom's fake-earnest question "Which one?" As if he knew the title to even one of Hardy's poems. Opening a can of tomato paste she had that feeling again that this was not the real moment, that she hadn't married him, that she and Peter didn't actually live here. It startled her, how easily reality could slip off her shoulders. She put down the opener and poured herself the damn drink.

After a few sips it was easy to make the paste into a sauce, put the water on to boil. She sat back down at the table, in her seat this time. She stirred the ice with her fingers, thinking of Davis Clay and that awful trick his wife played on him a few summers ago. She'd called people all over the country, childhood friends, aunts and uncles, even his ninety-two-year-old granny, everyone the poor guy loved, and they'd all snuck into his house while he was out playing golf and when he got back they surprised him not with a party but with accusations that he was ruining his life and his children's lives. They pushed him into a car and drove him to this place in Connecticut for a month, the remaining month of his summer vacation, to dry out. Vida never forgot the way the guy looked in September. Old Clay went to Auschwitz for the summer, Vida said to someone in the lunch line, and the joke traveled around school. He'd never recovered from it, as far as Vida could tell. He still had these gray hollows under his eyes, as if he hadn't slept since, and he'd completely lost his sense of humor.

These babies are going to be writing better books . . . She felt sorry for Mark Stratton, really. His wife had left him several years ago, taking their six-year-old son with her to Minnesota. He was a pitiful character, someone, despite the irritation he provoked, you had to feel sympathy for, a Robert Cohn. Perhaps she should have been kinder to him after his wife had gone. They'd only had one conversation about it, in the lunch line. He didn't even mention her or the kid, just that he missed his cat. Vida had earnestly commiserated with him, imagining if something ever happened to Walt, but she'd deliberately separated from him when they'd gotten their food, feigning interest in the salad bar. Now she wished she'd handled it differently, for clearly he'd wanted to talk that day. Carol had been one of his confidantes at the time, and though she and Vida used to gossip nearly every afternoon, Carol would never divulge the details of Mark's situation. Vida respected her for that, among other things. She acknowledged the familiar shame about Carol and the unfinished letter as it rose, but she didn't feel it, didn't let it overwhelm her as it often did. That was the beauty of a good drink at the end of the day.

On his rug in the corner Walt twitched and whimpered. Did he picture her in his dreams? How would she appear to him—in fragments? A pair of legs, a long hand, a soothing voice? Did he have nightmares about her, in which she transformed into a hollering, dog-kicking old crone? The thought of nightmares did not scare her right now. She could even think of her own without panic. The checked shirt, the mustard breath, and her chasing him down the hallway with only a book for a weapon. Every time she lunged for him he got smaller until, when she reached the room he'd veered into, Peter's room, he was gone. Only Peter was there, in his crib—he was always only a few months old in the dream—but when she drew close to check on him he leapt to his feet, agile, angry, no longer a baby at all despite the body, and grabbed her. She raised her book and smacked him off. She beat him and beat him until he was finally still.

Vida felt pain in her hands and looked down to see her finger-nails cutting into her palms.

She made the next drink stronger, then stirred the sauce with a fork. She wondered if the clock had stopped; it wasn't even quarter of seven yet. She thought of Fran on her sleepover in some bedroom right now with her girlfriends talking about their hair. She had had enough experience with teenage girls like Fran to know what little went on in their heads. She didn't understand it. The girl wasn't stupid by any means, but she'd never read more than a few pages of any of the books she'd loaned her. When she was Fran's age she devoured books. There had been no better feeling on earth than being under her pink blanket on a Saturday afternoon with a new book in her hands. No reality competed with the reality of those books. If her mother's hounding grew too persistent she took the book and the blanket to the car and locked herself in. She would spend days—a whole weekend and then Monday and Tuesday if she could convince her mother of a stomach bug—prone, engulfed, gone. She didn't understand a girl like Fran who found this thin life enough, especially after losing her mother. Why wouldn't she want to enter a better world every now and then, a world with a little more sense to it, where even tragedy had luster and resonance to it?

Her sister Gena had been like Fran, probably still was. California attracted that kind of person, social, unreflective. Gena had never spent a minute more in the house than necessary, always off with some pack of girls, or, later, boys. Their mother had despaired. She'd wanted good girls who would marry early and well, like Jane and Elizabeth Bennett. Instead she got one who never came home at night and another who never left the house. One of us finally got married, Mother, Vida said to the ceiling. Was it possible she hadn't even thought of her mother since before her engagement? Her mother knew everything, now that she was dead. It probably didn't feel so good to know everything.

She heard the thuds of car doors. She put the bourbon back in the closet. She didn't remember making a third drink but there it was and she polished it off. She put her glass in the dishwasher, and the spaghetti in the water. Half of the water had boiled off, but she pressed the stiff noodles into it with a spoon, cracking most of them. After they sank, the water became a white fizz. Vida leaned her face into the steam. It felt old and dry. Tom's voice rang through the house, calling her. There was no apology in it.

He and Peter came into the kitchen carrying big brown bags.

"Chinese takeout!" Peter said, as if he and Vida didn't used to pick up a meal from the Lucky Star on occasion, as if Tom himself had invented Chinese food.

"I made spaghetti," Vida said.

"Oh, no." Tom frowned, and she heard in his tone some facile expression like *A little trust goes a long way.* He'd said that one before. He slid his bag onto the counter, brushed the steamed hair from her forehead, and asked how it went with the computers. He was using a gentle, patient voice, the one he used with Fran or Caleb when they were on the brink of unruliness.

"Awful. They raised five hundred thousand dollars and hired that troll to burn it." Gone was the fellow feeling for Mark and his divorce. "It was a complete waste of my unpaid time." She felt her rage rising, with its insatiable appetite. She wished he'd stop touching her head.

"I'm sorry." But despite the soft voice and caress, he was quite unsorry. He seemed quietly accusatory.

"I wish you'd called," she said.

"I left this." He held up a piece of paper next to the flour canister. How was she supposed to have seen that? "Always check there first." Why was he speaking to her like this?

He bent over the stove. "Mmmm," he said to the sauce, and then, in one dramatic gesture, flipped the whole pan over.

"What are you—" Nothing spilled out. She'd forgotten to turn down the heat and it had caked on the bottom. The pasta, however, bubbled in happy ignorance behind it.

The food was, though she wouldn't say it, delicious. Chicken with cashews, shrimp lo mein, fried rice, beef and broccoli. She hadn't eaten since breakfast. Stuart was at the table, though when he'd come in she couldn't say.

"Earth to Ma." Peter never used to be so rude. "The rice?"

"How about an old-fashioned 'please'?" She never used to be so clichéd.

Tom and Stuart were already arguing.

"Tell me our military couldn't figure out a way to go in and get them if they wanted." Stuart spoke with his mouth full, his fork in his fist.

"They couldn't. They'd be bringing those people home in body bags if they tried."

"That is so naive, Dad. If we wanted them out we'd get them out. This is all about oil."

"Oil?"

"Yes. Don't you even read the paper? We need that oil. We don't want to jeopardize the sweet oil deal we have with them. That's why we've supported the Shah and his brutal regime for so many years. That's why we had to take him in last month."

"We took in the Shah because he needed medical treatment."

"Spare me the sob story. A lot of people say he's faking it. And would we take in Pol Pot or Idi Amin if they needed treatment?

No. We only take in the mass murderers who are selling us oil at a good price."

"Say you were head of the U.S. military, Stuart. How would you rescue those hostages? How would you go into the center of the capital and get inside that building without being seen? Because once you are seen, everybody's dead. What would you do, take an invisibility pill?" He was angry now.

They went on and on. Eventually Stuart put up two hands in mock surrender.

"Speech which enables argument is not worthy," he said.

"What?"

"These aren't the important things."

"What are the important things?" Vida heard herself ask. He was such a coward, the way he ducked at the last minute behind his mystic baloney.

Stuart put his hands in his lap. "The true self, the inner life, a harmony between heaven and earth."

This last surprised her. "Do you believe in heaven?"

"In a metaphorical sense."

"How is heaven metaphorical? Either it exists or it doesn't." He was like one of her weakest students, tossing up a big word and hoping it landed in the right place.

"Its existence is not the point."

"What is the point?"

"The point is"—he paused to look at each of them in turn, and it angered her to see how worshipfully Peter looked back—"not to care about the point."

"Spoken by a true Sophist."

"Sticks and stones, Vida."

"I'm not trying to insult you. I just think it's too easy to believe in nothing."

"It's not nothing. It's the opposite of nothing."

"But every time I try to coax a declarative sentence out of you, you twist away in a puff of smoke."

She saw how calmly he sifted through the words in his head. "To you it appears as smoke."

"But to you it's the truth?" She was aware of the absence of sifting in hers.

He nodded.

"Describe what it is you believe. In your words."

"That which is nameable is not the Tao."

"Those are not your words. But let me name it for you. *Crock of Crap.*"

Tom was hushing her but she didn't care. Someone had to stand up to this Buddhist bully.

"What do you believe in, Vida? In your words."

So he could get angry. She was glad to see she'd cracked the surface. She felt her own creed assemble easily. "I am a humanist. I believe in man's creative—"

"And woman's?"

"That's a semantic argument for another day."

"Are we having an argument?"

"Are you interested in my answer?"

Stuart bowed his head.

"I believe in the imagination and its striving toward truth and beauty, toward the ideal, through accurate and penetrating representations of our world."

"Our world? What is our world? We're here for two seconds. Blip. Blip. Then we're gone forever."

"I believe"—she was surprised by the pleasure she took from saying those two words—"there is a transcendence through acts of creation."

"You mean writers and artists can achieve immortality if they're good enough?"

"Not just them. When I pick up Tolstoy, for example, I am instantly connected with his world, his mind, and therefore both of us have transcended. And my world has become richer for the new layer his perceptions have added to it."

"The goal of the Tao is to detach from this world."

"Why on earth would you want to do that?"

"Because our attachments to it prevent us from seeing beyond it."

"You know, Stuart, I've heard a lot of stupid theories in my life, but that really takes the cake. If you want to believe that, be my—"

"What's so special about *your* world, Vida?" He had a way of saying her name that made it sound like she'd made it up. "Teaching books your students will never remember? Keeping them pinned to chairs they ache to get out of? Does that have meaning? Driving home. Making lousy dinners." He pointed to her glass. "Measuring out your precious bourbon. Fucking my father while you're—"

"Stuart, that's enough," Tom barked.

Stuart looked at his father and finished: "shit-faced. Is that the height of existence, of consciousness?"

A teacher needed at all times a face impervious to shock or insult, but twice in her career, a student had done or said something so unexpectedly awful that her skin reddened. Each time was a surprise—the prickling in her cheeks, then the pulsing heat—and she had resented it deeply. She felt it now; within a few seconds her face would be a flaming carnation. Far more than his words, what angered her was that he was going to make her blush.

"You're not going to find your mother this way, Stuart," she said.

True to his convictions, Stuart seemed perfectly detached. "I'm not trying to *find* her, Vida. I'm trying to let her go."

She watched Tom close up the white boxes of leftover rice and lo mein and carry them by their perfect wire handles to the fridge. He slid her plate out from beneath her without a word. He was pursing his lips, a sure sign that he was upset. She wondered why he didn't go have a talk with Stuart. He usually scampered so quickly back to the children's hallway if there was any tension at dinner. She hoped when he did that he wouldn't be too hard on the boy. An apology to her would suffice.

He was at the sink now, scraping and rinsing. She heard a huge plop into the garbage disposal. Someone had hardly touched the food. She wondered if it was her. Or Peter. Where had Peter gone? She couldn't even remember him sitting at the table. She collected what remained on the table and brought it to Tom. He dropped the forks he was rinsing and wheeled around to her.

"Where does all that anger of yours come from?" He grabbed the bottle from the pantry closet. "From inside here?" He shook it at her. She was surprised by how little was left. "Or is it in here"—he poked her in the bone between her breasts—"all the time, crouching, waiting?"

Vida was stunned. The scene was like the nightmare in which one of her best-behaved students hurls obscenities at her. The poke on her chest stung and spread.

"The boy is simply trying to cope."

"But he's filling himself with illusions."

"We're all filled with illusions."

"No we're not."

"Taoism is one hell of a lot less harmful than practically all the other ways of dealing with grief he could have latched onto."

"I'm not so sure. Actionless action. Blankety blank. He's negating himself from his own life. He's disappearing."

"Why does it upset you so much? It's just a way of looking at the world."

"It's a way of *not* looking at the world. You heard him. He wants to detach. You might as well give him a shotgun so he can blow his head off."

"Jesus Christ, Vida."

There it was finally, the glare, the tone of voice he'd been denying himself. He saw her now for what she truly was; he saw the waste within. She needed to get out of the house. She threw on a coat and whistled for Walt.

"I don't know why you're trying to push us away. All of us. Ever since you agreed to marry me, you've been—"

"Pinched and thin?"

"I don't understand what happened. I thought you were—"

"Someone else?"

"Stop it. Stop finishing my sentences. Stop looking at me with that smirk like you can see all around me, like I'm a character for you to analyze. You don't have to be a goddamn *English* teacher all the time. Just be *yourself.*"

"And who do you think that is?"

He looked up at the ceiling and shook his head. "I don't know. I think it's the woman I first saw at a podium, in tears, clutching a little silver cup. It's the woman, the first woman, who let me talk about Mary without feeling threatened in some way. God, what's happened to her? You've gotten so hard and closed and—"

"Let's leave our sex life out of it." She couldn't resist a little humor. And these memories of his—where did they come from? She certainly wasn't *in tears* at the podium.

"I'm not joking, Vida. I don't give a flying fuck about the sex. It's our marriage I care about. You have to work at marriage. It doesn't come easy to anyone. But it's like you've already given up on it. Before you even gave it a chance. You're like that student of yours who decides he hates the book before he's opened it."

"I'm going to take the dog for a walk."

"I'll come," Tom said.

He actually believed they could talk their way through it. "Screw you," she said, and slammed the door, nearly catching Walt's tail.

She wished she'd glanced at Tom's face. He'd probably never been spoken to like that in his life. "Little goody-two-shoes," she muttered, then laughed at her childishness.

It was freezing out. Walt looked up at her as if asking her to reconsider, then he bowed his head into the wind and they set off. The cold felt good; escape felt good. She was trapped, trapped like Dorothea with Casaubon, like the new wife at Manderlay.

"Ma!" Peter called from the front steps, yanking a sweatshirt over his head. "Can I come?"

He didn't wait for an answer. "It's cold," he said, his breath hanging white between them. The sweatshirt added bulk to his frame. His shoulders never seemed so wide to her before.

They followed Walt as he trailed a smell down the strip of grass inserted between the sidewalk and curb, carefully shifting his nose for oncoming trees and poles, then shifting back again. Her arm began to ache and she let go of the leash. They had to move swiftly to keep up with him.

"You've got some beans in you tonight, old man." Her voice was distant and unnatural. Nothing seemed recognizable out here tonight. She wasn't sure which street Walt had led them onto. Had they turned right back there, or left?

But Walt knew where they were going. He swerved into the same driveway they'd stood in that morning. The house was just a house being fixed up. The smell had retracted in the cold.

Peter stood beside her, too close. He had something to say.

"He asked you to come with me, didn't he?"

"Yeah."

"Why is that?"

"He was worried, I guess."

"Worried that what, I'd hang myself on a tree with Walt's leash?" She hadn't meant to be so specific.

"Worried you wouldn't come back."

"Oh for Christ's sake where am I going to go?"

"Ma—"

"I don't want to be called Ma. Stop calling me that."

She could smell the wood now, the new doors and floors. But it was mild, unmenacing. Now she could follow Walt up the steps, stand here and look at the sawhorses, breathe in the dust from all the new floors. None of it provoked any reaction. It almost felt like she was remembering someone else.

Walt disappeared through a doorless opening. Peter called to him, but not with the urgency Walt responded to. They waited for him on the porch. The street was quiet, with only the thin hum of a streetlight and a faraway squeak of a car frame going over a speed bump. She had a mind to tell Peter right here, tell him everything. Tell him about the porcelain sink and the fresh boards on the floor and the sound of the football game across the street rising and falling and rising again and how all the other teachers and even the workmen had left their work to see the last half of a close game, left their tools scattered in the hallway, the only witnesses to her steps from the classroom to the bathroom, her last fearless steps in life, one two three four five and her thoughts on the toilet as simple as hoping that her mother would be making chicken for dinner and the water running warm now from the sink—before the renovations there was only cold—and she kept her hands under it too long. At first she thought the lights had gone out, the way in the mirror the room darkened behind her. He brought her down quickly, smashing her chin to the sink, her lower teeth cutting clean through her tongue in two places. She heard a grunt as he turned her over, the clang of his belt buckle, the rip of fabric, then skin, her own gagging on the blood in her mouth, and a horrible boarlike snorting—but she never heard the sound of his voice. In some memories she is clawing, hitting, writhing, but in others she is perfectly still, save the blood pouring out of her mouth. Her dress was badly stained. I bit my tongue, she told her mother, who had in fact made chicken, when she got home.

"Walt!" she called, and he came immediately, head lowered by the sharpness in her voice.

Peter knocked the railing with his sneaker. "Tom loves you, you know. If you could just lighten up a bit."

So this is what he had to say to her. That she should lighten up.

Walt pushed the side of his face against her thigh, then, finding her hand, nudged his way in against her palm. The shape of his head beneath her hand was the most familiar object in her life.

Peter waited for her to respond but she didn't. That there was a burning hole in her chest was all she could have told him. He walked ahead of her and Walt, his gaze following the smoke rising from chimneys, following people as they flickered past their windows. He peered hopefully into every house, as if he were looking for someone he knew.

THE PARTY WAS OUT IN SUTTON, A FORTY-MINUTE DRIVE NORTH. IT WAS the first senior party Peter had ever been invited to. The entire upper school had been invited—Scott Laraby's parents had gone to St. Croix for a week.

Jason's sister Carla drove them. She was back from college and had brought her roommate with her. They were listening to the worst music Peter had ever heard, more breathing and talking than singing, with one screeching instrument in the background. When Peter looked up front to see what radio station would play such awful music, he saw that the two girls were holding hands.

Jason told Carla to drop them off at the end of the Larabys' long driveway. As they walked toward the light flickering through the trees, Peter asked about Carla and the roommate.

"Neither of them have boyfriends," Jason said, "so they practice with each other. That's what my dad says."

They continued in silence up the road. Peter could smell the stain on his hands, and he was glad. He'd spent most of the afternoon with Tom in the garage, helping him work on a table he was making for one of his assistants who'd recently gotten engaged. Peter had taken shop at school; he'd made a napkin holder and a stool the shape of a turtle. He'd never found any pleasure in the dry noisy room with Mr. McCaffy. He didn't like being around wailing machines that could cut off fingers or fighting with his classmates over the best scraps of sandpaper. He felt like stuff was always in his eyes. But with Tom it was different; it was peaceful. Fresh air came in freely through the open garage doors. People driving by saw them working together and waved. The brand-new sandpaper came in large sheets. They started with the coarse brown squares and finished with the soft black ones. The whole table felt warm and velvety smooth when they were done, more like skin than wood.

Tom threw out the used pieces of sandpaper and brought out the stain. He pried open the can, stirred it with a wooden stick, and placed two brushes beside it. There was a certain tenderness to each gesture, and Peter understood that he was in the presence of someone doing something he loved. He wasn't sure he'd witnessed that before. Most of his teachers had probably once loved their subjects, but their passion was hidden under layers of frustration, years of repetition.

Staining, it turned out, was even more satisfying than sanding. Stain had none of the stress of paint, which Peter remembered glopped and streaked and never went on as evenly as you hoped. It was hard to make a mistake with stain. Sometimes they talked; sometimes there was just the sound of their brushes. He'd never really been comfortable with a grown man before. Nothing was worse than being stuck alone with Jason's father, who stood with arms crossed over his broad chest and stiff black hair coming out of his nose as he assaulted Peter with questions. He felt awkward around all his male teachers and coaches; perhaps it was his less than stellar performances, or perhaps it was their knowledge of the absence of his father, their fear that he was looking for a substitute, or Peter's fear that they had this fear. He even felt uncomfortable in the presence of his great-grandfather's bronzed head in the vestibule. But with Tom after a while he just felt himself, the self he was when he was alone. Things just came out of his mouth; he didn't rehearse his lines first, as he often did with Stuart or before speaking in class.

"Peter," Tom said into one of their comfortable silences. "Did you ever meet your grandparents? You know," he added hastily, "your mother's parents?"

"No."

"Has she ever told you about them, or told you about her childhood?"

"She didn't like them much. They moved around a lot and my mother read in the backseat of the car. That's all I know."

Tom waited a while, then asked, "What was your mother like when you were little? Do you remember?"

"I don't know," he stalled. He knew Tom wanted him to say she was different somehow. "She played more games, maybe." He wished they didn't have to talk about her. He wished he just lived with the Belous without her getting in the way.

"Has she always had a few drinks at night?"

"No, not always. I think it was more on weekends, if she went out."

"Did she go out a lot?"

"Probably once a month." Peter kept staining, watching how quickly the wood absorbed the color.

Tom nodded, then asked softly, "And would she come home drunk?"

"Not drunk. Not like she couldn't walk or talk. Just kind of happy. She's actually a lot nicer that way." Ever since that fight in the kitchen, he'd wanted to tell Tom this.

"My father drank himself into his grave before he was fifty." Tom's voice was slow and hard and his mouth had fallen down into his chin. "I won't let that happen to anyone else I love."

The front door and all the first-story windows of the Larabys' house were open. As he and Jason crossed a circle of wet grass, the machinelike hum they'd hardly been aware of broke into separate human voices. Kristina. Kristina would be here. His heart thumped heavily. Peter could see people holding beers.

"Aren't they worried about the neighbors telling?" he said.

"What neighbors?"

It was true. The property was encased in woods; the last house Peter had seen was miles back.

"I'm going to get laid tonight," Jason said.

"Yeah, right." But Jason's confidence made him uneasy, and Peter worried that that was how you had to be to get a girl, even just to kiss a girl.

They stepped into the front hall, where a group of seniors leaned against paintings on the wall.

"Hey, J-man," Kent Scully said. "Keg's in the kitchen."

"Cool."

Peter wasn't exactly sure what a keg looked like. Jason was starting to know a lot more than he did. Peter watched him lead the way, greeting juniors and seniors, being greeted. There was no mockery in it anymore for him. Peter got the same twisted smiles and the funny voices he got in the hallways at school. "Does your mommy-mommy know where you are?" he heard someone say behind him. Peter had learned to block it out. Kristina was his only thought. It was the only thought he'd ever had since he'd started going to parties. And so useless. He'd heard that week at school that she'd broken up with Brian again, but even that, if he was really honest with himself, would never matter.

They passed a small den filled with kids from his grade holding plastic cups and trying to act like they'd been to senior parties before. Kristina, who certainly didn't have to fake that, would never be among them.

Scott Laraby, the host, lay spread-eagle and fast asleep on the kitchen table. A girl with a few of Scott's features, the same stunned eyes and pushed-in nose, was in the corner, operating what Peter guessed was the keg. It didn't need an operator—all you had to do was press a little button at the end of a hose—but she had put herself on a stool with the cups stacked between her knees just to be able to talk to everybody. It was the kind of thing Peter would do if he had the chance, and it made him instantly dislike her.

He and Jason got in line.

"Easy does it this round, sailor," she said to a guy in a blue-and-white-striped shirt.

When it was their turn Jason asked if she was Scott's sister.

She nodded at her brother, passed out on the table. "Some girls have all the luck."

"So why don't you go to Fayer?"

"Oh, it was decided long ago I'm not private school material. Red or blue?"

"Whichever's bigger," Jason said, though of course he knew the cups were the same size.

"You like 'em big?" she said.

"Always have."

Peter was left out of these kinds of provocative, senseless exchanges. He couldn't respond to them any better than he could initiate them. As if sensing this, Scott's sister handed Peter a blue cup without a word and poured. Other people, even girls, even now Jason, exuded something he did not. He was as bland as water, as unremarkable as air. He and his cup of foam moved on while Jason stayed at the keg bantering with the sister.

Peter had no choice but to head to the room of tenth graders. He took the long way around, glancing into the dining room. At the far end of the long table was Kristina with two guys he'd never seen before, older guys, maybe even older than seniors. She was holding a small pleated paper cup, the kind you rinse with at the dentist's, up to the mouth of a bottle with a fancy gold necklace around it. When it was full, she knocked back the liquor in one swallow. Her throat was much paler than her face and arms. The guys were smiling at each other. Peter knew what they were after; probably Kristina knew, too. She wouldn't want him to intervene. Although the sight disgusted him, something—that oval of pale skin, the already drunken shape of her lips—aroused him and he tugged down the front of his sweatshirt over the tightening of his pants.

He tried to imagine Stuart at this party, standing with his perfect posture. He'd drink water instead of beer and make it seem cool. In a half hour he'd be able to get any girl he wanted. Trying to invoke Stuart's spirit through the meditative techniques he'd taught him, Peter straightened his spine, became aware of his organs, and dissolved his tension. He took a long deep breath, a long gulp of beer, and vowed he'd fool around with someone, nearly anyone (it didn't have to be Kristina—it could never be Kristina), tonight.

When he turned away from the dining room, he noticed that the three most lusted-after junior girls were watching him. He tried to look at them the way Stuart looked at his girls through the window, pleased but unsurprised. They buckled, all three of them, to the floor in heaves of laughter. He retreated immediately to the den, grateful for the flat chests and sympathetic voices of the unpopular girls.

Jenny Mead made room for him in the circle. She asked about the game yesterday, and about the French test he'd barely passed. As she listened, she ran a finger around the lip of her cup. Did she have a thing for him? He could see her searching for another topic.

"Your mom's the hardest English teacher I've ever had," she said at last.

Everyone said this to him. "Really?" he said, stretching his spine as high as it would go. She was tall, and her bushy hair didn't help.

"I don't understand what she's talking about half the time." But Jenny had clear blue-green eyes and a small nose like a fawn's. It wouldn't be awful, kissing her.

"She probably doesn't know what she's talking about either."

Jenny snorted, her upper lip revealing too much gum. He looked away, at a funny kind of sofa across the room. It was like a figure eight, with the two cushioned seats facing in opposite directions.

"Are you close, you and your mom?"

Girls loved to ask him this. "I guess," he said. Then he looked at the little sofa as if he were just noticing it for the first time. "The guy who made that must have lost his job pretty quick."

Jenny laughed, though he could tell it was fake. "It's a Victorian love seat."

He'd been about to ask her if she wanted to sit in it, but he couldn't now that she'd used the word love. They stood there staring at it.

"Should we try it out?" she said. In the end, girls were so much braver.

Peter chose the seat that faced the doorway, in case Kristina walked by. It was far more comfortable than it looked.

"Hey." Jenny's face was unnaturally close. It was a Victorian make-out couch. Stuart would kiss her right now. Right *now*. But Peter couldn't.

Disappointed but not discouraged, she asked, "What kind of things do you talk about?"

"When?"

"With your mom?"

"Let's see." He knew it had to be provocative. "Marijuana, condoms, pornography—the usual topics."

She flung her head back, leaving her mouth wide open. He couldn't tell if she was really laughing now or just putting together all the elements of laughing—except the sound. When she tipped her head forward again, she said, "No, really. Does she ever talk about what she was like when she was our age? I mean, some teachers you can completely imagine as teenagers, but your mom . . ." Jenny's clear eyes widened as if she were staring into the pitch dark. "No amount of rationality can convince you that she was ever young."

He'd forgotten that if you talked to Jenny Mead long enough, her sentences would start getting weird.

He looked around the room for other possibilities. The handful of other girls were either unobtainable or unthinkable. He had this awful feeling that Kristina had left the party with those two guys. It was Jenny Mead or nothing. The thought of hinting to Stuart when he got home that he had gotten some action spurred him on.

"Of course my mother was young once. She was wild. She grew up in Skaneateles, New York."

"I thought she was from the South. She has that accent."

"She was born in New York, then moved away later. Her parents were so strict they wouldn't let her go to any parties, so she had to sneak out onto the roof and shimmy down a rope she hid up there."

"Why wouldn't her parents let her go out?"

"They were Christian Scientists." He couldn't remember exactly what Stuart had said.

"They go to parties. They just don't go to the hospital."

"Mormon. Sorry. Mormon."

"But—"

"Do you want to talk about religion or hear about my mother?"

He meant to be playful but it came out snippy, the way Fran was to him sometimes. He wondered if she, too, didn't always mean her snips. He remembered his conversation with Tom this afternoon, and his stomach rolled over. It wasn't just a little chat; it was a warning.

He saw the extent of Jenny Mead's interest and excitement only as it drained out of her face. Just as he was about to apologize, Kristina came into the den and flopped sideways in an armchair. Alone. Not just her lips but all around her mouth was red, like someone had been scrubbing it clean. Her cheeks were flushed in two bright splotches and her eyes moved around the room without latching onto anything. She was smashed. He remembered a time when she wasn't like this, when at parties they made lemonade from scratch and had cookie-eating competitions. He remembered Stephen Ball's birthday party and how she asked to be Peter's partner in the three-legged race and how when they'd fallen her hair had gone in his mouth and it tasted like pizza he'd said and they'd laughed because she'd actually had three slices of pizza for breakfast. He ached with a love for her that had existed for as long as he could remember.

"It was nice talking to you, Peter," Jenny said bitterly and rejoined her clique in the corner.

Peter remained in his side of the love seat, pretending to read the spines of the hardcover mysteries on the wall. He tried to catch Kristina's eye for a sort of comradely shrug about being alone in chairs at a party. But her eyes were three-quarters closed. He didn't know if she was actually seeing through the quarter that was left, though he remained prepared for anything.

Then one of the older guys from the kitchen was in the doorway. He was pointing Kristina out to someone else, some tall, thick-armed guy with lime-green hair. A swimmer. He crouched in front of her chair and whispered into her right ear. Her feet twitched, her stomach bobbed, then a smile came across her flushed face. It was like he was breathing life into her one puff at a time. When he straightened up and left the room she followed, holding on to his fingers in front of her with both hands.

The swimmer led her up a flight of stairs. It was easy to trail them. Everyone in the hallway and on the staircase was moving, shifting, craning necks in search of a better place or better companions. Peter didn't recognize any of them. The house was now packed with kids from other schools who had sniffed out a party. They wore varsity jackets from Sutton High and Whaley High and St. Andrew's Prep. As he climbed he became aware of tension down below. Scott Laraby was awake and asking people to get off the piano. It was a Steinway, he said apologetically. People were arguing in the kitchen. The back of the swimmer's shirt said *Beer: It's Not Just for Breakfast Anymore*. Upstairs the hallways were empty but there were small parties in each of the bedrooms he passed. Someone lying stomach-down on a bean-bag chair called out to Kristina. She didn't turn. In one room with a linoleum floor Peter saw an oven and smelled brownies baking. The swimmer opened the next door with one hand and pulled Kristina in with the other. The door shut quickly behind them.

Peter listened. The party below made it impossible to hear within. He gave them thirty seconds to come out. Then he went in.

The swimmer stood a few feet from the door. Peter expected him to be furious, maybe even to punch him, but he just shook his head. "She's really out of it, man. You can give her a try. I'm not into laying corpses."

"Get out of here," Peter said, but the guy was already gone.

Peter pulled the door shut and locked it. The bedroom was huge, with several mahogany bureaus the size of mastodons hulking around its edges. In the center of the bed, her head wrenched up on overstuffed pillows, was Kristina. Her eyelids were still lowered; her eyes didn't seem to follow his approach.

He sat, like a doctor, at her left side, one foot raised, one foot firmly on the ground.

At the sudden depression in the mattress, she tilted her head. Then she said his name. Her parents were Russian, and though she had arrived in this country with no English, not a trace of an accent remained. Except if you listened very carefully to her saying your name. Then you would hear a faint long o where the first e should be. Poter. If there was one sound he could take with him into eternity, that would be it.

"How's it going, Kristina?"

"I'm drunk."

"Yeah." Already, this was the most they had spoken all year.

"She wouldn't let me spend the night at Sarah's."

"So she's coming to pick you up?"

"My father," she whimpered.

"When?"

"Eleven-thirty."

He looked at the alarm clock. Sixty-three minutes. He saw there was an adjoining bathroom. Water. He filled the two heavy crystal glasses by the sink and she drank obediently. "I'm going to get in so much trouble."

He went to the bathroom for more. When he returned, she was sleeping.

"No!" He clapped his hands. "Wake up!"

No response.

He got on his knees beside her. "Kris." He'd never called her that before. It was reserved for Sarah, her best friend, and Brian. "Kris," he said again, and touched her arm. He meant to shake it, but once his fingers met the plushness of her flesh—how different a girl's arm was; was there any muscle at all?—he couldn't bear to disturb any part of her. Without letting go, he pulled his legs up under him and sat close to her.

Of course he knew she was pretty, but he had long since stopped being able to see it. He had loved her so much and for so long that when he saw her at school her whole body seemed encased in an iridescent haze, a sort of body halo so bright he couldn't see inside. But now with her eyes shut and her body so still, her light was diffuse and he saw everything. Her hair was blacker than he ever imagined, weakening only to dark blue where the lamplight fell on it. Between his fingers the strands were thick, horselike. He brushed her bangs sideways and found that, like her throat, her forehead was pale and unfreckled. She had a cluster of blackheads along the curve of her left nostril. The redness was gone from around her mouth and her heavy lips, pooled to one side, advanced and receded with the tide of her breath. He thought of that sonnet they'd spent so much time on last year, about the girlfriend's breath not being like perfume, and her cheeks not like roses and her lips not as red as something else. And then the last two lines—he wished he could remember them—that confessed the speaker's rare, unending love. At the time, he'd thought it was stupid like all the other poems and crap they had to read, but now it stepped out from the rest like a friend who had known all along about this night with Kristina, understood how beautiful she was here before him, more beautiful than she had ever been within her shining halo.

What was stopping him from lifting her shirt, taking a look— most likely his only chance ever—at what lay beneath? He knew it was neither respect for her body nor fear of shame if she woke up. It was something more like pride. He wasn't sure he'd ever used this word outside of English class before. But he knew it was the right one. He wanted the invitation. He would wait for that.

The numbers on the digital clock changed all at once. Eleven o'clock. How had he wasted thirty-three minutes? Gazing, touching, remembering poetry of all things. Her father was going to come banging on the door and Peter would never be allowed near her again.

"Wake up!" he shouted, shaking her with both arms.

Her eyes flashed open. Her lips tightened. "Jesus Christ."

"I'm sorry. I'm so sorry but thank God you're awake. Your father is coming in a half hour." He thought this news would alarm her into action, or at least panicky tears, but she just shut her eyes again.

"Kristina!"

He pulled her by both arms up to sitting, then pushed her to the edge of the bed. Her eyes were back to those inscrutable slits. He spun her legs around so that they were dangling with his off the side. "C'mon. Up you go." He slung her arm over his shoulder and fastened it with his hand like they did in movies. He put his other arm around her waist. "Let's walk."

The room was large enough that they could make a loop of about twenty paces. After his neck got used to the pain, he let himself enjoy the fact that he had her—he had her!—in his arms. She was unbelievably soft, as if there were cushions beneath her skin. He had no idea girls felt like this. No one had told him! He and his mother had hugged so rarely, but his memory of it was all bones, his fingers falling between the ribs in her back, his ear bent by her collarbone. A general thrill at the squishiness of girls momentarily engulfed the specific thrill of Kristina finally beside him. He caught himself in a mirror. He had never seen his face with such a smile.

He began counting their revolutions around the room. For the first twelve, she took very little responsibility for her own weight. Then, just when he began to give up hope, his load lightened.

"Poter, what're we doing?" Her head lifted from his shoulder; her legs, which had been dangling like a doll's, buoyed her up. The cessation of pain from his right ear all the way through to his elbow was instant, though the relief was not worth the loss of her hair against his cheek.

"We're getting you sober."

"Oh."

He waited for her to pull away from him, but she didn't.

They kept walking. In the mirror their eyes met and she burst out laughing.

"What?" he said.

"Did you ever read *Pride and Prejudice*?"

"No." He figured it was some story about a beautiful woman and a pathetic man who had no chance with her.

"Those people were always taking 'turns' around drawing rooms. They walked very straight and proper and they held each other like this. Look." Her words were clear, but she had a hard time slipping her arm through his like she wanted.

"What did they talk about?"

Her drunkenness seemed to come in waves now. She made a strange noise, as if several words had piled on top of each other. She hung on tight to him and tried again. "Lotsastuff. Secrets. Gossip. Whas rich, poor, pregnant."

He wanted to kiss her. He wanted to push her down on the bed. Even though she was carrying her own weight now, her whole body knocked against his as they walked. He had an erection but she wasn't going to notice and he was too overwhelmed by his good fortune to care.

"So what are *your* secrets?"

He was not above taking verbal advantage of her.

"Oh God. I have too many." She let go of him then and fell onto a corner of the bed.

"You've got to keep moving, Kristina." He slipped his arm back through hers and tried to lift her up.

"Cut it out!" She jerked her arm away, then brought the elbow back and sunk it into his ribs.

He cried out. He hated this kind of unexpected pain. He knew it was what kept him from being a better athlete and he hated that, too. But the thought of her leaving the room checked his anger.

"How about some more water?"

He brought her a glass from the bedside table. The clock read 11:16. She drank, then had trouble setting it on the floor. It spilled, but she didn't seem to notice.

"Tell me one of your secrets," he said.

"Okay. But you're hovering."

Peter sat down near her feet.

"Okay," she said again, "I'm going to give you a good one."

He nodded. He didn't care now how much he was smiling. He was happy; he was with her.

"Miss Whitmore tried to kiss me last year."

"Oh c'mon. It's got to be real."

"That is one hundred percent true. I swear."

"After a game or something?"

"No, in her office. She was taping up my stick after practice and showing me this little crack at the tip and when I leaned down she leaned up and I had to jerk away. It was incredibly awkward."

"You're lying."

"I am not lying."

"Did you tell anyone?"

"You're the first."

"Now that's a lie."

"You have serious problems trusting people."

"Why would you tell me of all people that story?"

"What do you mean *you* of all people?" She lay back on her elbows. From his angle on the floor her breasts nearly blocked out her face. Even when they were horizontal they were huge.

"We're not exactly close friends."

"What do you mean? We grew tomatoes and leeks together."

"That was in sixth grade."

"We canoed down the Pawcatiqua River."

"Piscataqua. In seventh. With everyone else in our class."

"But we collected firewood together the first night."

"We did?" Was it possible there was a moment with her he'd forgotten?

"And we got lost and had to sleep curled up next to each other all night for warmth."

"That definitely did not happen.'

"No, but I wanted it to."

"Really?"

"C'mere," she said, patting a space beside her. *C'mere, cutie* was what she said to Brian.

He lifted himself up onto the bed. His heart was cracking his ribs.

"Lie down," she said.

He lay on his side and she rolled over to face him. Their knees touched. He was trembling all over—even his lips were trembling—but she didn't seem to notice. The only way he knew she was still very drunk was that she would never be this close to him otherwise.

Her eyes hooded over. She had very thick eyelids. And Belou earlobes. A smile came to her lips. "Are you thinking about sex?"

Peter laughed. "No."

"What are you thinking about?"

"Earlobes."

He knew he could kiss her, should kiss her, but he wanted to wait till his nerves calmed down a bit. Otherwise he wouldn't feel it. And he might bite her or something spastic like that.

"Earlobes," she said without curiosity. Then her eyes opened and she tilted her head up. "You know what I think about sex? I think we only know a fraction of all there is to know about it. It's like in psychology, how Freud said our consciousness is only the tip of the iceberg. I think we only understand the tip of our sexual urges and how to fulfill them. What our parents' generation knows about sex, what they do, depresses me so much. Is that all there is? Kissing, feeling up, feeling down, then sex. Peg in the hole. Guy on top or girl on top. It's so completely limited. I think there's another universe—many universes—waiting out there for us, and we have to find them." She was breathing heavily now; all those words had taken a lot of effort.

He saw at that moment that they hadn't just taken different paths; she had traveled around the sun and the moon and was bored, while he hadn't begun moving yet.

"What do you think?" she asked.

"I think, with the right person—"

"Oh spare me. You sound like my mother."

"You talk to your mother about all this?"

"Of course not, but if I did that's just what she'd say. 'Brian's just not the right person for you. Wait for the right.'" She had slipped into her mother's accent. "'Then you know.'"

Through the mockery Peter could sense some hope that her mother's theory was true. He knew he should kiss her, that she was waiting, that she was ready to believe. But he also knew that he would fail. It would be like going to the Olympics with no training. Why hadn't he taken the practice when it had been offered to him—Jill at last year's class movie night, Amy at the fall dance? Even Jenny Mead on the love seat would have helped him practice for this moment. He hadn't because he was waiting for the right person. There had only ever been one right person but he never realized that when she finally lay beside him he'd wish that he'd kissed all those wrong ones first.

She was looking at him, though the alcohol made her eyes sink repeatedly down to his shoulder and it seemed to take a great deal of effort to raise them up again. Her breaths through her nose were short and loud. If he kissed her now, even managed to travel to another universe with her, she'd never remember it. He couldn't think of a time in the past two years when she hadn't been drunk at a party or a dance. It had started in eighth grade, at their very first dance. Billy Chesney had gotten his brother to buy a case of beer and leave it in the woods. He remembered Kristina coming into the gym that night. She looked so happy, like she'd just gotten really good news. He doubted he'd have had the the courage to ask her to dance, but he didn't even get the chance. She just went out onto the floor and started dancing. All the other girls stood around the edges waiting to be asked but Kristina just danced with whoever came to her. He knew she was different that night, but he didn't find out why until the next week when Lloyd discovered the empty carton in the woods. After that there was always drinking outside of school. He used to like watching her get happier, goofier. Sometimes he could even get her to smile at him across a room. But this year she seemed to skip the happy stage and go right to blotto. He doubted she'd even remember the swimmer or those guys at the dining room table tomorrow.

"Kristina?"

Her eyes swam up slowly toward him. "Mmm?"

Her hands were gathered under her chin. He took one out and held it in both of his. It was warm and sticky. "Do you think you might have a problem, a problem with drinking too much alcohol like this, at parties?" Oh God, why had he said it? She had a vicious temper. She would bolt.

But she didn't move. She just squeezed his hand hard. "Sometimes I think I might," she whispered. "Oh God, Peter, I don't want to be drunk right now. I wish I could just take a pill and feel normal. I don't know what happens. The idea of going to a party and not being buzzed—and now my father's going to come and—"

"Damn." Peter looked at the clock. "It's eleven-thirty-seven."

"Shit!" She sat up as he knew she would. "Holy fuck. He's here.

He's never late." She slapped her face. "And he's going to know. He's going to know."

Out in the hallway her name was being called.

"See? He's incapable of being late."

"There's a back staircase. There has to be. C'mon." He yanked her up, unlocked the door, and led her down the hall, away from the way he came. People were yelling her name outside and in. He released his grip on her arm and took her hand. It felt familiar already. Why hadn't he kissed her?

They came to a stairwell. He'd kiss her there at the bottom, before he delivered her to her father. With her free hand she wiped away tears and patted her face. "Sorry, I was in the bathroom," she said to herself, practicing.

The steps bent around to the kitchen. Sarah was at the bottom looking up. "Jesus Christ. There you are. Your father is having a shit fit out there."

Kristina let go of Peter, pushed past him, as if he'd been in her way this whole time. "Daddy, I'm right *here*," he heard her call out, irritated, as if the only trouble had been her father's eyesight.

From the front hall window, Peter watched them walk out into the driveway. Her father was examining her and she was pretending not to notice. When he had decided she was sober, he put his arm around her shoulder and guided her to the green Mercedes whose license plate, 210514, Peter knew by heart. She rolled down the window and waved to people on the grass as her father turned the car around. She didn't look toward the house. Perhaps she had already forgotten him.

Carla came at midnight, and when they got on the highway, Jason leaned into the front seat. "Can you turn it up a bit?" This meant he wanted to talk. He sat back and waited for Peter to ask.

"You and the sister?"

"An hour and a half in the poolhouse." Jason shut his eyes.

"Sounds cold."

"I was amazing."

"You were amazing?"

"I think she must have had fourteen orgasms."

"Wow."

"Yeah. Wow."

If Peter asked anything more specific, Jason would get prickly, so he kept quiet. Up front they were giggling. The roommate kept wiping the fogged-up windshield with what looked like a brown bra.

"So where were you?" Jason asked, expecting little.

"With Kristina."

"Kristina *Luhzin*?"

"Yeah."

"No."

"Yes," Peter said. A small elated laugh slipped out.

"Where?"

"Upstairs."

"In a bedroom?"

"Yeah."

"And?"

"We talked."

"Talked? I saw her. She was bombed."

"I was trying to sober her up. Before her father came."

"You were alone in a bedroom with her all that time and nothing happened? You got nothing off her?"

"A lot *happened*. I mean, I could have kissed her. She wanted me to, I think."

"But you didn't."

"She was drunk."

"Of course she was drunk. That's the *point* of parties. Girls get drunk because they want us and can't ask for it unless they're drunk."

"Kristina doesn't want me."

Even Jason couldn't argue with that. "Well, she asked for it tonight and you didn't have the cojones to do it."

"Fuck you."

"Fuck me? Try fucking her."

Peter had never hit anyone before, not like that. It didn't even feel like a decision—he just watched his right fist cross his chest and smash into Jason's face. Jason pummeled him four or five blows so fast he couldn't get another swipe at him. Carla was swearing at them in the rearview mirror and just when Peter was about to land another solid punch, he was shoved hard against the door handle. The roommate was sprawled above them like a hawk, one flat palm pressed against Peter's chest, the other against Jason's.

"Fucking cut it out." They were the only words he ever heard her say.

She flexed her arms, shoving him and Jason simultaneously slightly farther apart, then withdrew and settled in even closer to Carla.

Why *hadn't* he kissed Kristina? Why had just lying there talking to her been enough? Why hadn't he jumped her with the same unconscious passion and urgency with which he had just punched Jason? That's what it was like for other guys in love. In movies they leapt out of chairs, dashed across rooms, clutched and grabbed and pressed themselves against the women they loved. Why hadn't he had any of those impulses? Why was he so self-conscious, so controlled? What was wrong with him? Was he gay?

It was a long ride home. Peter told himself he wasn't going to say anything to any of them when he got out of the car, but a small "thanks" slipped out anyway.

The house had not been waiting for him, not the way his old house waited, the way it seemed glad when his feet touched the porch steps in the afternoon. When he lived there, he'd never really thought of it as home. Home was something in books and always had more than two people living in it. Home wasn't a borrowed gardener's cottage on a school campus, even if it had once belonged to his grandparents. But now he missed the smell of it, a blend of cheese popcorn and wet dog. They still bought the cheese popcorn, and Walt still smelled, but the Belou house had its own smell that he and his mother would never alter, no matter what they brought into it.

He could see that someone, probably Stuart, was still up watching TV. Normally the prospect of hanging out on the couch with Stuart would have cheered him, but tonight he didn't feel like talking to anyone. He shut the door quietly and headed to his room. But he felt bad, felt rude, not even saying hi, and he glanced over to give at least a wave. It was Fran on the couch, her head turned away from him, one knee drawn up to her cheek. And she was shaking.

"Fran?"

She shook her head. "Just go to bed, Peter."

He moved to obey, then heard a huge gasping sob, as if she'd been carefully holding it in since he'd come through the door.

"Are you okay?" He moved closer and sat at the far edge of the couch.

"She hates me. She hates me so much." She raised her head, and her mouth, readying for another sentence, opened then kept opening, far wider than necessary, and the lips quivered as she struggled and failed to get control of it. A long moan careened out instead, ending in sharp, short cries. After a deep breath she said, "I was just talking about this stupid book I got out of the library and suddenly she's screaming at me, wanting to know my 'position,' telling me to clarify and then going on about 'girls like me' and how our brains are jellyfish or something. God, Peter, no wonder you're so—"

"What book?" He couldn't bear to hear her adjective for him.
"*The Thorn Birds.*"

"Oh. She hates that kind of book."

"Aren't English teachers supposed to *like* books? My teacher last year used to cry when he read us poetry. All I did was tell her what it was about and before I knew it she was screaming at me." She broke down again and hid her head.

"You can't take it personally. It's how she is about stuff like that."

"I was trying so hard." She wiped her nose, which was red and wet, and then wiped her palm on her shirt. It made a long filmy streak. In someone else he might have found that a little disgusting but Fran was exempt in his mind from those kinds of judgments. She did everything with such self-confidence he didn't dare question her, even to himself. It was this composure that made her tears, her complete lack of control of her mouth, so disturbing to him. She usually operated with such coolness and detachment, like nothing could ever really bother her.

"Things began really well. After I put Caleb to bed, it was just the three of us and Dad seemed happy that I was there, hanging out." He couldn't help noticing that her shirt was tighter than most things she wore and he could see, against her thigh, the outline of her right breast. "Daddy told his story about breaking his collarbone on a date in high school and your mother was laughing. Then she told us about a straight-A student who always had to wear this white fur hat of his grandmother's during tests. But then we started talking about books and she just snapped." Fran's face twisted up and her voice creaked but she was determined to get her next sentence out. "My mother never ever . . ." The rest of her words got lost in another long moan.

Peter touched her back. She was crying so hard he wasn't sure she could even feel his hand. He gave her a few pats, then began stroking her slightly. Her spine was like a row of marbles down her back, nothing like Kristina's padded bones. The memory of touching Kristina made his stomach hollow. Why hadn't he kissed her? What was wrong with him?

"I don't think my father has the strength to deal with all her problems. He's been through so much already. It doesn't seem fair." She began to cry so hard now that she made no sound at all except a little click click deep in her mouth. Peter let his fingers drift up to the ends of her hair and, on the next stroke, to her head. It was hot and moist at the roots. His heart was pounding so hard, harder than it had even with Kristina. With her head still down, Fran said, "I don't understand her. She's not like any other mother I've ever known. She's lucky you're such a . . . good kid. You could have turned out really badly. You could fly to the moon and back and she wouldn't even know you'd gone. She doesn't wash your clothes or tell you to pick up your room or even kiss you hello or good night or anything. She just reads her books, mixes her drinks, and smokes her cigarettes so she can get cancer one way or another and die, too." Peter barely heard her through the racing of his blood, daring him, urging him. She was talking and he was touching and she hadn't told him to stop. He watched his hand disappear into the hair in the back of her head. Then he felt it rising up and she looked at him for the first time that night. His hand was still tangled in her hair. "You're bleeding," she said. And he kissed her.

It was wet and salty with tears and blood and when she opened her mouth Peter did the same and their tongues met and it felt slimy, like kissing Walt. It felt like being a tadpole more than being human, a tadpole with a tiny brain and a big mouth and everything wet and silty all around. A rattle of breath from her nose poured out onto his cheek and he was so focused on his mouth he didn't know what he was doing with his hands though they were moving the whole time. It was noisy, this kind of kissing, and the noise made him like it even more. And then, in an instant, that whole briny, underwater world became memory. She hit him hard on the upper arm and stood up, wiping everything off her mouth. She was still crying as she told him he was gross and shouldn't be kissing his stepsister. Then she disappeared down the hall to her room.

Peter waited a long time before he got up. In the bathroom, Mrs. Belou was stern.

I thought it might come to this.

I'm sorry.

She's my little girl.

I know.

You don't know. What do you or your mother know about anything?

Peter turned away from the picture to the mirror. No wonder you're so—What had she been going to say? Wimpy? Boring? Dense? "Unfocused" and "distant" were words that appeared regularly on his report cards. Was his mother somehow responsible for that? He'd never thought of his mother in this way. She was like a building to him, tall, brick, permanently adjacent and absolutely necessary, whose shape he had never questioned, whose shadow he had never noticed until he stepped back and stood with the Belous at a safe distance. Now he could see the dilapidated frame, the broken windows, the rotting roof.

He sat on the toilet cover looking at the thin hand towels with the embroidered bluebells and the jar of dried petals on top of the wicker cabinet—decorations his mother would never have chosen. She would have left all those places bare and ugly.

He thought of how, not all that long ago and for as long into the past as he could remember, he used to fear her absence, and how the sound of the Dodge pulling up beneath his window could make him whimper with relief. He doubted he could ever feel that way about her again and for a moment, as the great building was razed swiftly to the ground, he felt guilty and ashamed. Then he turned back to the picture and saw a deepening smile.

Stuart was not in their room, and he was relieved. In his bed in the dark his body reexperienced, in random order, moments of the long night. The bra on the windshield, the smell of stain, the salty metallic slippery kiss, the blue black of Kristina's hair in his fingers, Jenny Mead's head tipping back. His mind could find nothing to rest on, nothing that made him feel safe.

SEVEN

VIDA CIRCLED THE CLASSROOM SLOWLY, STOPPING AT EACH WINDOW, feigning interest in the bleakness below. Wendell was out by the pond, raking up the last of the slimy half-frozen willow leaves at its edges. Her freshmen were writing an in-class essay comparing "A Perfect Day for Bananafish" with "A&P." If she looked toward them and not out the windows, their hands would shoot up with a hundred useless questions—Can I use purple ink? Where should I write my name?—questions designed simply to bring her over to their side where just the presence of her body was comforting to them. But they were in ninth grade now, and they needed to be broken of those middle school habits.

Stepmothering, she realized, was not all that different from teaching. It was essential to keep their intellectual development in mind at all times. You couldn't get all wrapped up in their needs and whims. Stuart and his mysticism. Fran reading *The Thorn Birds*. They were too old now for that kind of material. A young man needed a hearty Byronic outlook, not this boneless Taoism. And if Fran began to believe in the characters in novels like that, real people were going to be a sore and sorry disappointment. She would have to, once again, urge Fran to read *Tess of the d'Urbervilles;* that would teach her exactly how far she could trust a man, even a seemingly well-intentioned man like Angel Clare.

Or Tom Belou, who had withdrawn since her blowout with

Fran last week. He was angry in a way she didn't understand—placid, wordless anger. He had behaved yesterday as if he couldn't see her in the room. She figured that all marriages, if they lasted, ended up here in the land of quiet regret. She and Tom had simply arrived a little early. She had predicted it, but even her own conviction that she would fail did not protect her from the discomfort of having done so. In bed last night she had tried, her heart thumping stupidly, to make a small advance: one brave hand reaching up over the curve of his hip bone and down into still unfamiliar and terrifying ground—but it was soundly rejected and she lay awake for several hours cradling her humiliated fingers.

She moved to the windows at the back of the room. A dog she didn't recognize trotted briskly up the driveway. A few years ago Walt would have charged out to meet it, smell it, inform it of whose territory it had trespassed. This morning she'd had to lift him up and hold him before his bowls as all four legs quivered and shifted desperately for a painless balance. He took a tongueful of water, then looked at her, confused by his lack of appetite.

Behind her Patrick Watkins cleared his throat. He'd let his raised arm fall unbent into the crook of his other hand just to let her know how long he'd been trying to get her attention.

When she was beside him he asked, "Is it okay if I call Seymour Glass Morie? I mean, just sometimes? My father's best friend from college is named Seymour but we call him Morie so I've kind of gotten used to calling Seymour Glass Morie in my head."

"That's not okay, Patrick."

"Really?"

As she weaved through the desks back to the perimeter of the room, she saw that Mandy Hughs was dotting all of her i's with daisies. She'd only written half a page for all the time it took to make the petals. "No flowers," Vida said as she passed. "Just letters." How did those middle school English teachers sleep at night?

Finally the bell shook the floor. Her students dashed off their last thoughts and tossed their pages onto the pile on her desk. Everyone was suddenly free.

Peace returned to her classroom. She realigned her chairs, picked up flecks of torn notebook paper from the floor. She gathered up the essays, each page puckered on both sides from the ballpoint ink pressed on hard and nervously. If she were focused, she could get through half of these, then glance at the pages her sophomores read over the weekend before the next bell. But focus had eluded her lately. She was behind on her grading, and had been less than inspired in the classroom. Her students rattled her in a way they didn't used to. And the material, once so easily intellectualized, seemed to writhe under her inspection of it. Even Hardy, whose theories on Darwinism, religion, and social codes were as cold and straightforward as mathematics, was becoming a sensualist, with all those disgusting passages she'd never noticed before about the oozing fatness and rushing juices of summer, the dripping cheeses in the dairy where Tess takes refuge after her baby dies and meets Angel Clare.

"Vida."

A wild yelp came out of her as she spun toward the voice. It was Tom. Fuck him for sneaking up on her like that.

"I was just hoping . . ." he said, looking around, making sure they were alone. "I called to find out when you had a free period, and I thought we could talk."

She couldn't speak for the sudden thrumming of her heart. She'd heard nothing, no scuffle on the stairs, no crack of an old board in the hall. Fear, unable to hear reason, flooded her body.

"Is there someplace we could go? Someplace"—he looked around the dim, cavernous room—"smaller?"

The scare had heightened her perception yet dulled her reaction. She could smell the vinyl of his station wagon on him, but it took her a delayed moment to turn and lead him to her office.

He sat on the ratty green sofa and she moved to take her seat behind her desk. He patted the cushion beside him. It was the first attempt he'd made to be physically close to her in eight days, and she gave in. She regretted it instantly; the springs were shot, the cushions nearly featherless. She felt trapped in a rabbit hole.

How often, in September and October, she had conjured him up in this room as she worked at her desk. How often she had stared at the empty couch and wondered who he really was, and what he wanted with her, her blood churning at the memory of the slightest gesture from the night before. And now he had come and it seemed perverse to think back to that other time when his lips shook against hers, when he said things no woman should ever let herself believe.

"I came here to try and talk." The sound of his voice in this tiny room that had been for fourteen years reserved for the dispassionate talk of books, made-up people's blunders and heartaches, not her own, disturbed the very molecules in the air.

"Okay. Shoot," she said, feeling the gulf between this smooth, teacherlike response and the mayhem inside her.

Disappointment flickered in his face. He began again. "I think we need to air out a few things. I came here because I thought it might be easier for you to talk in your own element." His eyes traveled briefly around the room, which after all these years bore little evidence of her presence. The books on the shoulder-level shelf across from them could be found on the shelf of any high school English teacher in any state across the country: Norton anthologies, the Riverside Shakespeare, Melville, Dreiser, Brontë, Hawthorne, Cather, Faulkner. Nothing contemporary, nothing edgy, nothing out of print, nothing in translation. Not even a slight leaning toward a theme, a preference of gender or time period. The passionless shelf embarrassed her.

"All right," she said, straining for the appropriate tone to cover up the hollowness she felt, as if all her emotions and the words for her emotions were scurrying to the farthest side of her brain where she couldn't reach them. Years ago, her first year at Fayer, Gena had flown in for Christmas wanting to talk, wanting to know what had happened, why Vida had left home so abruptly, and though she'd planned, that whole fall, to tell her sister everything, when the time came her mind went blank. She had let Gena hold Peter, feed him a bottle, walk him around the pond in her arms, but she was never able, not even with an easy lie, to explain his presence.

Tom began talking. He had a lot of things to say, rehearsed phrases that he'd clearly refined over the course of days and maybe even weeks, phrases like "off on the wrong foot" and "between the sheets." Her years at Fayer, with all their assemblies, banquets, and dedication ceremonies, had made her an expert in the art of not really listening. She let his clichés roll easily over her. She did not let their eyes meet, and instead looked at the cuff of his dress shirt, a wedge of which poked out from beneath his jacket sleeve. His clothes did not have tags. They were softer to the touch than regular men's clothes; their colors were unique. The tweed of the jacket he wore today had bits of scarlet, bits of turquoise, though looking at it from a distance you'd never guess it had anything but shades of brown. And the jacket fit him in a way that men's clothes off the rack wouldn't. Even though he was sitting down, there was no bulge at the back of the neck. He was pleasing to look at, pleasing to touch, without trying to please at all. His clothes fit because he had been making them for himself since he was nine years old. There was something she resented about the comfortableness of his clothes, the comfortableness of his body in this world. Even now on the green sofa beside her he seemed to be pretending to be nervous, pretending to be awkward and wary of her reaction to his words, pretending to care about who she was and what would become of them. But no matter who she turned out to be, no matter what happened to them as a pair, if they could really call themselves that, he would be fine. In his soft tagless clothes in his little mouse house (he was talking now about the house, how it was a challenge, merging families, merging lives) with his precious, badly educated children, he was going to be just fine.

"Hey." His eyes, squinted, fierce, accused her of not listening. He clutched her two hands, his fingernails stinging the flesh of her palms. "Please talk to me. Please."

"I really don't know what you want me to say."

"I want you to share yourself with me. I want you tell me how I can make things better for you."

"I'm fine. You don't need to do anything for me."

He dropped his face into his hands, rubbed, and then sat up again with a red forehead. "I keep going back to certain moments. At Emma's, remember that night? It was the first time I'd spoken of my children, really. You had so many questions, so many insights." He went on and on, each date, each conversation.

He was right. She'd been good at talking; she'd been good at listening. She had that English teacher's ability to communicate, to draw out meaning, to produce the larger picture. She had taken great interest in his children as characters. But he had expected more from her when they became flesh and blood.

"Everyone said to take it slowly but I couldn't. I just couldn't. When I saw you go up to that podium last June I knew. Honestly, it was all I needed to see. I felt I knew you, and I wanted to be with you."

"I can't be that person you saw. You've got to forget about her. She existed for a few minutes and then she sat back down."

"But Vida—"

"That morning my friend Carol's son hung himself in an apartment in Boston. My favorite class was graduating. It was an emotional day."

"And you're saying you'll never be emotional again?"

"It's not something I can turn on and off."

"Just turn it on. Forget about off."

He took her hand with the rings on it and cupped it in both of his. It quickly warmed to his temperature. She wished they could just stay like that. Why did relationships have to be so verbal? All day long she dealt with words, adjusting them, negating them, praising them.

"I know you've begun drinking to stop it from turning on."

"Begun drinking?"

"From what Peter says this is pretty new."

From what Peter says.

"When I was a little boy I watched my father disappear every night. He came in from the shop joking and laughing and by the time dinner was over that man had died. And a bitter disappointed man was in his place."

Oh Lord. She couldn't bear the cliché of it. Had he plucked it directly from one of Fran's books?

"I can't watch that happen all over again in my house. I know where it leads. I'd like to ask you to stop."

"Stop drinking?" She was still incredulous.

He nodded.

She laughed. She couldn't help it. "Oh God. You're way off track."

"Am I?"

"I'm a hell of a lot better with a few drinks in me." Didn't he at least understand they'd never have sex again if he cut her off?

"I don't think so."

"Trust me."

"I don't, Vida. I don't trust you at all."

And then, like the junior boy who'd sat on this couch last week begging for a better grade, he began to cry. He made no attempt to stop his tears or cover his face or turn away. Her eyes, which had been locked on the sleeve of his jacket, drifted up toward his, and when they met she felt a shifting of the weight inside her and she could feel how it might be to speak about the falling falling falling feeling she got sometimes even when she was drunk and Tom was touching her, a feeling as close to feeling like you don't exist, have never existed, as you can have in this life, like the whole universe is a joke, an enormous joke and you're finally being let in on it, and how somehow this feeling was worse than the terror she had felt in that bathroom that afternoon all that time ago. How a memory could be worse than the thing itself made no sense but it was the remembering she was scared of, and if she unplugged that memory for him it would always be there between them. It would spread everywhere; it would spread to Peter, and then her life would truly be over.

Once she got ahold of herself again she grew bored by his performance. She had the impulse to get up and grade a few papers until he had finished. Then she understood that he wasn't going to stop until she stopped him.

"All right," she said. "If it's so important to you."

"Not just to me. To all of us. Stuart, Fran, Caleb, and Peter."

"Peter has nothing to do with this."

"Peter has everything to do with it."

"I'll see you at home." She got up off the couch, sat down at her desk, and swung the stack of freshman essays around to face her.

When she looked up again, he was gone. She was soothed again by the sensation she'd had in her kitchen the day he proposed, that this was practice, and that the real event, the one that counted, the one that would be graded and put in the book, would happen later, when she had studied harder and knew her lines.

Her sophomores were in the midst of some intrigue. She could tell at once by the sound of their feet, which were clustered together and moving quickly as if trying to keep up with the pace of their gossip. Even the boys were in on it, their voices cracking with surprise. By the time they reached her door they had all composed themselves somewhat, greeting her with their usual blend of resentment that people like her existed and reassurance that the world, dastardly as it was, had not changed over the weekend. Peter seemed out of the loop. He was the last to enter the room and took his regular seat, which was removed from the froth of gossip. She admired him for this, and tried not to think about Tom's words.

Whatever it was had gotten them all stirred up, and they took longer than usual to get settled. Lindsey scribbled something and handed it to Brian, who giggled like a third grader.

Karen was the only one who'd gotten out her book. "God, Mrs. Belou, why did she tell him?"

"Why did who do what?" She wished she'd had time to review last night's reading.

"Tess! Why'd she have to tell Angel?"

So they had gotten there already. "All right," she said to the most agitated corner of the room. "Give it a rest now. Why don't you take out"—the commotion stopped and she could hear them breathing, waiting—"your book."

A ripple of relief spread through the room, though there were a groaning few who had read carefully in hopes of a quiz to boost their grade.

"Brian, could you give us a little summary of what happened last night?" she said. Then, as an irritating little grin grew on Brian's face, she added, "In the book."

"Well," he began, clutching the unopened novel like a football, "after a lot of talking talking talking Tess finally agrees to marry Angel. On December thirty-first, which I think is a really weird day to get married. And then she tells him about the Alec dude and the baby and it's all over."

Vida was surprised he'd understood that much of it. "Anyone want to add anything to that?"

"She tells him because after the wedding he tells her about some woman in London he was with for a while and he asks Tess to forgive him," Harry said. "She is so psyched because she thinks now it will be easy to finally let out this secret she's been keeping from him, but when she tells him he has a completely different reaction."

"What does he say?" Vida felt an energy returning to her, an energy she'd begun to suspect she'd lost. Lately, she found herself vacillating between anger and lassitude, unable to find the vigilance and rigor she once had. But today she would talk about the ill-chosen location of the honeymoon, the crumbling d'Urberville mansion, and how Hardy plants his Darwinian theories of social determinism in the faces of Tess's two ancestors on the wall (paintings built into the wall that cannot be removed), one representing treachery, the other arrogance.

"At first he wonders if she's joking or going crazy, and then he gets mad."

Helen raised her hand. "He doesn't get mad, exactly. He's kind of in a state of shock. He tells her that he can't forgive her because the woman he has been loving is not her, but another woman in her shape. It's just like that poem we read by Hardy last year—about the guy who meets that ghost on the road."

"'The Well-Beloved,'" Vida said quietly, wondering exactly who she was, that woman Tom had seen going up to the podium in June.

"I think she was so stupid to have told him. They could have gone to a different part of England and he never would have found out," Kristina said.

"But it would always be there in her heart, eating away at her," Helen said.

"I think it was selfish of her. She like ruined this guy's wedding night."

"*He* ruined it. He couldn't forgive her."

Vida interrupted the two girls. "You have to understand Angel's point of view. Tess was a poor, uneducated, unreligious girl. Purity was her only asset, the only way he could justify her to his parents."

"She wanted to start the marriage honestly, no secrets."

Vida was sick of Helen's whining. She looked to the back, careful to avoid Peter in the corner, who actually seemed to be paying attention. From what Peter says. She felt a burning on the underside of her arms. Caroline was beside him and hadn't spoken in several days. She caught the girl's eye. "What are your thoughts, Peter?" Peter? Had she truly said Peter?

Caroline, whose mouth had opened slightly in preparation, turned in relief to her left.

"I don't think you can have a real relationship with someone without being truthful."

"But Tess's 'truth' isn't true, Peter," Vida said calmly.

"What's that supposed to mean?" He glared at her, defiant.

"The subtitle of this book is *A Pure Woman*. Tess is no less pure for her encounter with Alec d'Urberville. In fact, it is what she learns from her experience with Alec and losing her baby that makes her so intriguing to Angel. He doesn't love her for her innocence. He loves her for her depth of feeling and knowledge, which comes from her experiences. 'Tess's corporal blight was her mental harvest,' Hardy writes."

"But she was miserable, Mrs. Belou!" Vida let Helen override any noises Peter had begun to make. "She had to tell him. She was never going to be happy otherwise." It was the first stupid thing Vida had ever heard come out of her mouth.

"Well she sure as hell ain't gonna be happy now."

"Don't tell us!" several of the girls squealed.

"This is what is known as a tragedy. It says so right there on the back of your book. I don't teach fairy tales, folks."

"Does something terrible happen to Tess?" Karen asked quietly.

Peter's neck had splotched up. He was still glowering at her.

Vida nodded, then pulled on an invisible rope around her throat as her head fell limp against her shoulder.

"She dies?" they gasped.

Helen's voice was cold and serious. "But you said she wouldn't die."

"Of course she dies." She looked down at their faces and for a moment she couldn't have said who any of them were or how she knew them; even Peter fell away from memory. All she knew was that she wanted to hurt them somehow for all they didn't know. "We all die."

The lunchroom of a high school is a disturbing place. Everyone's neuroses gather here. The combination of food and voluntary seating releases uneasiness into the air like a gas. At Fayer Academy, the teachers suffered no less than the students. Of the sixteen tables in the lunchroom, two were designated for faculty. Brick always came to lunch first and stayed through all three periods. He sat at the table closest to the door, making it, for the twenty-four years he had been headmaster, the desirable table. The rules of the lunchroom seating for faculty had never been uttered, yet every teacher, within days of arriving at Fayer, understood where he or she belonged. Somehow, without words, Brick made it clear who was in and who was out. In the course of one's career, adjustments were made. Mark Stratton, when he was a part-time geography teacher, would have never dreamed of sitting at the first table, but the computer revolution changed all that. Davis Clay had sat at Brick's table for years until he stopped drinking and lost his sense of humor. There were more teachers popular with Brick than there were places at the table, but room was always made, chairs borrowed from other tables to accommodate them.

Today Vida arrived for the second period of lunch. As she stood in line, pressed between students she had never taught, she was not aware of discrete thoughts but of an inaccessible roar that tossed up every now and then, as if from the depths of the sea, some image or phrase to antagonize her. The bright flecks in Tom's jacket. We all die. From what Peter says.

Vida looked down at her tray. Shepherd's pie, wax beans, and sponge cake. A meal like this was perhaps the most humiliating part of her job. But at least she hadn't had to make it herself. She was hungry and moved swiftly to the faculty corner.

It happened so quickly that later she wondered if she'd imagined it all. She approached the crowded table, knowing she'd already been seen: Brick and Cheryl Perry and Greg Massie had all been looking in her direction while she'd been filling her glass from the teat of the milk vat. But now, at the moment for hellos and scootching over, her tray hovering over the table, no one looked up. So this is how it's done, she realized. Without breaking her pace, she traveled the arc of the table to the one behind it, joining the librarian, the substitute Spanish teacher, the school nurse, the head of development, and the entire math department. They all stared at her as if she'd dropped down from Neptune.

"Mmm mmm good," Vida said, lifting the first bite of the pie to her mouth. "And people wonder why there's a shortage of teachers in this country."

"Actually," the librarian said, "I read three days ago that a large percentage of teaching positions will be cut at the end of the year."

"I read that article, too!" Bob Crowse said, pressing his small chest into the table in his excitement.

"You did?" The librarian blushed.

Vida looked around for someone to share her cynical mirth, but these misfits were either unnaturally engrossed in their meal or smiling jealously at the coincidence.

At the other table, Brian Rossi was whispering something in Jerry Poulk's ear. Jerry frowned, tossed his napkin on his tray, and stood abruptly. Vida, watching his surgeonlike urgency with amusement, was startled when, as he passed, he said, "Heard there's been a lot of drama in your classes lately. Tryouts are coming up—we could use you." This last sentence was tossed over his shoulder, his absurd little ponytail flipping into the air. If she'd had a retort, he wouldn't have heard it.

Halfway through her sponge cake, she felt a familiar pressure on her arm, then Brick's ranch dressing breath at her neck. "Swing by my office when you're done, will you." Before she could give an answer he, too, was gone.

"Vida," he said, manufacturing surprise while sliding a slip of paper beneath his fingertips toward the center of his clutterless desk. "Have a seat."

Every April, before the next year's contracts were distributed, each teacher was called into this office for what Brick called "The Chit Chat." Carol, who had to type up the notes from these meetings, called it "The Shit Shat." It was an evaluation of sorts, though Brick had trouble complimenting people and relied on oblique references in the passive voice. "Word is," he said to her last year, "you're only getting better." But it was not April yet and Vida sensed the word was no longer good.

She stroked one of the gold tacks pressed into the leather of the chair she'd chosen while Brick warmed up.

"How have you been, Vida?"

"I've been fine, Brick." She mocked his unnatural earnestness with her own. He didn't like that, and took a moment to rethink his strategy.

"You and Tom have been married how long now? A month?"

A quick, quivering pain traveled through her at the sound of his name. Though she knew it wasn't April, she couldn't think which of the other months it was. "Something like that."

He removed his fingertips from the yellow piece of paper and leaned back in his larger leather chair. "Marriage is a curious institution, isn't it?"

She knew this was how he behaved with students in deep trouble; he took the time to indulge them, to pamper them, like drawing a warm bubble bath before tossing in the toaster. Vida had always thought this a cruel tactic until now, when to her surprise instead of barking at him to cut the crap, she egged him on. "It sure is," she drawled.

"It is quite frankly the most challenging experience any of us will ever face. As you know my daughter Betsy got married last summer. A nice fellow. We'd waited for what seemed like decades for him to ask her, and then when he did, suddenly I felt she was too young and what was the rush. I'll be honest with you. They've had a rough year. He never told poor Betsy about his allergy to cats."

"Cats?"

Brick looked disappointed, as if Vida, having known Betsy since the girl was eight, should be able to fill in the blanks. He took a deep

breath, not having wanted to stray this far from the point. "All her
life, Betsy has loved cats. She begged for one every birthday and
Christmas. But Charlotte was firm. She always told her, 'When you
marry and you have your own house, you can have as many cats as
you like.' So on the first morning of their honeymoon in Paris, Betsy
went out and bought a kitten. Brought it back to the room. Within
minutes, that husband of hers, his eyes puffed up and his windpipe
shrank and, well, they've had a rough time of it." He looked at Vida
expectantly and again seemed disheartened. He shifted in his chair.
The leather cracked. He took another breath. "Charlotte and I have
certainly had our differences. I don't play bridge. She doesn't like
cake. Twenty-three years and a cake has never been baked in my
own house. But we've made our allowances, shifted our priorities,
relaxed our ideals a bit." He paused, pursed his thick lips, then said,
"I've never betrayed her, not once."

But not for lack of trying, Vida thought, remembering the lick
on her neck and the many other equally inept passes he'd made at
other teachers over the years. Who did he think he was talking
to? But he needed soothing now; this confession had made him
vulnerable.

"There aren't many men who could say that, I imagine," she
said.

He puffed up instantly. "No, I can assure you, there are not."
He looked at her with a mix of love and confusion. Where was he
headed? He remembered, and aimed perhaps a little too directly.
"Is Tom treating you well, Vida?"

Had he orchestrated this? Had he arranged for her to be laughing privately at him and his self-deception when he zinged her here?
It was the first time anyone had asked her such a specific question
about her marriage. "Yes, of course," she answered, too automatically. Even she heard the falseness of it, but she could think of nothing to add to change the effect.

Finally he spoke. "You are one of the very best teachers we've got here, Vida. And you haven't seemed yourself lately. And since the only change I've known about is your marriage, I just assumed. But perhaps there's something else."

Let's have it, Vida thought. "How haven't I been myself?" Was anything more foreign than this self other people believed you could maintain?

"Frankly, I haven't noticed all that much myself, but there have been reports." Careful not to glance down, he folded his hands atop the yellow sheet. He was still willing to negotiate. If she would just confide in him; he'd much rather be daddy than boss. He prodded her with sleepy sympathetic eyes. It might feel nice to say a few things out loud. She could be careful not to reveal too much. What a relief it would be to utter a complaint or two to somebody, even if it was Brick. And it would make him laugh, the accusation that she, whom he had always teased for not being able to keep up, had a drinking problem. A warm bubble rose in her chest and she waited for it to settle before she spoke.

But Brick saw her fighting laughter and decided he was through waiting. He'd given her more than enough time. His hands separated and he read out the list in the stentorian voice he reserved for his worst offenders. "'November sixth: allowed discussion of abortion to go unchecked in the classroom.' We've got Catholics here, Vida, in case you've forgotten. 'November eighth: gave ten demerits to Julie Devans in study hall for picking her nose.' Ten. To the daughter of a trustee. 'November thirteenth: referred to Mark Stratton's computer lab as Jonestown and asked students if they had enough Dixie cups.'" Brick's mouth curled slightly after this last one, but the next sobered him. "'November sixteenth: told American lit students that,' and I quote, 'God is in my underpants.'"

"Apart from this last, I simply see a bad attitude. I can accept that. I understand your resistance to the computer and the weekly lab day, which Mark tells me you haven't once shown up for. It's nearly the end of the term. I'm sure a lot of us are giving out some negative vibes to our students. I'm sure each comment had its context. But Vida, I've thought long and hard about this and I cannot imagine any context for 'God is in my underpants.' A teacher, especially a female teacher, should never, not in any situation, be talking about her underpants.

"I should fire you. Anyone else with this sort of a list and they'd be out. But you've been here too long and I like you too much. So as of right now, you are on probation. One more report like this and I'll have to inform the board."

Vida gave Brick the solemn nods he required, and was released.

Climbing the two flights to her office, she had that brittle, eviscerated feeling she normally didn't get till the end of the day. When she reached the top she smelled the must and mold that everyone always complained about. She opened the three windows in her classroom and a violent wind cut through the room. She erased her nearly illegible words from the board. God is in my underpants. She laughed out loud. Had she really said that? In American lit? She imagined her juniors in their seats, then she remembered. A discussion of transcendentalism had turned into an argument about the role God should play in one's life. John Swiencicki said he liked Emerson's idea of trying to achieve unity with the universe, and Gretchen O'Hara asked what was the point of believing in a God that isn't separate from you, that isn't in every part of your life, controlling everything. Vida had suggested then that there be God-free zones. "For example, I don't want God in my underpants." That's what she'd said. Not that He was in her underpants, but that He *wasn't*. Her first impulse was to go down and clarify it with Brick, but she knew it would only stir him up again.

In her office she looked down at a pile of junior quizzes. She fished out her best student, Henry Lathrom's. He'd scrawled his name at the top of his paper, as they all did, though none of her students needed to label their work anymore; their handwriting was more familiar to her than their faces, and far more expressive. Henry's letters were minuscule and virtually without curves, so that an essay looked like thousands of tiny sticks painstakingly laid out. She read a sentence three times, then shoved the quizzes away, threw on her coat, and drove down to the gym. This was Fayer Academy's newest monstrosity, with two sets of locker rooms, nine offices, a tennis bubble, a swimming pool, a volleyball court, a weight room, and three turquoise basketball courts. Peter was practicing at the farthest of these. Vida took a padded seat in the bleachers.

They were doing drills. A pair of boys were released from the center, one dribbling toward the net, the other flapping away in front of him, guarding him. Then, when the dribbler approached striking distance of the basket, another boy came shooting out from the side to take the pass.

Gary Boyd coached the team, the thirds. His Fayer sweatpants were barely held up by a brown necktie and billowed out at the knees, even when he was standing straight. Vida doubted they'd ever been washed. Gary lived alone in an apartment above the post office in Fayer. In the nine years they'd worked together, they'd never spoken more than a few sentences at a time, and always about a mutual student, but when word of her engagement leaked out, he'd given her a forlorn congratulations one night in the parking lot, holding her hand a few seconds too long, as if there'd been an understanding between them she hadn't quite understood.

When he noticed Vida in the bleachers, he slapped his hands together a few times and called out, "This should be easy, offense. If you're not making the points, there's something wrong with you." This encouragement made the next two groups miss their shots.

Peter stood in the line at the side. She knew from the way he'd shifted his torso away from the bleachers that he'd seen her. He had a large dark bruise on his upper arm. Had he been in a fight? He was doing what all the other boys were doing, letting out a hoarse grunt when a basket was made, then slapping the guy on the back as he sauntered past. Vida enjoyed seeing him like this, in a group, barely distinguishable from the nine others in dress or gesture. Here, he was just a boy, not her hefty personal responsibility. He was looking to someone else to tell him what to do and how to do it. He did not need her. He sprinted out now for the pass. He caught the ball badly, then took a shot. It fell far short of the rim. She was only making things worse by being here. She stood, then sat again. It wasn't even four o'clock. Where was she going to go? She couldn't be alone in her office one more minute today. She missed Carol. She tried to remember where she'd put all her notes for that letter. How was it possible she still hadn't sent it? Tonight she would find the papers, pull it all together. By now Carol would know about her meeting with Brick. What a good laugh they could have had about it this afternoon. *God is in my underpants.* She knew Carol would be hooting at that one.

Gary blew the whistle and hollered out another drill formation. He glanced up at the clock on the scoreboard in the corner, and his face sank a bit. Fifty more minutes till cocktail hour, she felt like yelling out to him. He liked his martinis, she knew that. Every teacher on this campus was going to be able to sit down to a good healthy drink this evening. Every one of them—except her and Davis Clay. An unfamiliar tingle crept up her arms and settled in her chest. She breathed deeply, and paid closer attention to the scene below.

The boys now stood in three lines at one end. Every ten seconds or so, Gary blew his whistle and a set of three was released. The boy in the middle passed the ball to the boy on the left, then ran behind him and took his place. Now the one with the ball was in the middle and he passed to the right, then ran behind that boy. Like this they weaved quickly and fluidly down the court. She didn't watch Peter when it was his turn. She didn't have to watch him to know he was the weak link, that a pass to him had to be exact, and a pass from him would be unpredictable. She saw how the two other boys, younger boys, compensated without annoyance, and felt grateful to them. She'd hoped with her being there he'd try harder, which he did, but trying harder didn't translate to playing better. Again she felt the impulse to leave and half stood, then worried that her departure would be interpreted as disgust, and sat. She'd slip out once he made a basket. But even though Peter had three turns to make an unopposed layup, he missed each time. Then Gary called them over, tossed half of them red pinnies, and they all took their places for the jump. Vida was surprised to see Peter on the court and not on the bench. Before he threw up the ball between the two tallest boys, Greg flashed an eye at Vida and she realized he'd put Peter in solely for her benefit.

She could endure it no further. Finally she gave her legs the unambiguous signal to stand and they carried her off the bleachers, back along the narrow sidelines, and down the fire stairwell to the parking lot, where she sat in her car with her tingling chest for the remaining twenty minutes.

But removing herself from the scene, putting a windowless wall of concrete between her and Peter, didn't prevent her from seeing him. His feet were fast; he had no trouble getting free of an opponent. He would be darting in and out of the key, always open, gently calling to the teammate with the ball, "With you, with you," his eager arms out and ready, always ready. His hair would have fallen over his eyes but he wouldn't brush it away, wanting to keep his arms out for the pass. His mouth would have that desperate, beseeching shape to it as it became clear to him that his teammate was stalling, dribbling in place, until someone more reliable broke free.

He was the very last boy to emerge from the locker room. He walked out well behind Jason and a few others. And it was only at that moment, when she did not feel the urge to tell those boys to include him, that she realized how angry she was that he was in cahoots with Tom.

Without a word, he opened the door, kicked down his knapsack to make room for his feet, and breathed flatulently through his nose. She did not, as she had done every day since he started prekindergarten, ask him about his day. She did not offer him a greeting at all; she simply turned left out of the school driveway and headed fearlessly toward the great test of her character they had plotted together.

Like any decent protagonist, she would pass it. But that, she told herself, did not in any way mean they would have won or gotten the better of her.

By the time they reached Larch Street, their silence was no longer tentative but an established fact. As they approached the house, Vida saw that Tom's car wasn't in the driveway yet, which meant hers would be blocked in when he came home. Like the carpet cleaners, like gloomy Mrs. May, she parked alongside the curb. She could feel Peter wanting an explanation but she didn't give it. They walked up the driveway single file.

From the smell of the house Vida knew that Fran and Caleb had snacked on raisin toast and Stuart had a girl in his room. She heard the window in his bedroom shudder shut; now the girl would be creeping off behind the house. Seemingly oblivious, Peter headed down the hall to his room, which would be thick with sex and incense.

She whistled for Walt. When he didn't appear, she called, "Here, baby." She thought she could hear his front paws scraping the floor of the kitchen, trying to get up, but the kitchen was empty. So was the backyard. She checked under the table and in the pantry. Her new bottle of bourbon, still three-quarters full, was there. Walt was not. Stuart had probably taken him into his room as some sort of seduction accessory, but she headed to her bedroom first. It was an unlikely place to find him. The room was dark, and it took her many seconds of stroking the wall to find the light switch. He was lying right in the spot where he had usually lain in their old house: beside her bed, waiting for her to wake up. Perhaps he'd been waiting there all day. Such a long awful day. She thought of the bourbon on the shelf. Just as she was about to call to him, she saw that his head was at an odd angle against his right paw. For a moment she thought it was another dog, some sort of prank of Stuart's, some misunderstanding, some confusion in the universe. She crouched beside him and swung his head, his beautiful head, on her knees.

He was stiff, even his hair felt stiff, but she knew she could pull him back. She heard herself crooning in his ear, luring him home with sounds that weren't her words but new words, a sort of dog talk, like in her dreams about him, that she was finally fluent in. He would listen. He'd always done anything she told him to. Such an easier child than Peter, never recalcitrant, never moody. Walt was her best friend, her partner, her lover. She heard him laugh. Don't laugh, she told him in their language; it's true. You are my love, my deepest love. She began to laugh with him. She pressed her face to his, though his eyes were looking off toward the nightstand. Didn't you know that, baby? Didn't you know? I found you at a gas station. I rescued you. And you rescued me. We drove across the country together, just you and me. What would I have done without you? Where would I have gone?

She was still trying to coax some movement out of him when she felt a hand on her shoulder. At first she thought it was Brick, asking her to have another talk.

"He's gone, honey. He's gone."

"He's just so tired."

"He's dead." He said it as if he enjoyed the word.

"Please, just go get Peter."

Peter stood several feet back. "What happened?"

Vida wanted to raise her head and reach for him, pull him down beside her, but she couldn't bring herself to let go of Walt's head.

"What happened to him?"

From far off, Tom said, "He was old and in pain. His heart probably just gave way."

She felt Peter's fingers on her back briefly. "I'm sorry, Ma." That's all he said. He did not squat down with her, mourn with her.

He left. After a while Tom left, too. She thought of the bourbon on the shelf. She continued to talk to Walt in their language. She wanted to cry but he wouldn't like it. She shut his eyes and stroked the velvety fur of his eyelids. She apologized again and again for not having been home, not having been on her bed when he came in to find her, to spend his last minutes with her, his only love. He had never warmed to Peter. Peter had never loved him. They'd never had that boy-dog thing.

Occasionally there were voices behind her. "He was a nice dog," she heard Fran say.

"He's finding his new form now," Stuart said. "Something more elegant and powerful."

He's perfect the way he is. She didn't know if she'd said this out loud. She caressed the length of Walt's body, her hands remembering how strong it once had been.

Tom stood at the door and spoke of dinner. Later it was Peter, urging her in to eat. But she was so tired. Maybe it was time for her to die, too. She was so very tired. She could hear them at the table, clattering, chattering. All their voices chittering along, while she sat on aching knees with her dead dog. I need a goddamn drink, she told Walt. If she'd married Brick they'd have a minibar in the bedroom.

Then they were all there, surrounding her with their platitudes and garlic breath. Tom had, of course, formulated a plan.

"He needs to be buried. We could call the vet or we could just bury him here."

"Here?" Fran said, disgusted.

Tom shushed her. "Which would you like to do, Vida?"

"I just want to pat him."

"We can have a little ceremony. I'm going to start digging a grave out back."

"You can't do that," Fran screamed as if expecting this all along. "Not in my mother's garden."

"To the side, near the compost."

"You'll break all the roots of her lilacs. You will."

"I won't. I'll be careful."

Fran followed him out of the room. "It's just a dog, Daddy."

Vida wanted to scream at her, but Walt told her to not to bother.

In a few minutes she heard them in the back, rummaging through the shed, calling out to each other, laughing.

"That's a snow shovel, you dingbat."

"We should rig flashlights up on our foreheads like coal miners."

"How much do you think grave diggers make an hour?"

They were all outside.

She placed Walt's head carefully down on the carpet. Neither of her legs could hold her weight so she leaned on the bed, then the doorknob until she could get herself down the hallway alone. The bourbon in the pantry was gone.

It wasn't that she needed a drink. It was the principle. It was not getting bossed around. She had a boss, a boss who'd put her on probation after sixteen years of indentured servitude. No one else was going to push her around—not tonight.

He would have hidden it somewhere. He was such a Yankee he wouldn't have been able to throw it out. In the basement she groped around for the string that hung somewhere near the washing machine. She was always helplessly searching for the goddamn lights in this house. Her finger brushed it briefly, then it was gone again. "Fuck it," she cried out. At that moment there was no one she wasn't furious at. She was even pissed at Walt for dying on this lousy day. Finally she felt the soft twine in her hand and yanked. The string snapped off the chain, but the light was on. She went through every cupboard, every box, everywhere except the one place she guessed he'd put it. Finally, she had to look there, too.

She unzipped the garment bag, separated the flaps, and reached in. The dresses parted easily, as if they'd been expecting her. She ran her hand along the cardboard bottom. On one of their dates, probably that date at Emma's he'd been going on about, Tom had read her what Fran had written for her mother's funeral. It was a poem, and he kept it in his wallet. "She smelled like hyacinths and rain" was one of the lines. Vida remembered asking afterward if Fran had been reading T. S. Eliot at the time. She remembered, too, that this response had disappointed Tom and she didn't understand what he could have expected. She'd never known Mary, had yet to meet Fran, and Tom himself was hardly more than a stranger who'd taken her out to dinner a few times. She didn't know until now, until she'd buried her head in a rackful of Mary's clothes, how accurate the description was.

But there was no bottle of bourbon.

She went back to the kitchen, trying not to think of poor Walt abandoned on the bedroom floor, to get Tom's keys. The only place left was his car. She still had the goddamn string in her hand, and when she went to put it in the trash she saw it. Neck-down, nearly buried. She lifted it out. It had been drained and tossed out. Not such a skinflint after all.

She rummaged around for her old mushroom-colored raincoat beneath the pile on the hook and went out the back door. The padded right shoulder of the coat bobbed at her chin. She made straight for the half-dug grave.

Tom was in the hole up to his waist, crouched, spraying up dirt. Above the grave, they'd tied a flashlight to a tomato post. Fran stood beside the post, still shouting about roots. She stopped when Vida stepped into the flashlight's faint outer ring.

The first thing Vida noticed when she stopped moving was that it was not raining. It hadn't rained all day. The sky was clear and full of sharp stars. She had added this detail. In books it always rained while graves were being dug. Or perhaps it was Fran's poem. Hyacinths and rain. She looked at Fran now, in her silver-studded jean jacket and fake fingernails. She hardly seemed capable of such a line.

Tom raised his head. He looked as if he'd been shoveling the dirt directly into his face.

A part of her wanted to laugh. Are you the First Clown or the Second, she might have said. But it was overruled by the anger that pinched and clawed with every molecule of her body. She didn't know where to start.

Fran glanced at her with her usual disdain. "Your coat's all twisted."

"I don't give a shit, Fran."

She'd been so good up until now, but she was done being good, trying to squeeze into the little box they wanted to keep her in.

Tom leapt out of the hole as if she were holding a gun.

"Get the fuck away from me!" She remembered Helen on stage a few weeks ago, hollering, throwing pots. It felt great. It felt grand, stepping out of character in front of them all.

"Vida, come here. You're upset." He was reaching his arms out for her, arms that he'd withheld for so long now, tucking them tight under his body in bed in case they tried to wander. She wished she could chop them off.

"You fucking touch me I'll kill you."

She was aware now of Stuart, Peter, and Caleb staring at her from across the grave. Caleb had been crying. But Stuart and Peter had obviously been having a mud fight; their clothes were covered in splats of dirt. They had played like insensitive beasts while a grave was being dug.

What was her point? What had she come out to say? They were clustered together now, bewildered together at the edge of Walt's grave, this family she did not belong to. She swung back toward the house. Her bag was by the front door. Keys on the hook. It was so simple to leave. She'd never been able to leave Peter before, never let herself fantasize, even momentarily, about leaving. But that feeling of wanting him away, that wretched feeling of him inside her, stuck to her, had always been there. Wanting to leave him was one of her most familiar but unrecognized impulses. Perhaps all these years of fearing she would kill him in her sleep were all about getting free of him. Exhilaration flooded her as she moved toward the front door. There was her car out on the road. She pressed her face against the front window. Had she known she would do this? Had she known it even when she issued her bewildering yes to Tom's proposal? Had it been there all along, a tiny hopeful seed in the cold ground?

First stop would be O'Shea's on the way out of town, where Tom had taken her once, back when he didn't fuss about her having a drink. She hoped the same Irishman would be behind the counter. "What'll do you?" he'd said. She loved that accent, right out of *Dubliners,* though he'd never read it, never even heard of Joyce, poor man.

Good-bye, Walt, she whispered and shut the front door. Her feet took her swiftly across the grass. She felt like one of Stuart's girls, young and weightless, with nothing but mysteries ahead.

EIGHT

IN HISTORY CLASS PETER LIKED TO SIT IN THE BACK BESIDE THE WINDOW. From that angle he could see their old cottage and the playing field behind it, a patch of land he still considered his own backyard. That field looked now as it always did in winter: abandoned, soggy, the lime lines ravaged, one goal having fallen in a storm. The cottage, with its tidy yellow clapboards and shimmering black shutters, sat on the knoll above. A light was on in Peter's old room, a baby's room now. Peter, too, had been a baby in that room. He had been every age in that room with the sloping ceiling and crooked windows and the closet with the old wallpaper he used to peel when he was angry. What had he been angry about then? He couldn't remember anything more specific than a dull thudding *wanting* feeling. He thought her marriage to Tom would quell it and for a little while it had, but the sensation was back again. Only now he didn't simply want another change; he wanted to step out of the very skin of his life and into another.

His mother hadn't come home last night. Tom had driven him to school and they'd barely spoken. Peter guessed Fran had probably told her father and Stuart about the kissing. They wouldn't want him around for much longer if his mother didn't come back—or even if she did.

When Tom had pulled around the circle to the front door, he'd said, "If anyone asks," and seemed unable to go on.

"I'll just say she's sick."

"Good. Okay then. Have a good one."

There had been something about shutting the door on his step-father, leaving him to drive away alone, that seemed cruel. Peter had stood on the pavement dumb and inert for an awkwardly long time. He'd wanted to say something encouraging to bring color back into Tom's gray skin. Peter didn't know his mother this far out of her orbit. Anything could happen now. "You, too," he offered, then let the door go, softly.

He'd forgotten, until he entered this classroom, that most of his grade had stopped speaking to him. They were working in small groups today, pretending to be landholders from 1749 working out their income and assets. Peter's group was ignoring him. The truth was, even when he wasn't being ignored, he didn't contribute much to group work. Group work was just a way for teachers to get another free period. By this time of year Mr. Hathaway had given up the pretense of visiting each group, listening with fake interest, and moving on. Now he just worked at his desk, scratching out his illegible remarks at the bottom of each of their take-home tests from last week. When he looked up suddenly, Peter turned back to his group and nodded. Sarah, Kristina's best friend, shot him a scowl and he had nowhere to put his eyes but back out the window.

Kristina had told her friends that he'd locked her in that bedroom in Scott Laraby's house, that he'd tried to have sex with her. She even claimed to have cuts and bruises. Jason had not come to his defense.

He remembered how big that JV field used to seem to him, how when he was four or five he'd watch the games at dinnertime, kneeling backward on their couch, a plate of fish sticks balancing beside him. His mother hated the games out the window and always went to her room and shut the door. Those boys he had watched, so hard and tall and serious, with smoke rising off their skin into the cold fall air, were no older than he was now. He'd played on that field this fall, though only once, when a Fayer victory was certain, and even then only for a few minutes at a time. He'd never known what those boys he'd watched had known— the red steaming face, the burning chest, the ache to win, the ability, he saw now, to become with his others teammates one victorious organism. Looking at the field was making him feel worse than looking at his classmates ignoring him and just as he was about to turn back to them he noticed a mark at the far side of the field, a sort of gray-brown gash in the turf. Who would have dug a hole in the soggy grass? A dog? A fox? He thought of the military term "foxhole." Was this what a foxhole really was?

"Mr. Avery, I'm sure your groupmates would appreciate those penetrating thoughts of yours," Mr. Hathaway said, not even noticing how his group had shut him out of their conversation, which had quickly moved more than two centuries beyond the issues of 1749 landholding.

As soon as Mr. Hathaway's attention fell away, Peter returned to the hole in the field. Now he couldn't determine if it even was an indentation; at certain moments it seemed to be something on *top* of the grass. It was like that trompe l'oeil when the little girl's shoulder becomes the witch's hideous chin: first it was a hole, then it was a clump. It was part of the earth, part of the torn earth, he was certain, until it moved and then suddenly he no longer needed to see— he knew. The coat. The hair. It was his mother.

He was nearly to the door before Mr. Hathaway looked up.

"I'm going to throw up," Peter said, capping his mouth.

"Gross!" a chorus of his enemies exclaimed before he shut the door on them all.

He took the absurdly curved and elaborate staircase three steps at a time.

"This is not the Indy Five Hundred," a teacher called out above him, and he slowed obediently for a few seconds.

Now he was in the front hall. A portrait of his great-grandfather hung over the fireplace. A lot of good you can do me from up there, he thought, crossing over to the back staircase. The side door of the boiler room would be the quickest, most discreet route to the field.

Coming up those stairs at an erect and steady clip was the photography teacher. No sophomore had a free period this early in the morning, but Mrs. Dilworth simply said "Hello, Peter" under her breath. Her viewing room, Peter remembered, had a large picture window that framed the field. Was she coming up to report his mother to Mr. Howells?

He took hold of the thin banister and leapt, his feet touching down lightly only once before the bottom. The boiler room was to the right. When he was younger and his mother had an after-school meeting, he'd come down here with Lloyd and play slapjack at a little table he used to have in the corner. It was down here that you really felt the age and the immensity of the old house. It took three oil furnaces to heat the place. And the noise they made, the shuddering and screeching and hissing that went on all day and night. It was creepy alone—he'd never come down here without Lloyd. Jason had told him junior and senior couples snuck down here to make out. He wondered as he cut through the dim enormous room if somewhere in the shadows hands and mouths were momentarily suspended. He pushed on the bar of the far door and was outside, running now, not directly toward her but down the back driveway to the dirt road to their old place; then, making a wide circle around the house, trying to blend in with the pines, he followed the tree line around to the far side of the field. She was still there, still facedown, unmoving. He thought for the first time today about the way Walt's body had fallen into the grave, like something that had never been alive at all.

"Mom!" He hadn't meant to cry out; his voice an ugly squawk.

His knees were cold and soaked the minute he hit the ground. He rolled her over, half expecting, half sickly excited by the expectation of a gray face and blue lips. But it was just her, a little grass on her cheek. Since she never wore makeup there was no shock in the morning, nothing like seeing Jason's mother at breakfast. She was breathing evenly.

"Ma," he whispered, calmer now.

She continued sleeping. He looked toward school and was surprised how close it was when from that second-floor classroom she had seemed so far away. The mansion, so dark and cavernous from the inside, appeared to be all windows. How many people had seen, were watching him right now? They would send an ambulance. Mr. Howells would follow in his car, and at the hospital the examiner would tell them that she was simply inebriated.

"Get up now. C'mon, Ma. Get up." He gave her a shove. It should have hurt—he'd shoved harder than he'd meant to and his wrist began to ache—but she was out.

He had so little time. The bell would ring in five minutes or so. He had to get her off this field. He pulled her up to sitting, her arms through the coat so thin and free of muscle. When had she become so small? When was the last time he'd put his arms around her or been so close to her face which hung contentedly now against her shoulder?

"Ma, please, let's get out of here."

He heard a voice and looked up with dread, his mind spinning an excuse, but it was just Mr. Mayhew at the circle, his back to Peter, calling his retriever Buckeye, who always wandered.

Peter hoisted his mother over his left shoulder. He expected her to be lighter, or at least more manageable. But she was so long. Her feet seemed to be dangling somewhere down by his ankles. He felt one of her shoes, then a few steps later the other, knock against him and fall off, but he couldn't stop. By the tenth step there was no part of his body that didn't ache—and how many more sets of ten were there to go? Hundreds, maybe thousands. And first there was a hill. He'd never, not even when he was a little kid, considered this incline up past the cottage as a hill. Even when he was three, he'd taken his sled to the real hill close to the main road. But now, with his mother draped across him like something he'd just shot in the woods, this patch of grass was his own Kilimanjaro—without the snows. Everything hurt: his ankles, the backs of his calves, every single muscle in each thigh, lower, middle, and upper back. And his neck— the whole weight of her seemed to be pressed against his neck. Even his lips hurt from how his teeth had clamped them shut from the in-side. It was such a myth, the weight of a woman, the way in the mov-ies men were always tossing women over their shoulders and running here and there with them. And what about that short story they'd read last year, the one about the boy and his father who go out hunting and the father dies and the boy has to carry him out of the frigging woods. Imagine how heavy a father would be. And that boy was only nine or ten. It was a bunch of bullshit, everything he'd been taught.

He made it to the top, but there was no reward in that be-cause he had to keep moving, even more quickly now as he'd heard, though he didn't know exactly when, the first bell, which meant everyone in school would be changing places, glancing out win-dows. What would they look like, he and his mother, from one of those windows? Would they be identifiable, if not as particular, familiar individuals then even as humans? Wouldn't they seem more like a lurching beast, shifting its shadow among the pines, barely upright, staggering so slowly to the dirt road which thank-fully sloped (he'd never noticed that incline before either) down to the faculty parking lot. He just had to hope none of the teachers had scheduled midmorning dentist's appointments or concocted some other strategy to liberate themselves.

He himself was not conscious of his mother, at this moment, as human. The pain of carrying her had changed from individual aches to a general burning so distracting that he was simply aware of her as a pressure, unlocalized, neither from within or without. Later he would wonder why he had not had to fight off thoughts of dropping her, of letting her roll off his shoulder onto the needled ground, as he did in subsequent dreams.

Finally the Dodge was within view, and the second bell rang and the faculty lot, thank God, was empty of everything but the aging cars of teachers. Peter swung open the back door and bent himself and his mother inside her car, then slumped her off his right shoulder onto the seat. He watched the extra blood that had pooled in transport drain from her face. She made no movements of her own, save breathing. He had so rarely seen her sleeping. Her expression was entirely different in sleep. He'd always thought the severity of her jaw and brow was due to the shape of her bones, but now he saw it was from the way she bore down on them.

He'd anticipated, the whole time he was carrying her, stashing her in the car, then returning to school. But now he saw he couldn't leave her here. He'd have to drive the car off campus, to the gas station on Sea Street, then walk back to school.

He found the keys in her coat pocket. His only driving experience had been at Jason's house when his father let them loop around the campus driveway. He thought that at the sound of her car's engine Vida would hurl herself upright to yell at him. She'd never allowed him to so much as fit the key into the ignition. But all was quiet behind him. He knew he had to back out without drawing attention to the car. He pulled down on the gearshift, matching the red line with the R just like in Jason's father's truck. But he'd never driven backward before. He couldn't manage to get it to move in a straight line. Instead the car sashayed out of its spot, knocked over a garbage can, and shuddered to a stop. In the cafeteria, Olivia and Marjorie stood in the window, looking down. What could they see from up there? He restarted the engine, threw it into D, and pulled out of the faculty lot. Now he was on the main campus drag, a long smooth strip of new asphalt. How easy it was to drive, to leave in a car. How powerless those colossal maple trunks were to stop him. Even Mr. Mayhew, still calling and clapping for his dog, now peering into the car with a scowl, could not stop him, no matter how much he waved his arms in the rearview mirror. In a car you were invulnerable.

He sailed past the hockey rink, the girls' fields, Mr. Howells' little house on the hill. In the mirror Mr. Mayhew was running back to the mansion, which was just a big white house, like any other place you could just drive away from.

At the intersection with the main road, Route 26, he didn't make the left toward the gas station, toward Norsett. He turned right instead, toward the northern causeway. He was sure that the sheer unnaturalness of this turn would rouse his mother, but there was nothing but silence behind him. He pressed down on the accelerator, felt it resist a moment, then give way. The car quickly picked up speed.

On either side of him, the land, once a forest he used to trample through, had been cleared, roads had been cut, and houses—whole neighborhoods—stood in various stages of construction. It had been a long time since he'd been out this way. Signs for the mainland and the highway directed him left. He drove over the water, careful not to look at it, keeping his eyes on the space between the white lines, and soon he found himself on an entrance ramp with a brown van on his tail and a steady stream of commuters ready to sideswipe him. He tried to slow down but the van honked and he thrust himself into the fray and waited for the crash. Somehow, however, he had been accommodated, accepted into this adult workday morning as if he, too, were racing toward the city. Except that he didn't want to go into the city, and took the next exit to the turnpike and all points west.

Driving was perhaps the most exhilarating thing he'd ever done. And he was good at it. He was a natural. So often as a child he'd pretended to be the one driving, stamping down on a pretend brake when his mother stopped. He knew how to center the car between the lines, how to pass a Sunday driver safely. "You're doing a good job," he whispered. It was the first time he'd ever said such a thing to himself.

Behind the wheel the world was a different place. He was nearly sixteen, and things were going to change.

By noon he needed gas. In his mother's wallet he found several hundred dollars, more money than he'd ever seen in her wallet before, and he wondered if she'd been planning this escape all along. It bothered him that he might be doing right now exactly what she wanted, that even lumped in the backseat she was somehow pulling his strings. He filled up the tank and with the change from the twenty bought five packs of gum. She hated gum. He stuffed several pieces in his mouth at once.

The woman at the drive-through across the street was the first person to look at him quizzically. He hadn't pulled up close enough and had to get out and walk to the window for his food. Gum bulged out his cheek.

"How long you had your license—a couple hours?"

"Yeah," Peter said, his voice full of the defensive sarcasm he used when he had no comeback—which was all the time.

"Whatcha got in the back there?"

"My mother," he called before he shut himself safely in the car again. The woman's mouth broke into a laugh she didn't expect. Peter felt his throat tighten as if he might cry for the pleasure of making a lady in a drive-through window laugh. He forgot to release the key in the ignition and the engine made a long terrible racket. He didn't look at the lady again.

He held his breath and merged back onto the highway without a collision. He didn't recognize the names of towns on the signs. He wasn't sure what state he was in anymore, though it all looked the same—same food and gas logos, same plateglass office parks with their big half-empty lots. He tossed the gum out the window, peeled the foil from his hamburger, and ate quickly, ravenously. When the highway forked he alternated between west and south; he liked the sound of both. He drank from the Coke wedged between his knees. He began to shiver and realized he didn't have a coat. He turned the heat on full blast. He drove and drove. He would never tire of driving.

A sign read *Pennsylvania—The Keystone State*. He whooped quietly. Pennsylvania. He looked at the clock on the dash. His entire grade would be in study hall right now, but he'd driven to Pennsylvania. Kristina would be in the back left corner of the library. He realized how hard he'd been trying not to think of her. All he'd wanted to do was help her. That's all he'd ever wanted to do for her. When she came to Fayer in sixth grade in the wrong clothes with the wrong accent he'd felt sorry for her and chose her as his science partner. The braid down her back. The way she said Poter. Things like that hollowed out his insides, even in Pennsylvania, even after what she'd said he'd done.

At the Exxon station a kid Peter's age filled up the tank and didn't even notice a body in the back. But through the doorway of the mini-mart, eating a pink coconut cupcake, a cop was staring right at him. As imperceptibly as he could, Peter tried to lift up his rib cage and harden his expression. He did not catch the cop's eye again, but looked straight ahead with preoccupation, as if while waiting for his tank to fill he had many adult thoughts to untangle.

Behind him, his mother was stirring. A long swish.

Not now Mom not now he was thinking but didn't dare move his lips. Peter checked the digits on the pump; it wasn't even half full. The cop pushed through the door. When he paused to hike up his trousers he left pink sugar fingertip marks on either side. Then he headed directly toward Peter. He put a hand on the roof and bent his head down at the window. Peter fumbled to unroll it.

"I suppose you've got your driver's permit." He said per*mit*.

"Yes, sir."

The cop leaned in farther and addressed the back. "I assume you're over eighteen and in possession of a valid driver's license, ma'am."

In the mirror Peter found his mother upright, open-eyed and nodding.

The cop patted the roof of the car. "Hope you folks enjoy your visit here."

The kid, who'd been waiting behind the cop, took his place at the window to collect his money. Peter could barely remove the bills from his mother's purse, his hands were trembling so wildly. The police cruiser pulled out of the parking lot and headed away from the highway. The kid didn't have enough ones in his pocket and said he'd be right back, but Peter got his hands around the key and took off.

He waited for his mother to speak, to holler at him, and when she didn't he glanced and saw she'd shut her eyes again, her face clenched as if sleeping hurt.

It took a long time for the shaking to stop, but when it did he felt good. He felt great. He remembered the radio and turned it on. A sign read *You Are Leaving Pennsylvania* but there was no sign to tell him which state was next.

The sun, which had been flickering through the trees, disappeared. He was hungry again but didn't want to risk a stop. He sang along to the music and tried not to think about food. All at once the earth seemed to open out and he could see in the dusk long swathes of land and a farmhouse miles and miles away, with a light on. It was like looking across an ocean. He could see the curve of the earth. In that one glimpse of distance he understood so much more about everything he'd ever studied in school: Western expansion, cyclones, *O Pioneers!* Instead of shutting you up in classrooms for twelve years, why didn't schools just put you on a bus and show you the world? He'd never known how cramped and ugly New England was until now.

At the risk of waking his mother, Peter rolled down the window to let in this new air. It was much warmer than he'd expected and he stuck out his whole left arm and let his fingers rattle in the wind. There were no other cars on the road and even though it was paved and occasionally signposted, it was easy to pretend he was the first person to travel across it. The exhilaration of freedom coursed through him like a drug. He remembered similar moments, like the time Jason's sister Carla, before she went to college, picked them up at the movie theater with a hitchhiker in the front seat. They'd driven the guy to an intersection a few miles up the road where he could catch a lift to Canada, he said. He had no bag and no shoes, and when he got out a wave of envy and wanderlust had passed through Peter. That his mother would eventually rouse herself fully and demand he turn around, that he had a geometry exam tomorrow and a history paper due on Friday was information this swell of freedom could not contain. This was his life now; he was a driver heading for parts unknown.

The road began to dim. Then he remembered headlights. He pulled the silver plug and the road ahead glittered. The dotted lines came fast on his left and he tried not to let them distract him. The sky, which had been a vast dome with deep purple clouds, was now close and black and indistinguishable from the land.

Within minutes the dark eroded his exuberance.

"Ma!" he said and got no response. He had the feeling that something terrible was about to happen, that this was how death happened to everyone: a few hours of joy and then you're snuffed out for good.

An eighteen-wheeler passed on his left, buffeting the Dodge with its wind. The car was flimsy, no longer the haven it had been all day. He felt himself growing younger. He needed to eat, to pee, to sleep. He needed to be taken care of now. But in the backseat his mother just rolled over.

NINE

FOR A LONG TIME SHE HUNG ACROSS WALT'S BACK, HIS PACE SLOW AND rhythmic. They didn't speak. She was drunk and he was dead. He placed her on a small sofa. Her face stuck to the cushion. My legs are too long, she cried, but he had gone. She smiled and nodded at a policeman. It was one of the few things her mother had taught her, to smile and nod at the police. But never seek them out, never call that kind of attention to yourself, no matter what has happened. She taught her that, too.

All the chairs were being taken out of her classroom. Students she didn't recognize hoisted them, seats down, on their heads and carried them off. She made a barrier with her arms and legs in the doorway but they passed right through her. Fran passed through, too, reading aloud from a yellow sheet of paper, though there was only one word on it: *Mom.* All the while there was this tugging at her mind that she had forgotten something, but when she strained to remember, the feeling disappeared. For a long stretch of time she dreamt only of the word *blunt,* the b and the u and the n, a sort of visual onomatopoeia, she decided, over and over.

There was pain in her hip, her shoulder; her lungs were sore and she could only take in shallow breaths. She smelled grass. She was in her bedroom with the fading buttercup wallpaper and her mother was handing her a book. "I just got it out of the library. It's about a woman who gets—" Vida knew what she was going to say next and lunged, smashing her hand against something hard.

She is walking down an unfamiliar street, searching for clues to where she is. Ahead is a sign but everything is blurred. She hears a voice, a Cockney accent. She's in London. London! But she can't see it, and she's waited so long to get here. Someone takes her arm. It is Carol. Carol who finally read all her notes has forgiven her. They are walking swiftly now, through a huge house full of people. Carol leads her upstairs and down a corridor to a long narrow room. She shoves her in and shuts the door. Her vision clears. In the window a boy is hanging from a necktie. It is Peter. The thing she's been trying to remember. She is flooded with the pleasure of remembering. Peter. He is dead, but she has remembered him.

"Poor Tess," someone says behind her.

"Tess? That's not Tess. That's my son, Angel."

She is aware, occasionally, of a door slamming, of a shoulder beneath her, of darkness but not silence. For a few minutes at a time she is lucid. She is in the backseat of a car, her car. She recognizes the roof, the pinpricked vinyl. She remembers Walt's grave, the countertop at O'Shea's. Someone must be driving her home from there. Her heart races. When he stops the car he will expect something for his trouble. She returns eagerly to the buttercup wallpaper, the thin curtains rolling in the breeze. She is on her stomach reading. It is a Saturday and no one is home but her and there is a big bowl of peanuts on the table beside her. She eats them one by one, sucking off the salt first, then biting gently so it splits, then letting the halves nestle in either side of her mouth before chewing. It is morning and she can stay up here all day. Downstairs a door slams. He is on her before she registers his feet on the stairs, his weight pressing the air out of her chest, his arms knocking the book from her fingers. She has no air to scream with. She is overwhelmed by the familiarity of the act, the belt, the grunts, the blood in her mouth, as if it has happened not once before but hundreds of times. It is not anger or sadness or fear that she feels, just a habitual acquiescence. Yes, this is what happens to me, her body seems to be saying. When he is done he thanks her. She is not surprised by the voice or the thin ponytail resting on the collar of his jacket as he turns to go.

TEN

APRIL WASN'T SURE WHAT AT FIRST CAUGHT HER EYE. USUALLY SHE WAITED for the customers to see her, need her attention, and she liked to toy with them, dragging her eyes slowly up off her magazine to their eager faces. But these two she was watching even before they came through her door. The driver got out first, scanned the street, then opened the back. He leaned in all the way and April expected him to bring out some sort of jacket or bag, but instead it was an old woman, stooped and shoeless. They stopped outside the door, admiring the ribbons. April was in charge of tying fresh bows, twenty-five of them, every morning and replacing the ripped, faded, or stained ones. She hoped Billy Hughes, who'd never eaten here as far as she could remember, had seen a picture of her work. Could they get mail over there? Probably not.

The old lady raised her hand and ran it down every ribbon like a child. April almost called out to her to stop but then wondered if the woman was retarded and let her finish. They finally pushed through, the young fellow struggling a bit to keep the woman upright and the door open. She'd been all wrong about their ages. The driver was a mere boy, and April didn't know a state in the union that let fourteen-year-olds drive. And then the old lady: she wasn't much over forty, a good deal younger than April. She could tell by the hair. Nothing stiff or brittle about it. It was young hair, even if the face was a bit trashed.

"Y'all two?"

The boy seemed confused by the question. April held up two menus and pointed to a booth. He nodded, and followed on behind her.

She heard him whisper at her back, "Is it all right that she has no shoes?"

There was something special about this boy. The way he tipped his head up to her when he ordered, the way he maintained eye contact even though it seemed to pain him.

"I'm losing my marbles," April muttered as she threaded the order up into the rod on the other side of the window.

"You just figuring that out now?" Dave said, snapping up the ticket, then groaning about the onion rings.

April went back to her perch at the register. She could see the boy's profile from there. He was talking but the woman wasn't talking back. She was bent over her cup of coffee, her hair everywhere, the barrette in back useless. She was a sight. When he gave up, his eyes drifted around the restaurant, though his mind seemed caught somewhere else entirely.

Dave grunted, and she spiked their ticket and brought them their food.

"Thank you so much," he said for both of them.

She looked at the photo of Sgt. Billy Hughes on the wall. He'd always seemed so innocent. All these weeks she'd been staring at his face and she'd never noticed the hint of arrogance in his eyes, the mischief in his mouth. April bent her head and prayed for God to forgive her those last thoughts and deliver all the hostages home where they belonged. She raised her head and there was the boy standing on the other side of the counter, wanting to know about the restrooms. She pointed and he signaled to the woman and they went down the hallway together. April cleared their dishes. His plate was clean, but she'd barely taken a bite. As she moved to the kitchen, she heard a commotion down where they'd gone. She peeked into the dark hallway. The woman was clutching the boy with both hands. "Please don't make me," she whispered. "I'll be right out here," he said, calm and steady. "Let's not go through this again." "I can't. I can't." She had slipped to the ground. The boy finally gave in and the two disappeared into the ladies' room.

"Where y'all headed?" she said when he reappeared at her counter with the bill and a twenty, trying to maintain the incurious tone she usually had with out-of-towners.

"Uh." The boy looked at her desperately. He was the kind of kid who seemed incapable of a lie.

"You're just heading out," she said dramatically, sweeping her arm westward. She shrugged up her shoulders, turned down her lips, and said, "Maybe all the way to California."

The boy laughed. "Maybe," he said, and then with the first animation she'd heard in his voice, "Maybe!"

He took the change with another smile, shoved two dollars into the tip jar, and called out, "C'mon, Ma."

It was rude to not even call out good-bye, but she felt like she'd been punched in the chest, hearing *Ma,* knowing now this was that sweet boy's mother. Why hadn't she guessed they were related? Because there are just some women who you know have never raised a child. It's in their eyes. April herself was one of them. That woman, she'd have sworn, was another.

Just before they stepped off the curb, the boy tried to take his mother's arm. But she jerked away fast, as if his touch would burn. She lay down in the back, disappearing from April's view. With the engine running, his hands on the wheel, the boy sat stock-still, his face set and his mouth so pale it seemed to disappear.

April wiped her tears quick away. Dave would make such fun if he saw.

ELEVEN

CALIFORNIA, THE LADY HAD SAID. SHE MADE IT SOUND SO CLOSE.

He'd been driving for three days. For a few hours each night he'd gotten off the highway and found an empty parking lot. In one of the far corners, he'd park, lock the doors, and sleep. Then he'd find some doughnuts and coffee and be off again.

He loved coffee. He loved driving. There were long stretches each morning when the road was empty, the music was good, and he didn't even care about his mother behind him. That time of day, the coffee zinging inside him, he could think of anything without defeat. He relived his night with Kristina, the shape of her sleeping lips, the weight of her against him. And his kiss with Fran, the sound of which he often replicated with his mouth on the back of his hand. And when those memories made him too horny (if he were alone in this car he'd be masturbating round the clock), he just let his mind drift to other pleasant times. The consequences came later, in the afternoon, when the caffeine had gone and he was light-headed with hunger. He rarely stopped for lunch. Lunch places were always crawling with cops. They had early dinners at remote diners. He wished he could leave his mother in the car—she never ate more than a french fry, and without shoes or a brush or an interest in speaking, she called so much un-necessary attention to the two of them. But she couldn't be anywhere by herself. And she was always terrified they were driving through Texas. After hours of silence, she'd suddenly rise up from the back and demand to know where they were. After he reassured her, she slept. She dreamed. She yelled out things he couldn't understand. She kicked at the back of his seat and he had to scold her. He turned the radio up louder and louder. He'd almost left her in Nelson, Missouri, and Silverthorne, Colorado.

California 174 mi. He thought the sign was a joke. But then, an hour later, California *110 mi.* He had thought it took weeks to cross the country. California. Gena. He'd never written her a letter but he knew her address by heart. 363 Pajaro Way, Santa Lucia. He began to follow signs for San Francisco. Her town, Gena had told him at the wedding, was just south of there.

There were long stretches of time in which she believed she was in the Oldsmobile, her father behind the wheel, her mother foraging through her purse. She could hear them bickering, not the regular bickering about when to eat or which road to take but the helpless flailing sound of their disillusionment with each other. They would be moving again. "On to the next wacko scheme," her mother would say, slowly poisoning her father's optimism with her presentiments of doom. Vida often thought that if her mother were the man and her father the woman they would be happy together. If her mother didn't have to conceal from the world her intelligence and ambition, if her father wasn't expected to squeeze money out of his dreams, there might be peace. But pressed up so close to their pain, Vida learned that true life was in books, life that was, no matter the foulness and misery, beautiful and symmetrical and comforting. *The Portrait of a Lady* from Virginia to Albuquerque, *Madame Bovary* from Albuquerque to San Antonio.

She was aware of having left the highway, of being on slower roads, of the car moving with sudden purpose: a left turn, a long straightaway, a right turn. The car hit gravel and stopped. All she could see was the upper half of an orange house, a small strange house, a playhouse maybe that had been shaped from clay by a child. She shut her eyes.

One thing she admired about Hardy was the inevitability of his tragedies. He was right up there with the Greeks, the way *Tess* for example picked up steam. You felt the first spasm of motion in the very first scene, then with each subsequent scene the tragedy gathered power. But life itself was nothing like that. In life the lack of inevitability—the lack of any design at all—was the tragedy.

"I told you you wouldn't call first." She knew that voice. "Didn't I tell you that?"

Gena. No! She kicked the seat in front of her. But Peter was already out of the car, his feet scuffling through the gravel. No! Not here. Please dear God not here. She tried to get back to her thoughts— she still had something more to think about Hardy and design—but Gena was crying, then snuffling, then saying, "Come in. Are you hungry? Come in."

And Vida was left outside in the car like a dog.

"You're not all that surprised we're here," Peter said.

"Tom's been calling about every hour practically. All we could do was hope you'd turn up somewhere."

Peter was aware of a strange lack of disappointment in not having surprised her. It just felt good to be here.

"Though I didn't expect *you'd* be the one driving."

He laughed.

"Sit," she said, pointing to a foldout chair, the only chair at the small kitchen table. Gena stood at the sink, looking through the window. "You really think she's asleep?"

"I don't know and I'm not sure I really care at this point."

"It's been a rough few days, hasn't it?"

"Yeah.

"Has she eaten?"

"About six onion rings and a french fry."

"Water?"

"A few sips."

"Alcohol?" Tom must have told her about that.

"No. But she was drunk when we started out." Peter felt the room moving past him, like a highway, and stood up. "I don't want to get in a car for a long time."

He went into Gena's living room. For all the sunlight outside, the house was buried in darkness. He felt like turning on a light. He walked around the room slowly, though there was little to see, just a brown flowered chair facing a television. He heard scratching beneath it and squatted to lift the skirt of the chair. It wasn't a cat that bolted out past his feet to the kitchen.

"What was that?"

"You'll have to meet all my babies." She scooped up something brown and white at her feet. It was a guinea pig. "This is Fluffanutter."

Peter tried to stroke the top of its quivering head but it quickly tucked itself into Gena's elbow. "They're all going to be a little shy at first."

It was too much of an effort to stand, so he sank into the brown chair. Gena dragged the metal chair from the kitchen and sat beside him.

"Either you drove a hundred miles an hour or you didn't sleep much."

"I didn't sleep much."

"I should call Tom. Do you want to talk to him?"

Peter shook his head. He didn't really believe the Belous still existed. That chapter of his life was over. He knew he should get up and check on his mother; the car would be getting pretty hot. But he didn't have the strength. He shut his eyes and highway lines rushed past. Someone laughed, Fran or Stuart. A huge yellow ribbon was being tied in a bow. He was in history class, in the front row, away from the window, and Kristina was unzipping his fly. His erection jerked him awake. But Gena wasn't looking. She was on the phone in the kitchen, facing the window. She was speaking quietly but not whispering. He heard ". . . exhausted but otherwise fine . . . yes . . . yes, I know."

He remembered Stuart's trip with his mother, and Tom's worry back at home. He wouldn't be feeling anything like that now, not for a wife of a few weeks, not for a boy he'd done a little woodworking with, that was all. He'd been so stupid to think the Belous would become family, that you could press people together and they'd stick. Look at him and his mother. They'd been pressed together all his life and they still weren't a family. He'd always thought that was because two was too small a number for a family, but that wasn't it. He knew now that wasn't it.

"Oh God," he heard Gena say. "Peter. Here." She held the phone out as far as it would reach.

"What?" He didn't want to get up.

"Talk to him. I've got to go get your mother. She's walking away." She put the receiver down on the counter and went out the door. He could hear the gravel being thrown in the air behind her as she ran.

He lifted the phone to his ear. Out the window he saw his mother, still in her trench coat, hobbling toward the road.

"Hello?" he said as Gena caught up to her.

"Peter?"

"Yeah."

"You're okay. Thank God you're okay." There was all sorts of emotion in Tom's voice. He pressed the receiver closer.

"I'm fine." His mother kept walking and when Gena tried to take her arm she flung it away, just as she'd done to Peter for the past few days. But she was no match for Gena, who stood in her path and clutched her by both shoulders.

"Are you still there?"

"Yeah. I'm just watching." He was so tired. He hadn't meant to say that.

"Watching what? TV?"

"No. Gena and Ma. I've never seen women fight before."

"They're fighting?"

"Wrestling."

"Wrestling?"

"They're in a sort of lock right now. Gena's heavier so you'd think she could just shove her down, but Mom's got the height."

"Peter, is your mother okay?"

"I don't know. I found her on the JV field that morning. I had to carry her."

"I'm so sorry." From the way he said it, Peter could tell he already knew that part.

"They're down."

"They're done?"

"Down. On the gravel."

At first Peter thought his mother was laughing. Her mouth was open wide and her arms were wrapped around her stomach as if so much laughing hurt.

"What's she doing now?"

"She's laughing."

After a long time, Gena led her into the house.

"I'm going to run your mama a bath."

"All right," he said loudly, cheerfully, hoping his mother would look up. But she didn't. She was watching her feet move along the floor. Her tights had holes in the toes now. Her trench coat was bent up in the back. Her whole body seemed as delicate and precarious as a dried leaf. He wasn't on the phone with Tom anymore, though he didn't remember saying good-bye.

From the flowered chair he could hear Gena's voice above the rush of the water into the tub. The faucet stopped running and there was only the sound of water tinkling as his mother stepped into the bath.

Gena's face was pink and glistening. She sat on the metal chair again and put a hand on his knee. There were no more noises from the bathroom, not even a few drips from an arm reaching for soap. Could you really drown in a tub? Wouldn't your head, after you went unconscious, bob up automatically and gulp for air?

"She's going to be all right, honey, she really is."

If his mother died would he start looking for his father? Whenever he thought of finding his father the same image always came to mind, of a man outside a small unpainted house, raking leaves. The man had a kind flat face and wore a wool sweater. He was lonely and distracted, and even in his dreams Peter couldn't get his attention when he called to him.

Was there somewhere among his mother's possessions, somewhere he hadn't checked in all his years of rifling through her things, a clue? He'd forgotten until a few minutes ago how Gena always said *your mama.* Mama was such a cozy word, absolutely the wrong word for what he had.

In the bathroom water thundered out of the faucet again. He pictured her huddled up near it. She wasn't like those women in ads who could sprawl out under a blanket of bubbles. His mother didn't know how to relax. He thought of their trips to York Beach, her pile of books, her dash to the bookshop when she got halfway through the second-to-last one. She huddled on her towel on the beach just like she'd be huddling now. She never swam, never wanted to play Ping-Pong in the rec room. After dinner she might agree to a game of Scrabble, but never Monopoly or Stratego. And she took it so seriously. He tried to think if he'd ever seen his mother having fun. Even her wedding was more like a dentist's appointment to her, the way she'd put on her dress at the last moment, and let out a big "uhhhh" when they reached the church parking lot. There was only one time he could think of, years ago, when she'd had people over to the house after he'd gone to sleep. He'd awoken to the sound of the blender and talking. He listened at the top of the stairs to his mother imitating people, other teachers who weren't there. Suddenly she turned and ran up the stairs, giggling to herself. She ran right past him without even noticing him, into her room. Then she went downstairs again, wearing a wig, and everyone exploded into laughter.

The water was still running. He needed to get out of this house. Gena looked relieved when he said he was going to take a walk.

Her street, though narrow and quiet, extended perfectly straight in both directions. He went left because there were more palm trees that way. He'd never seen a palm tree before, and was surprised to find on the sidewalk long stiff straw-colored fronds that cracked under his feet like regular leaves. He didn't recognize anything else on the sidewalk, not the smashed purple berries or the hairy red stalks. There wasn't a cloud to be seen and Peter kept expecting to get hot and sweaty beneath the uninterrupted sun, but it just seemed to keep everything at room temperature. A car drove by, fast, with many people in it playing music he didn't know.

All the houses were small and sunless like Gena's, all made out of the same smooth clay. After about ten blocks they started to get fatter, their grass shorn, their driveways more elaborate. Some had gates with a keypad. There were beat-up trucks out in front of many of these houses, and small groups of men bent over a cluster of shrubs or flowers. They spoke in Spanish and did not look up when he passed by.

He had thought that the dark rim of blue on the horizon was part of the sky, but as he got closer it became the ocean. Stuart was right: it was so blue it looked fake. Gena's long street dead-ended into a path that led down a steep incline to a strip of sand. Waves boomed against walls of rock on either side of the beach. He was too scared for some reason to go down there alone.

He wondered where on this coast Stuart and his mother had been. Perhaps one day they had stood right here on this cliff. Mrs. Belou, knowing what she did, might have held Stuart's hand or put her arms around him, her chin on his shoulder. She might never have wanted to let go. She might have hidden her tears, pretended it was the wind coming off the ocean as she caught them on her fingers. She had loved her son, and she wouldn't have been able to imagine saying good-bye.

Peter felt his own eyes begin to fill. Stupid, he said aloud, wiping them with his sleeve. Stupid, he said again, angry, unable to stop the tears or the clutch in his chest that was forcing them up. He squatted in the long grass as if there were people around, as if he had a cramp. He wasn't a crier. He took pride in that. Even in grammar school, even when he got struck in the back of the head with a softball, he managed to get up and say he was okay. But now he was crying about a woman he never knew. Then he was crying for Stuart not knowing about the cancer and for Fran trying on her dresses and protecting her lilacs and for Caleb in his huge reading chair and for Tom on the phone asking, "What's she doing now?" And then after a while it was just for himself and all that driving and his mother who was nothing, nothing like a mother, whining and complaining from the backseat but never explaining what she was doing on that soggy field, never explaining anything.

It wasn't just her silence for the past four days but her silence all of his life. She'd drawn him a goddamn picture of his father and that was it. And she didn't even know how to draw. She drew like a child, worse than a child. He could have done better than that, better than a few lines of hair and smashed-in mouth. There wasn't even a nose. Maybe that would have been fine if she had made up for it—Mrs. Belou would have made up for it—but she hadn't, she couldn't, she didn't like him. His own mother didn't like him. It was true and he'd never seen it before. All the ways he disappointed her. His very first memory was her saying he needed to grow up. You need to grow up. It was her refrain. Until it happened and then she'd get angry when his pants were too short or he'd walked to the gas station alone for candy. Only those nights when she'd tiptoe into his room and sit on the side of his bed and listen to what he'd watched with Lucy on TV did she seem to accept him the way he was. She'd stroke the hair off his forehead and sometimes, maybe twice, she'd told him that she loved him. He should have convinced Tom that she was better off drinking.

The tears had stopped and he was sitting in the grass, whose tips rested at his shoulders. His head had begun to pound and his shirt was wet in front and around the neck. His whole face felt swollen. The sun had fallen toward the ocean, darkening it, and the waves still smashed into huge white fans against the rocks below.

Gena would worry if he didn't get back. He followed the path out to the road, crossed it, and began the long walk to her house. In the weaker light, the unfamiliar vegetation seemed sinister. He hadn't known that a life could run amok so quickly. He wondered why he kept walking toward Gena's. In the movie of his life he wouldn't do that. He wouldn't ever go back. He'd make a left right here on something called Caballo Way and head toward the pink and blue lights of a strip of shops he could see at its end. He still had fifty-six dollars in his pocket. He wished he could be that kind of boy they always read about in school, the kind who trusted his luck. If there was one thing Peter didn't trust anymore, it was his own luck.

Gena's house seemed smaller than he remembered. She'd put a light on outside, above the door. The Dodge sprawled in the small driveway at the same angle he'd pulled up in. His mother would be in bed; Gena would be making dinner. She'd feign relief at his return, as if she didn't know he was incapable of anything else.

TWELVE

WHEN I MAKES TEA I MAKES TEA AND WHEN I MAKES WATER I MAKES WATER. Buck Mulligan imitating that old lady—Old Mother Gowan? Grisby? —and she couldn't get it out of her head. It was a habit from childhood, letting a senseless cluster of words get lodged like that. She tried to concentrate on the hummingbird whirring its wings against the screen across the room as it tried to push itself into the long tube of a white flower. Water I makes water. She wondered what a cup of tea would taste like. She'd always been a coffee drinker, never understood the teachers with their delicate cups of tea, the little paper tassel hanging off the side. Davis Clay had switched to tea. Not right after that summer his wife sent him off but a year or so later. Coffee's an addiction like any other, he'd told her. His wife had probably flown people in for that, too. Tea drinkers were like that. Sheep. Look at the Irish and all they put up with for centuries. Then again the English themselves were obsessive about their tea. In novels they packed it in their suitcases with their toothbrushes when they went abroad. Anger spiked down her arms. Why was she getting so worked up about tea? Could there be anything more innocent than a poor cup of tea? And when I makes water I makes. She heard, beyond the closed door, voices, soft, companionable. She should have given him to Gena and he could have been raised among guinea pigs. And then that feeling again that these choices were still ahead, not behind. It had always been a comforting sensation, a protective nook where she took cover. She remembered her mother throwing a dish towel at her father's face and her father taking her mother's head in his hands and knocking it five times fast and hard against the wall then walking out of the room and Vida laughed even though her mother was in the bathroom crying because she knew when this exact moment happened again, her father wouldn't do that and her mother wouldn't cry. How did you go about convincing yourself that this instant right now was real and solid when it felt so flimsy in your hands, bleeding into the next, porous, full of holes and puckers, and the mind was so bad at recording anything correctly? How did you make this moment right here with the hummingbird moving now onto the flat yellow flower and the voices dwindling toward the kitchen and her own quick breaths pushing up against her hand—how did you cut that into a granite block and slide it perfectly into place beside all the others?

Did Gena know how to do that? Isn't that what she'd always been so envious of, the way her sister had always known how to live? Their whole childhood she was the one the phone rang for, the car outside honked for. She was the one with the plans and the dreams. She had gone to Africa. Vida hadn't been aware that she had formulated a picture of Gena's life here until she walked into it however many days ago and nothing was as it should be. Where was the furniture, the bright fabrics, the plush cushions, the strange art? Where was the bulletin board crammed with photos and phone numbers? Why didn't the phone ring more often? She could hear their mother's voice full of vicarious titillation, "Gena, it's for yooooouuuuu!"

When she and Peter arrived, Gena had had to go out to a shed for two more chairs for her kitchen table.

Outside her window she heard Peter and Gena, their voices approaching and receding as they walked around the house.

"Someday I'd like to plant things out here." Gena was saying.
"I can help you," Peter said.

A few days later she heard Peter say, "I really thought I was in love with her."

Another time, as they lay in the grass after lunch, he said, "Just looking at a palm tree makes me happy. Isn't that weird?"

She heard Gena tell him about a dream she'd had about her boyfriend in Senegal. "And he pulled up into the driveway, just like you did, and I went running out to him and I was crying and laughing at the same time and I said, Look, look at my beautiful scars."

If they were outside, Vida walked about the cool house, made a bowl of cereal, spied on them through the small windows, but when they came in she retreated to her room. She found a sketchbook and a charcoal pencil in a drawer, and remembered how well Gena had drawn as a child. But all the pages were empty. Vida sketched the tree outside her window, a tall palm with spears for leaves. When they checked in on her, she hid the book and pretended to be asleep. Sometimes she did doze during the day, but at night she stopped sleeping altogether. Her old fear had new power now and she lay in the dark, blindsided by panic. Her heart vibrated, its beats barely separate. She couldn't get enough air; her skin felt like it would peel off. She turned on the light and focused on the pillow, the faded blue flowers and their sprigs of leaf. She tried to put Joyce back in her head, When I makes tea, I makes tea, but it wouldn't stick. She could not get her pulse to come down. She was going to have a heart attack, a heart explosion.

She dreamed about the mansion. The appendages were gone—no hockey rink or tennis bubble or science wing. She drove up to the front door, Walt in her lap, a puppy again. Her grandfather came out, carrying the bust of himself. He didn't see her. He followed a path along the side of the house to a garbage can, and he dropped the head in. Then he went back into the house and shut the door.

Down in the fields girls in white dresses were holding hands and dancing, some raising their arms high and others dipping their heads through, making intricate tangles then pulling back out to a large, perfect circle. The May Dance, she thought, looking for Tess but seeing, at the crest of the rise beyond, Angel Clare. He was walking away. No, she cried out. Not again. Not again. The sound of her own voice woke her up, but still she could not stop screaming.

On their eighth day in California, Gena drove her to a shrink. In the corner water bubbled over black rocks. Toward the end of the hour, Vida managed to say it out loud.

"I've always been scared that I'd kill him in my sleep." She waited for the woman to call the police or the nuthouse. They locked up people who said things like that.

Instead the woman said calmly, "What feels truer than that?"

Vida felt a small loosening in her body. This was what she was always asking of her students, to see beyond the words on the page.

"I'm so scared," she said, and even just saying those words shrank the feeling slightly, "of losing him."

The next day she agreed to go to lunch with Gena and Peter. "It's just a few blocks away," Gena reassured her.

She trailed behind Peter and Gena on the sidewalk. It was hot and sweat soaked into her turtleneck and the waistband of her skirt. She'd left her tights behind, and the canvas shoes Gena had lent her scraped the skin off her swelling ankles.

Gena pointed out a house and said the owners were extremely peculiar, as if she herself didn't live alone in a dark empty house with guinea pigs.

"Why did you come to California?" Peter asked.

Gena looked around. "I suppose it reminded me of Africa."

"Africa? Really?"

"Something about the flatness of the light. At dusk the sun just sets, like a light being put out. No afterglow, no in the gloaming." She glanced back at Vida, who decided to play her part.

>"*In the gloaming, Oh my darling!*
>*When the lights are dim and low,*
>*And the quiet shadows falling*
>*softly come and softly go . . .*'"

They both smiled at her encouragingly. She had a stab of paranoia. Were they scheming something? Was Tom going to be at the restaurant?

But the restaurant was nearly empty, every booth along the wall free. Through the doorway in back was a bar.

"Everything's yummy," Gena said, "But the soups are their specialty. Perhaps I've mentioned the spicy artichoke—"

"Yeah, I think you did," Peter said. "About a hundred times." They were smiling at each other. They already had their little jokes.

The waitress came and went, a tiny creature in turquoise ballet shoes. Stuart's kind, more sprite than girl. She couldn't stop the great chasm of failure, of shame, that opened up beside the thought of Tom's children. She pulled herself quickly from it.

Peter peppered Gena with questions: did she know how to surf, did she like the Giants, did it ever snow? He got her to describe her work at the nursing home and what an earthquake felt like. And yet their voices were too animated for the context; they were saying other things beneath their words. They shared a secret, an anticipation. Vida forced herself to look each time someone came through the door. He was coming; they had asked him to come. She was sure of it.

Gena was right. The soup was good, but Vida only brought a few spoonfuls to her mouth before she lost the energy and interest. Peter and Gena polished their bowls clean with the thick slices of sour bread from a basket the poor little waitress had to keep running back to refill. Vida slid her soup over to them and it was gone within minutes. Then they ordered ice cream sundaes, enormous goblets with chocolate, caramel, and pineapple sauces cascading down the sides. Peter giggled and raised the long spoon to the top. Gena said, "We've concocted an idea," and Peter put the spoon down again.

"I could tell," Vida said. Was Tom at the house now? What was happening?

"How about Peter stays with me for a while?" Gena said. Her round cheeks were red as apples.

It wasn't Tom. It was all about them, all the excitement in the air.

"Gena says there's a good school just a few blocks from her house."

Everything was a just a few blocks from her house, it seemed. In Peter's eyes, in his voice, was the same enthusiasm he'd had just before she'd married Tom. She'd misinterpreted it then. Now she understood. Getting away from her had always been the goal.

"That's fine with me."

They had been ready for a battle; their list of reasons twitched on their fingers. She needed to be away from them, in the bar through the beaded doorway.

Stools turned when she came in. She looked each one in the eye, the blond in flowered shorts, the old guy with the pink cap, the two college kids hoping she'd be someone else. They might not have seen many gaunt English teachers from New England, or turtlenecks, but she knew them, each one of them. She knew the feeling that brought a person to a strong drink at noon on a Thursday.

The bartender raised his eyebrows and slid a coaster her way.

"I'm just—" She glanced up at the TV in the corner. A bearded, blindfolded hostage was speaking into an old-fashioned microphone. It was Day 43. "I'm just looking for the bathroom."

"Right through there."

It was a dark little hallway. She looked back at the glasses pyramided on the bar, then rushed to the door with the W and bolted it shut behind her.

The soup came up yellow and bitter. She spat it into the sink and wiped her face slowly in the mirror. She didn't know how to fight for him. She'd never fought for anything in her life.

On the way back Gena and Peter veered into a store. Vida stayed outside, looking at the books in the window. There were a few classics in paperback. *Daniel Deronda,* which she'd never read. But she wasn't tempted. Gena and Peter came out with Parcheesi. They opened it as soon as they got home, hunkering down on the floor on their stomachs like little kids. The phone rang when they were into their second game. Gena went into the kitchen to get it. She spoke in a low murmur, her back to them. Peter was left alone on the floor, Vida on the brown chair. It was the first time they'd been alone since the car. He was sitting up now, sideways along the board, one knee bent, one arm straight as a pole to the ground. With the other arm he rolled the dice over and over, unsatisfied with the numbers. His sprawled body seemed enormous, the dice and the board tiny beside him. He was done with her. Every thud of the dice told her that.

Gena held out the receiver. "It's for you."

Vida shook her head but Gena shook her head right back at

her. "I can't put him off any longer, Vida." She wouldn't back down. Vida could see that in her face.

Maybe it was Brick, she told the blood rising to her face. It was just before five back there. He'd have come home, made himself a cocktail, put himself in the mood to deal with teacher truancy.

But it wasn't Brick. "Are you really all right?"

She remembered the sound of his voice from their first phone calls. Her heart would be slamming just like this and she'd wrap the ringlets of cord around her finger and half of her would wish he'd cancel the date they were making and the other half wanted to talk to him all night long. His voice was deep and always a little hoarse, like an old reed instrument hitting the low notes. "I think I'm okay."

"Vida, I—"

"I imagine you've spoken to Brick."

"I told him you'd call when you were ready."

It felt like a rug burn, the tight heat in her chest. A calendar hung by the phone and Gena had made a diagonal line through all the days that had passed, just as their mother used to do. It had always depressed her, that habit, as if each day were a task to be crossed off a long list.

"I want you to do exactly what you need to," Tom was saying, and she thought of that night in June when, after having dinner with the family of Tom's goddaughter, they'd split off from the rest, taken a walk to the Norsett town landing, then back to Tom's car. Nothing had happened between them on that walk; she couldn't remember what they'd spoken of, and Vida had decided that if he asked her out again she'd say no. But on the way home, for no good reason, her whole body began to shake. It was a warm night in June but she was shaking and couldn't stop. He didn't ask why. He just turned the heat on for her. When she didn't stop trembling, he turned it up higher, even though he'd begun to sweat in his suit and tie.

"I'm here," he was saying. "I'm not going anywhere. I'll come to you and Peter the minute you say the word."

She thanked him and then, unable to form more words, hung up.

"How did that go?" Gena asked from the doorway.

She pushed down all that was rising and found her usual flatness. "About as well as one might expect."

A guinea pig scuttled out from beneath a chair, paused, and kept on toward Gena, who scooped it up and cooed into its ear.

"Aren't they supposed to live in cages?" Vida said.

"Oh no. They grow much bigger and stronger if they're given room to roam."

"But they're not house-trained." She pointed to the small yellow puddle it had left behind.

"No more than a squirt of liquid here, a pellet or two there." Tucking the creature under her armpit, Gena folded a paper towel into a square and pressed it with two fingers into the urine. The whole thing saturated quickly. She tossed it into the trash and returned to her game with Peter.

She'd always believed Gena was the stronger of the two of them, the sister who was meant to flourish and thrive.

Vida went back to her room. She drew more palm trees. At night she slept. She awoke early, well before dawn. December 17. The date had been traveling through her dreams. It was a familiar date, a date printed somewhere. On flyers. At school. She had it now. The spring musical tryouts. Helen.

She picked up the pad and charcoal pencil by her bed. It didn't take her long to remember which of Jerry's girls corresponded to which year, as if her mind had been keeping a careful inventory without her knowing it.

1973 Janet Blake
1974 Audrey Beale
1975 Beth Zaccardi
1976 Nancy Goff
1977 Amelia Crane
1978 Bonnie Steadman

It felt good to match the names with dates, as if she were tidying up a small part of her brain. She wrote the letter out three times, one for Brick, one for Lydia Rezo, one for the board of trustees.

On her way out, she passed Peter sleeping on a narrow mattress in the living room. He'd kicked off his blankets and curled one leg up to his chest while the other stretched out straight behind him, as if he were taking a great leap into the sky. He'd slept in this position all his life.

She found envelopes and stamps in a drawer in the kitchen. Then she put on Gena's canvas shoes and left to find a mailbox.

THIRTEEN

HE AWOKE TO THE SOUND OF THE TRUNK OF THE DODGE SLAMMING SHUT.
Was she leaving? He waited for another sound. Nothing.

When his mother finally left, he'd move into her room, to the double bed. He'd never slept in a double bed. And palm trees out the window. He wanted to see the beach again today. Gena wanted to take him over to the school. The idea of a new school was only good in theory. Look how badly he'd fared with kids he'd known all his life. What would happen when he was a complete unknown from the opposite end of the country?

He fell back asleep.

"Peter." It was his mother, whispering. "Are you awake?"

"Kind of," he said.

"Shhh."

"What's going on?" He wasn't going back, if that's what she wanted.

"Let's go on a picnic."

"A picnic? What time is it?"

"A breakfast picnic."

He pushed himself up to sitting, his head still thick with dreams. Beside him sat a wicker basket with a wooden lid. The stalk of a banana kept it from closing all the way. Beside that squatted his mother. She'd combed her hair and put on a dress.

"Come with me," she said.

The dress was yellow with short sleeves and a full skirt that lay in folds on the floor. His mother, even in the summer, didn't wear tiny sleeves like that. She didn't wear yellow, ever. The whole thing—the dress, the basket, the secrecy, even the word "picnic"—was far stranger than any dream.

"Okay," he said, too curious to feel like there was a choice.

She waited for him out by the car.

"It's not far. We could walk," he said.

"I'll have to leave these behind then." She tossed Gena's shoes into the bushes by the door. "They've shredded my skin."

The dress could not have been Gena's. It was the exact shape of his mother. She walked, as she always did, a little ahead of him, her upper body tipped into an imaginary wind. The morning was overcast but warm, and the plants and trees had resumed their exotic, unmenacing aspects. The picnic basket swung on her arm like something from a fairy tale. He offered to take it but she shook her head. It was very light, she told him.

Soon this road would be his road, this sky his sky. He thought he should buy a notebook and write some of it down. Up ahead a car with surfboards strapped to the top pulled into a driveway and honked, then honked again. A kid in a red wet suit—the body was pressed so flat he couldn't tell if it was male or female—came out, shoved another board on top of the pile, and got in back.

The ocean was a softer shade of blue today beneath the clouds. His mother cut straight through the tall sharp grass to the edge of the cliff. Her hair and her dress blew in the same direction. She stood there for several minutes and if he didn't know better he would have said she was praying.

The path down was so steep you didn't really have to take steps; you just slid on your heels through the sand. The cliff seemed far larger from down here. Peter bent his head up the enormous rock face to where his mother had just been standing. It was probably sixty feet high. They were protected from the wind down here, and the clouds had begun to burn off.

His mother chose a spot on the dry sand a few feet up from the tide line. They sat and did not speak. Waves broke in great thuds and splatters against the rocks, and the foamy water rushed through the narrow passages to shore, then jerked back into the pull of the next wave. Peter was hungry but his mother had tucked the basket up in her lap, stretched her arms through the handles and around its sides so that it was now part of her belly. She was looking at her toes, or maybe a few inches beyond them. He'd never seen her sit still before, without a book or a stack of essays, without some purpose. When she raised her face to his, it was as if she'd pulled back the air itself, like a curtain he'd never known was moveable.

"Here," she said, unthreading her arms and hoisting the basket off of her. "Open it."

He raised the lid. On the top, beside two bananas, was a charcoal drawing of a man. It was elaborate, with shading in the cheeks and around the eyes, the cross-hatching Miss Conley was always trying to teach them.

"I thought I owed you a better likeness."

He recognized him. Even from the hasty sketch he'd demanded of her so long ago he recognized him. The thin hair, parted on the right, the small eyes, the uncertain mouth. It was an angry face, but whose anger was it, his father's or his mother's? He could hear his mother breathing unevenly through her nose. He figured he had one question, maybe two. What was most important? He knew he should ask the man's name, but something stopped him. It was both too little and too much. He held the drawing out to her—he didn't want those narrow eyes watching him anymore—but she flinched back and would not take it. He couldn't think of the words for what he wanted. Not another fucking drawing. He crumpled the paper and tossed it at the sea. It landed in the wet sand. Within seconds he regretted it and wanted to get up and grab the picture in case the water came up and carried it away, but it remained stubbornly in place. He heard her breathing and knew that he didn't have much time. One question maybe two, right now or never again.

"Tell me." It barely belonged to him, this voice from the clenched depth of his stomach.

She recoiled, pulling up her legs and wrapping the yellow dress over them. She rested her chin in the dip of fabric between the knobs of her knees.

"Tell me who he was and why you married him and where he is now."

"We were never married."

He waited for her to go on but she didn't. He felt like shoving her right over into the sand. "Tell me."

"I lived with my mother then." Her voice was so faint he had to lean toward her, but imperceptibly; too much interest and he'd scare the words away. "She was a . . ." A wave smothered the rest.

"I can't hear you!" he yelled into the sudden hush of the water peeling back.

She didn't react to the shrillness of his voice the way she normally would. She just pushed the basket away with her feet and slid herself closer to him. She did this not with her usual teacherlike alacrity but with the creepy deliberateness of an old person. "My mother was a true matriarch. She was that imperious blend of insecurity and strength that Faulkner and Lawrence capture—"

"I don't care about Faulkner and Lawrence right now, Ma."

She nodded and pursed her lips and he figured he'd lost her. He'd gone too far. What was wrong with him? Why was he behaving like this when he was so close to getting some answers? But she started speaking again. "I lived with my mother and liked to spend as little time around her as possible so I often stayed in my classroom until evening, doing my work."

"Where was this?" He regretted his own interruption immediately.

"Solano, Texas. It's a small town about a hundred and fifty miles from the Mexican border. My father had bought a cattle ranch there, but the land was better for spinach and sorghum. We were there for a year, then my father died. We stayed because my father couldn't push us on to the next place anymore. I went to a two-year college, then started teaching at the school there. My mother converted the whole ranch to sorghum and finally started making some money."

What the hell was sorghum? He didn't know and he didn't care, and he held his tongue this time.

"There was one afternoon at school. Normally other teachers were around." She curled and uncurled the hem of her dress and the thin cloth quivered in her fingers. "But everyone had gone across the street to the football, an important game, division something or other. The whole county had turned out for it. I could hear the roaring at my desk. I was planning to catch the second half, after I finished my grading. I had a few students on the team and I'd promised to show up. Everyone was gone. Even the construction workers— the schoolhouse was being renovated that fall—had permission to watch the game. There was one of them I had a terrific crush on. He used to visit me in the afternoons. He was too shy to get close to my desk so he'd circle the edges of the classroom, examining whatever was up on the walls, asking 'Who's Menalaeus?' or 'What's synecdoche?' He was so curious. His name was Eric. He always reminded me of Levin, that wonderful scene when he takes Kitty mushroom picking and—"

"Is Eric my father?"

"No." She shook her head, which she'd tucked down into her neck like a goose. "Eric went to the game. I did my work, gathered my papers, and stopped in the bathroom on the way out." She was talking with her eyes shut now. Peter could see the raised pupils jerking from side to side beneath their lids. "I was at the sink, washing my hands." She stopped there, and he waited. He didn't ask why she was talking about washing her hands when he wanted to know about his father. He took a deep breath. A pale-eyed dog trotted past them on his way to the water, two halves of a coconut shell wedged loosely in his mouth. "Sometimes it helps to think of Leda and the Swan." She was whispering now. "To think of Io, Persephone, and Europa."

Maybe there was a part of him, a cluster of cells somewhere in his small brain that knew, that was trying to tell the other parts that would not listen, but he needed her to say it, not in code, not in references to people that were only real to her. He didn't need this shit. This was the shit he'd gotten all his life. Leda and the fucking Swan.

He stood up. "Forget it, Ma. When I have my Ph.D., maybe you can tell me. But I'm going back now. Gena's showing me my school today."

She leapt up and grabbed him before he could take more than a few steps. "Listen to me, Peter Avery." Her nostrils flared white but the rest of her face was a purplish red, raw and ugly as a slab of meat. "I'm going to tell you what you want to hear, but I'm going to tell you my own way, the only way I know how. Now sit." She stood over him with her back to the roiling sea. "A man came into that bathroom." Her voice broke on the last syllable and she looked straight up to the sun behind him, breathing hard. There were streaks down the sides of her face, though he hadn't seen her crying.

"Whenever I thought about telling this to you I always thought I'd find in that moment some beautiful way of constructing it so that it would seem somehow magical to you. I know that's crazy but it happens. It can happen. The right words can transform even the grossest brutality. But they're not . . ." She dragged her fingernails across the inside of her wrist. "They're not coming to me now. A man came in. A stranger to me. He came into that bathroom while I was washing my hands." Her face twisted and she looked at Peter helplessly, as if she herself could not believe what she was about to say. "And he raped me."

The crumpled paper rocked in the sand near her bare foot. Leda and the Swan. He remembered it now. The Swan was Zeus, swooping down to rape a mortal girl. He'd gotten an erection in class when they'd discussed the poem last year: the loosening thighs, the shudder in the loins.

She dropped back down onto the sand beside him. He wished she weren't so close. He wished she had the sense to leave him alone.

"A few months later I got in my car and drove away."

"To Fayer?" he heard himself ask, though he didn't care, didn't want the rest.

"Yes, though I didn't know it at first. I just drove east and that's where I ended up. At my grandfather's house."

If Peter hadn't just done a similar thing in the opposite direction he'd have thought she was lying.

"And you were . . ."

She nodded. "I was pregnant."

He wanted to stop her now. But she was not to be stopped. It would have been like trying to stop one of those waves.

"It was eerie, discovering the house had become a school. I turned around before even going in the driveway. And then that night I saw in the paper they were looking for a substitute. I was so curious to go inside the house. I never thought they'd actually hire me. The faculty then was nearly all male and they were so stodgy. And I was a pregnant woman from Texas. But they did, and I rented an apartment off campus. Then when they offered me a full-time position, I moved into the cottage. Summer school was in session. My water broke while I was walking in the woods with Walt." She lifted her hand to her mouth to pull out hair that had blown in, but her fingers were shaking so much she couldn't trap it and gave up. "The pain was immediate. I thought it would be more gradual. It took me so long just to get back to the house. By then everything was confused in my mind. The pain and the fear seemed to trigger it all again. I knew I needed a phone but for hours at a time I thought I was back in that bathroom in Texas. And he was there and there was no phone and I was just screaming and screaming and no one heard. I couldn't see the phone in my own kitchen with the doctor's number taped to the wall and then I was pushing and I couldn't stop myself from pushing, and even when I knew where I was and I could see the phone on the wall plain as day, I couldn't bear the thought of some doctor coming in, some other man hovering over me, so I just pushed." He saw the tears now, sliding down quietly. "I remember your warm slippery head in my hands and how I felt like both an animal and a god at the same time and I lifted you up and you were screaming and I was still screaming and then it felt like my whole insides drained out onto the kitchen floor and I lost consciousness. I woke up in the hospital and Carol was in a chair beside me, holding you. I think I always thought of her as an angel after that.

"I used to have these dreams, after you were born, in which he'd come back. To steal you. And I'd fight him off. I'd kill him. I'd wake up standing rigid next to my bed or in the hallway. Every night I stood guard. Then once I dreamed"—her voice was growing thinner and thinner—"he was inside of you, inside of your little baby body, and I killed you both." He could just barely hear her now. "After that, I was so scared, so scared of myself." She covered her face from him, and only cracking sounds came out of her throat.

He hadn't known that the truth would feel like this, like having limbs pulled off. All these things he'd thought he wanted—her mar- riage to Tom, a night with Kristina, the story of his father—turned

out to be corrupt in some way. He had been created by the opposite
of love, had been the opposite of wanted. It all made too much sense.

"I dreamt I killed you once. Because you wouldn't tell me all
this." He put his arms around the little ball of her. Her whole body
shook and he shook with it. He thought of the lurching beast they'd
been on the field at school. Now they were something else. He didn't
know what.

She was terrified he'd take his arms away. Stay stay stay. He was the
only skin she had. Everything else was gone. Stay. She had no more
words, no more energy left to push them out. This was the last time
he would ever come near her, she was sure of it. He'd never truly
forgive. He was Angel, she saw now, like in her dream. He would
leave her. Stay, she cried. The sun rose higher and hotter and the
waves grew even larger, rising to thin tremulous ridges before smack-
ing the rocks. And Peter stayed.

"I'm sorry, Mom," he whispered. "I'm so sorry this happened
to you."

He'd come out of her like a slimy blue fish. She had forgotten
her own animalness.

After a while, a group of teenagers came down the path loudly,
carrying surfboards to the far end of the beach where there were
fewer rocks.

"I'm hungry," she said, and straightened up, permitting Peter
to let go. He would feel embarrassed, hugging his mother in public.

She dragged the picnic basket around. They each ate a banana
and a hard-boiled egg.

When they were done Peter said, "Should we go feel the water?"
and stood with his hand out to help her up. She was far too depleted
to move, but when she placed her hand in his and was lifted to her
feet, she felt a rush of life. A wave broke and sent cold foamy water
across the tops of her feet.

"It's freezing!" Peter cried and leapt away.

"It's the 'scrotum-tightening sea!'" she screamed and waded in farther, lifting her dress up over her knees.

"What!" Peter said, laughing.

Perhaps it was for this moment that she'd been remembering Joyce all week.

She lifted her feet up off the bottom, her dress billowing in great air pockets around her, her face to the sky and its strange California blue, a blue so deep you could almost see the blackness of space beyond. She'd forgotten how easily a body could float in saltwater. All she had to do was move her hands in nearly imperceptible little flaps below the surface every now and then, to glide along.

Couldn't his mother feel how cold it was? A huge wave began to swell behind her. The water at his feet retreated, sucking the sand out from under the edges of his feet. The wave grew and grew, hovered, then curled over with a thunderous crash and spray. His mother had gone under, near a cluster of rocks. She could have banged her head. He'd never be able to find her in all the foam, and churned-up sand. He took a few more steps into the surge and scanned the murky bottom. Then he saw her, bobbing in the chaos, her hair pressed down around her face, her mouth open, laughing, saying something to him that the noise of the sea carried off. She was young, he saw now, with freckles across her cheeks. In all his imaginings he'd never guessed that his mother had gotten hurt. Always in his mind there had been love on his father's side, and sadness when she could not love him back. There had always been that man in his yard, raking leaves and waiting. Peter saw now that maybe that man was himself. Maybe he was the one who'd been waiting.

On the way back to Gena's he said, without rehearsing it, almost without knowing he was going to speak, "I like it here."

"I do too," his mother said, to his unexpected relief.

FOURTEEN

October, 1980

THE TRIP FROM GENA'S TO BERKELEY WAS LESS THAN AN HOUR. PETER WISHED it were longer. When the bus wheeled into a slot in the terminal, he didn't look out the window at the trickle of people coming through the heavy doors to greet them. *Stuart says there's an eleven o'clock bus and you should be on it,* Fran had written. The driver was opening up the luggage bin below him. Why was he so nervous? He'd had far more nerve-rattling days than this. In the past year he'd started a new school, called up three different girls for dates, and read two of his own poems aloud at assembly.

He was now the last person on the bus. He forced himself to stand. It was Fran he dreaded most. Stuart would intimidate him, reduce him. But Fran would bring back the shame of that night he kissed her and disgusted her so thoroughly. He didn't know why she had written, why she'd wanted to include him in her visit with Stuart. He wondered if Tom had pushed them into it.

They were right there at the bottom of the steps, as if they were about to get on the bus themselves.

"We thought you'd blown us off." Her voice brought back breakfasts at the green table.

"I didn't," Stuart said. He was fuller, not fat, just inflated to the proper size.

They didn't hug.

"It's weird to see you guys," Peter said, aware that he was only looking at Stuart. He hadn't seen Fran yet, just heard her voice and felt the vague mass of her body to his right.

Fran and Stuart agreed but Peter could feel the old lopsided attachment. He wondered again why he had come. He felt tired already from the effort the day was going to take.

"How's Caleb?" he asked as they walked through the terminal to the street. It was the most innocuous place to start.

"He's moved into your guys' room," Fran said.

"What?" Stuart yelled.

Your guys'. His mother would have a fit over the expression, but Peter marveled at it for other reasons. He'd only been in that room six weeks. Was it really still partly his?

Fran laughed at her brother's outrage. She'd probably been saving this piece of information since September, to deliver it in person for the reaction. "He's painted all the lightbulbs different colors and he lights the incense and has his little friends over and they recite all that crap on the walls."

"What is one is not one," Peter said.

"And what is not one is also one," Fran finished.

"Does he have girls tapping at his window at night?"

"Watch it, Pete." Stuart gave him a shove with his shoulder and Peter bumped into Fran.

"Sorry," he said to the sleeve of her red jacket.

"You're different," she said, too quietly for Stuart to hear.

"Where are we going?" Peter asked, hopeful now, for different could only mean improved. They'd been walking fast and purposefully down one street, across to another, and were now headed up a hill.

"I've got class in ten minutes," Stuart said. "I thought you guys could drop me off, then we can grab lunch after."

"How long's your class?" Peter asked, too quickly, not conceal-ing his panic.

"An hour and forty minutes."

Holy shit, he thought.

Soon Stuart veered up a long flight of stone steps and was gone.

They were in a large quad that had been drained of people within seconds. A clock at the top of a tower struck the quarter hour.

"College," he said, thinking of Stuart's imitation of Tom, and the great relief Tom must feel now, thinking, too, what a mystery it was to him, this kind of life.

"Yeah," Fran said uneasily.

They walked toward a fountain in the center of the quad.

"I never got it," she said, "why Stuart dragged his feet about all this. But now that it's my turn I feel like I'd be abandoning her. My mother, I mean." But Peter knew who she was talking about.

He nodded. "She's a pretty powerful presence."

"What do you mean?"

"Her love. It was really strong. She loved you so much."

Fran's eyes filled even though she was smiling. "She did," she whispered.

He could tell she knew he was going to hug her and she let her chin fall heavily on his shoulder. She smelled like the shampoo they all used to use, and he remembered what it felt like to stand in the bathroom after a shower looking at the picture of her mother. He wondered if there was a word for missing something you never had.

When they stopped hugging, he said, "I'm sorry about the kiss."

"Oh God. Don't be. I wanted you to kiss me."

He thought about reminding her of what she'd said. Instead he kept quiet, and they sat on the rim of the fountain, shoulders touching.

A guy wearing sandals with thick noisy buckles trudged past, looking at all the buildings, then back down at his map.

"That's going to be me next year. Completely clueless," she said.

He thought of how his mother was taking a training class to teach self-defense in addition to her English classes at the community college. "Go help him."

"What?"

"Go help him find where he's going."

"I've been here a day."

"He's got a map. How hard can it be?"

"Peter."

"Do it."

"Shit," she said, and pushed herself off.

He watched her in her red jacket smoothing down her hair just before she reached the guy and tapped him on the the back. He spun around, and a smile bloomed. Together they looked at the large map. Fran turned it around for him, and pointed to the clock tower. The guy laughed and shook his head. Peter remembered the way Fran could make pancakes, bacon, toast, and scrambled eggs and have it all arrive hot on the table at the same time. And when Tom brought home a game for Caleb, a three-tiered maze for marbles that had loops and pulleys and zillions of tiny plastic pieces, Fran put it together without taking the directions out of the box.

They were talking now. Peter watched the guy's eyes dart to her face, wondering how he'd see her again, daring himself to ask.

It was all about courage. To live even a day on this earth required courage. All these things they read in school—*The Odyssey, Beowulf, Huckleberry Finn*—were all about courage, but the teacher never said, You may not have to kill a Cyclops or a dragon but you will need just as much courage to get through each day.

They shook hands and Fran came back carrying a corner of the map.

"His phone number?"

"Address." She was flushed and happy. "We can be pen pals, like your mom and my dad. He asked if you were my boyfriend."

"What'd you say?"

"I said you were my little brother."

Peter punched her. It was exactly what he'd hoped she'd say.

Stuart emerged in a thick wave of people and stood at the top of the stairs for a few minutes talking to a girl. Others joined them and Stuart broke off, descending the stairs alone.

When he saw Peter and Fran, he didn't hide his pleasure that they were still there, waiting for him. He had that wide smile from the cube of pictures in the living room. He led them off campus and down a side street to a tiny shop. He disappeared inside and came out with a bag of sandwiches. Then he turned up a path off the crowded sidewalk and soon the street was far below them. It was a steep incline, with thick tree roots bulging up out of the damp earth which smelled like old flowers and toothpaste.

"So who was she?" Fran asked.

"Who?"

"The girl you were talking to."

"Her name's Mary. She's in my Mandarin class."

"You didn't want to introduce us?"

"That was our second conversation ever. It might have seemed a little odd to her."

"You're worried what she'll think of you. You like her."

"I do."

"Of course her name's Mary."

"Me and Oedipus." He crossed his fingers. "We're tight."

They kept walking.

"Your mother's not stringing my father along, is she?" Fran stopped and turned back to face Peter. "I mean, he really believes what she writes."

"What does she write?" He wanted to keep moving, but Fran sat on a boulder.

"I don't know really, but he goes around humming and giggling after he gets a letter."

"My mother," he began, but he suddenly felt too dispirited to continue.

"What do you mean, Fran, 'you don't know really'?" Stuart said.

"I don't read them. I swear I don't. I'm dying to. But I don't. He reads parts to us. The funny parts. But I think there are definitely juicy parts because he's always trying to cover up the back of the page he's reading from."

Peter started walking again, and after a little while he heard them following behind. He wasn't going to try to explain his mother to them anymore.

They came abruptly to the top, which was a patch of grass overlooking the cities: Berkeley, then Oakland, then San Francisco across the glossy water. They sat in a line facing the view. Stuart passed out the sandwiches.

"This should be interesting," Fran said as she unwrapped hers.

Peter took a bite. The flavors were unrecognizable, but not awful. It was the texture that was challenging, so dry and mealy it sucked the moisture from his tongue.

"Gross!" Fran spat her bite out on the grass. "That is definitely the worst yet."

"I've been stretching her palate since she got here."

"'Stretching my palate'? You've been trying to kill me. Can we get a jar of this stuff for Caleb? God, Peter, you're not actually eating that, are you?"

He shook his head and spat his out, too. "I think it was trying to eat *me*."

They all laughed.

Peter noticed that Stuart's sandwich had regular lettuce in it. He snatched the other half and opened it. "Ham and cheese!" he yelled.

"Bastard!"

Peter split the half with Fran.

They ate and looked out at the foreign landscape, the valleys and hills covered in buildings and asphalt, the sea vacant.

"What do you think our real purpose is here?" Stuart said.

Fran groaned. "Can we have one day when we don't have to talk about the meaning of life?"

"I don't think we ever talk about anything else. It just depends how honest we want to be about it."

"I want to ask Peter about his life out here, about Vida, about when my father is going to get to see her."

"You want to know how much meaning Vida finds in her correspondence with Dad."

There was something different in the way they said Vida, something more hopeful.

"I bought my mother *The Thorn Birds*."

"You did not."

"I did. And she read it and she cried like a baby when Ralph died."

"You have to be lying," she said, grinning.

"I think she's hoping Tom will come out in January."

He could feel Fran relax beside him. "Good."

There had been talk, if visits went well, of Tom's moving out here with Fran and Caleb by summer, but Peter saw they didn't know that yet. They were all ready for a change, Tom had said.

They shoved their wax paper back in the bag and stretched out on the grass. There were insects gnawing on something nearby.

Stuart, placing his hands on his bony knees, said, "Heaven and Earth and I were born at the same time, and all life and I are one."

Chuang Tzu, Peter guessed. "I've missed you," he said. He hadn't meant to. It just blurted itself out, and he blushed.

"I've missed you, too." Stuart put his arm around Peter's neck and didn't take it off until they all stood up.

Before they left, they went to the edge of the drop down to the city. They stood close with their arms brushing and Peter smelled Fran's hair again and heard Stuart's familiar deep slow breaths in and out. It felt good to be with them, but it would feel good to be on the bus in a little while. His mother would be waiting at the stop for him and she would know the effort it had taken for him to see them and he would know the courage it had taken for her to be there, standing in the dark with strangers.

FIFTEEN

January, 1981

SHE WAITED FOR HIM OUTSIDE. IT WAS POINTLESS TO TRY AND BE ANYWHERE else. At first she sat in the orchard, as Gena called it, which consisted of the four fruit trees they'd planted last spring: a lemon, a lime, and two avocados. For her birthday, Peter and Gena had given her a wrought iron table and chair and she'd placed it between the avocados. She'd written to Carol at that table finally—without notes or quotes, just her own small words. And all her letters to Tom.

From the kitchen window, Peter watched his mother wander in the grass beside the driveway. Occasionally she stopped without knowing it, her mind caught on some snag. He could tell she was nervous from the way she scratched the inside of her wrists.

"I can't remember what he looks like," she'd said last night. "All I can picture is the mustache."

"Sometimes I can hear it against the receiver," he'd said.

"Yes! Scritch scritch." The guinea pig in her lap had leapt off at the sound. "I feel like I never really *looked* at him."

"Tomorrow's your chance," Gena had said. She'd tried to sound cheerful about it, but she knew that change was afoot, and she liked things the way they were.

A silver rental car pulled in the driveway. Vida stood in the grass in her lucky dress, barefoot, her wrists scraped red.

Tom didn't bother parking properly or shutting the door when he got out. He just went to her as if she were dying, the way Peter himself had gone to her that morning in the field, leaving his pencil and his history books on the desk. And when Tom reached her they sank into each other like neither could have taken another step without the other and even Peter felt weakened by watching, a bit like he'd felt two nights ago when they'd seen the fifty-two hostages come off a plane and fall into the arms of the people who'd waited for them. They'd been given parkas with enormous fur-trimmed hoods and they came down the set of metal stairs in groups of twos and threes, then separated as their families found them. A little girl in a red coat leapt into the arms of her big brother; a mother kept kissing her middle-aged son's hand over and over as they walked away. "What's the first thing you're going to do when you get home?" a reporter asked a man on the tarmac. "Take my wife in my arms." They'd been sitting down on the new couch, but by the time all the hostages had disembarked, he, Gena, and his mother were all standing a few inches from the screen, clutching hands without knowing it.

He smelled, even in California, of maple syrup. Vida held him and let him hold her. She felt herself opening, her whole being spreading not just over Tom but over the yard, over the orchard behind her, over the palms clicking in the wind. Over the Dodge which had carried her so many places. Over her son, her very own son, watching at the window. She pressed her mouth to the warm stubble on the back of Tom's neck. Desire rose easily. He'd waited, and had come when she asked. And yet she did not feel as Tess had felt when Angel finally came. Unlike Tess, her urge was not to die. *This happiness was too much,* Tess said. *I have had enough.* But Vida had not had near enough. Oh God, she thought, nearly unable to reckon with the vastness of the moment. This is it and I am right here. This is what there is.

ACKNOWLEDGMENTS

EVERYONE IN MY LIFE HAS HAD A HAND IN HELPING ME WRITE THIS BOOK. Thank you to each one of you. I would still be stuck in chapter nine without the extraordinary help of Judith Burwell, who opened all the doors and windows. I am grateful for the support and encouragement of my writers' group: Susan Conley, Debra Spark, Anja Hanson, and Sara Corbett. I am indebted to the following people for all their help: Sue Loomis, Fabiola Parra, Alix Bowman, Tina Barber, Paula Price, Nidia Restrepo, Holly Adams, and Hannah McCain. I'd also like to thank my mother, Don Lee, Maryanne O'Hara, Ann and Jack Cobb, Anita Demetropoulos, Cornelia Walworth, Cammie McGovern, Lisa Adams, and Becky Dilworth. And I need to acknowledge a real-life high school English teacher, Tony Paulus, who introduced me to both literature and creative writing, and without whom I would never have begun writing stories. I am blessed with a fantastic agent, Wendy Weil, and an exceptionally talented editor, Elisabeth Schmitz, who speaks my language, only better.

I need to give a special thanks to Susan Conley who, in a true act of friendship, somehow managed to read my manuscript twice in one week despite her responsibilities as teacher, writer, and mother of two small boys. Her feedback was invaluable to me. And to my husband, Tyler, who listened, and read, and made me go on when I wanted to give up. And to my daughters, Calla and Eloise, for their love and understanding, and for the expression on their faces when they took turns holding the pile of pages that night I finished.

The English Teacher

Lilly King

ABOUT THIS GUIDE

We hope that these discussion questions
will enhance your reading group's exploration
of Lily King's *The English Teacher*. They are
meant to stimulate discussion, offer new viewpoints,
and enrich your enjoyment of the book.

More reading group guides and additional information, including
summaries, author tours, and author sites for
other fine Grove Press titles, may be found on
our Web site, www.groveatlantic.com.

QUESTIONS FOR DISCUSSION

1. At the heart of the novel is the quest of Vida to find truth through fiction. The epigraph for *The English Teacher,* "Life is beginning. I now break into my hoard of life," is from Virginia Woolf. How would you describe Vida as an English teacher? What are her strengths? What are her dramatic limitations? What distinguishes an English teacher from other teachers? Does living in the world of books hamper Vida, or does it expand her experience? Do the students of an imaginative English teacher—and readers of good books—suspend disbelief in order to grow or live on multiple levels?

2. Why does Vida hate teaching *Tess of the D'Urbervilles*? Why is she afraid of Peter reading it? (See pages 33–38.) What is perverse about her students' taking the book to their hearts, adding it to Mrs. Avery's legendary status? How does the teaching of the novel continue to correlate with events in the book? See the last page, for instance.

3. Peter is largely resistant to his mother's obsession with literature. He feels held at arm's length by her retreats into poetry and fiction. Is that a fair assessment on his part? Describe one time when he, too, understands something better, more immediately, by recalling a poem.

4. "Memory does its work underground. Beneath consciousness, a past moment finds its kin all at once. Like a fish returned to its school, it frolics in remembered waters, and stirs up others. . . . Yet even awful, unlivable memories want to be relived; the fragments yearn to be whole once more" (p. 103). For Vida the "unlivable memory" is always near the surface as well as beneath consciousness. Does the passage evoke other characters, too? Have you known people who, like Vida, are disabled by earlier traumas? (For instance, there has been great attention recently to people's retrieved memories of childhood abuse. Do you give any credence to those who say, "Let it go—just get on with your life"?) How is Peter an inciting force for Vida's dealing fully with her rape?

5. "'Vida's a hoot, isn't she?' Peter heard Tom's brother say to him at the door. 'She is,' Tom said, confused, like he'd bought an appliance with too many features" (p. 94). How does Tom try and fail and then ultimately succeed in understanding and winning the complex, educated, and wounded Vida? What are the qualities that serve him in the end? Can you think of particular moments that show his generosity and strength? Think of his burying Walt, sharing his workshop with Peter, confronting Vida about her drinking. Others? What about the yellow dress?

6. "She figured that all marriages, if they lasted, ended up here in the land of quiet regret" (p. 152). We remember that this is Vida's first try at marriage. What have been her observations about the institution so far? About her school

colleagues? About her own parents? It is their strains that drive her to find a new reality in books. Vida is tantalized by the Hardy poem in which a young man is lured by his ideal of love, "not by the poor girl he has been projecting his illusions onto" (p. 105). Vida feels Tom is always asking, "Why aren't you who I thought you were?" (p. 104). Is Tom unrealistic in his hopes for Vida? Are there other characters who idealize someone in the book? Does King suggest that bedrock reality (disillusionment?) is a requirement for a strong marriage? Or is it a starting point for a mature relationship of any kind?

7. What is Peter's preoccupation with Mary Belou, the phantom mother in his new house? (Peter also wonders if his own mysterious father is dead and waiting for him—when that figure is not raking leaves!) What is it that Peter needs from the now mythologized Mary? (See page 101.) Is there some resolution for him later?

8. Recall some scenes of both lively humor and poignancy. For example, think of Peter's getting trapped in the nuptial bedroom (p. 28), wild to escape this lunatic moment. And Vida, true to form, in her schoolroom faced down by Tom, "grew bored by his performance. She had the impulse to get up and grade a few papers until he had finished" (p. 148). Can you think of other funny moments, all the sharper because they ring true to human nature?

9. What is it about the hostages that both compels and reflects the characters in the novel? It is one of the few issues that gets the family involved in something beyond themselves. How have the characters themselves been held hostage? For instance, when they are fleeing across the country, Peter reflects, "It wasn't just her silence for the past four days but her silence all of his life" (p. 209). How does it take many levels of diplomacy, perseverance, and perhaps luck to release the hostages that are the people in this book?

10. Discuss the varied angles of vision in the novel. How do we learn about Vida, for instance, other than through her own thoughts and actions? We know that characters perceive external reality through their own lenses and needs. Give some examples. How do we know whom to trust? One surprise is the diner waitress who observes and reflects on a young boy and an old woman. How does this section add to our knowledge of Peter and Vida's odyssey? Elsewhere, which are the most interesting shifts in points of view?

11. How is Walt a touchstone for the family? Older than Peter, where did he come from? And how is he important to the pivotal events of chapter seven?

12. Would you say that perhaps the central drama, the conflict that needs to be resolved, is the one between Vida and Peter? Is it this relationship that finally allows others to fall into place?

13. King is unorthodox in many ways, not intimidated by convention in her novel. Does Vida reflect this originality, particularly King's gimlet eye? When? What

other characters show odd and fresh human reactions? For instance, when Tom is questioning Peter about Vida, the boy "wished they didn't have to talk about her. He wished he just lived with the Belous without her getting in the way" (p. 127). When else does King reveal dead-on observations or memories of what it's like to be a teenager, in school, at home, or at parties?

14. Mary Karr, writer of memoirs and poetry, has defined a dysfunctional family as "any family with more than one person in it." Is that definition apt for King's book? How do parents and children fail one another in *The English Teacher*? What do they have to risk to grow closer? What are the added challenges of the stepfamily? Is this ultimately the way it is with families: intricate webs, interwoven, fragile, tenacious, voracious, and beautiful?

15. How does style reveal substance in chapter twelve (pp. 213–15)? Does Vida's internal dialogue, recollecting Joyce, put us inside her breakdown? And what about her aimlessness, paranoia, and nighttime panic attacks? How does she begin to work her way out?

16. What does California represent in the book, as opposed to Texas or New England? How is it important to Gena? Stuart? Peter? Vida? Fran? Tom? When do you begin to suspect that freedom is a central theme? (Is it logical that Vida's fear of killing her son is tied up with her own need to be free? Of what?)

17. How well do we know Stuart and Fran? Is it mostly through Peter's eyes? Do the brother and sister change in the book? Remember the scene where Peter revolves the picture cube in the living room, trying to find out who Stuart is. From early days Peter longed for siblings, to be part of a family. He hoped his mother's marriage "meant, ultimately, a real union, a true synthesis, without any loose ends" (p. 27). Is this goal achieved in the end? For everyone?

18. "It was all about courage. To live even a day on this earth required courage. All those things they read in school—*The Odyssey, Beowulf, Huckleberry Finn*— were all about courage but the teacher never said, You may not have to kill a Cyclops or a dragon but you will need just as much courage to get through the day" (p. 236). What are times when courage is particularly required of people in this book? Is it a quality that can be learned? Do characters help each other find it?

SUGGESTIONS FOR FURTHER READING

Tess of the d'Urbervilles and *Far from the Madding Crowd* by Thomas Hardy; *To the Lighthouse* and *Mrs. Dalloway* by Virginia Woolf; *The Evening of the Holiday* and *The Transit of Venus* by Shirley Hazzard; all books by Alice Munro; *Pride and Prejudice* and *Sense and Sensibility* by Jane Austen; *Light in August* and *Absalom, Absalom!* by William Faulkner; *The Scarlet Letter* by Nathaniel Hawthorne; *A Room with a*

View and *Howards End* by E. M. Forster; *The Gate of Angels* by Penelope Fitzgerald; *Independent People* by Halldor Laxness; *The Man Who Loved Children* by Christina Stead; *The Centaur* by John Updike; *Beloved* by Toni Morrison; *Dusk and Other Stories* by James Salter; *Disgrace* by J. M. Coetzee; *Atonement* by Ian McEwan; *Bel Canto* by Ann Patchett; *At Weddings and Wakes* and *Child of My Heart* by Alice McDermott; *Housekeeping* by Marilynne Robinson; *Amy and Isabelle* by Elizabeth Strout; *The Solace of Leaving Early* by Haven Kimmel; *The Pleasing Hour* by Lily King